"It's a love song,"
Marco said.

"But it sounds so sad," Anne Marie whispered.

"Because it is sad. He is singing of his lost love. He remembers her hair, like dark clouds . . ." Marco leaned across the table and took a strand of Anne Marie's hair between his fingers. "Like yours."

She swallowed hard. It was just a song. But Marco was real. The heat from his body, the sound of his voice, and the touch of his hand—they were real. She should stop him now, before she was lost in those dark eyes or got hypnotized by the sound of his voice.

"Her skin was as pale as marble," Marco said, so softly she had to lean forward to catch the words. He traced a line on the inside of her bare arm to her wrist. She shivered in the warm night air, and her heart thudded wildly. "As soft as velvet, and her lips were kissed by the morning dew."

Anne Marie knew what was coming next, and her lips trembled in anticipation. . . .

That's Amore

CAROL GRACE

POCKET STAR BOOKS

New York London Toronto Sydney Singapore

This book is a work of fiction. Names, characters, places and incidents are products of the author's imagination or are used fictitiously. Any resemblance to actual events or locales or persons, living or dead, is entirely coincidental.

An *Original* Publication of POCKET BOOKS

 A Pocket Star Book published by
POCKET BOOKS, a division of Simon & Schuster, Inc.
1230 Avenue of the Americas, New York, NY 10020

Copyright © 2003 by Carol Culver

ISBN: 0-7434-6760-4

First Pocket Books printing July 2003

10 9 8 7 6 5 4 3 2 1

POCKET STAR BOOKS and colophon are registered trademarks of Simon & Schuster, Inc.

For information regarding special discounts for bulk purchases, please contact Simon & Schuster Special Sales at 1-800-456-6798 or business@simonandschuster.com

Front cover illustration by Larry Rostant

Printed in the U.S.A.

This book is dedicated to my matchless critique group—Barbara Freethy, Lynn Hanna, Candice Hern, Barbara McMahon, and Kate Moore— who have vision, humor, insight, and best of all, always have the answer to the eternal question—"And then what happens?"

Acknowledgments

Thanks to my family, Craig, Nora, and Andrew, for their good company, their witty banter, and their jesting and joshing that helped ease jet lag and culture shock during our trip to Italy.

Special thanks to Linda Kruger, agent extraordinaire, and to my editor, Micki Nuding, whose enthusiastic support helped turn my dream into reality.

Chapter 1

She was lost. All the streets looked alike, and all the street signs were in a foreign language. Perspiration dripped down the side of Anne Marie Jackson's face as she pulled her new Samsonite suitcase through the back streets of Sorrento. Though it was early September, by ten o'clock the Italian sun was so hot her money belt was plastered to her waist. The guidebooks warned of petty theft; thieves were everywhere, they said, looking for innocent tourists. Tourists like her, dragging suitcases, weighed down with visas and passports and Italian phrase books and still unable to say more than a few words to anyone.

She heard footsteps behind her. With a swift glance over her shoulder, she noticed a man in a dark suit with a long loaf of bread under his arm. She made a quick turn down a narrow cobblestone street with laundry hanging from a line above, and prayed he wouldn't come after her. But he was right there behind her, slowing down when she slowed, speeding up when she sped up. Her heart pounded. Even if she knew the word for *help*, the street was empty—who would hear her? He might take everything she had—cash, traveler's checks, and credit cards.

After all, there would be no witnesses. No one to see him drag her body away, where it would lie in an alley for days until stray dogs gnawed at her bones. And who would ever find her and notify her family? Her family, which now consisted only of her eighteen-year-old son.

Two little boys in tattered T-shirts came around the corner, bouncing their ball off the cobblestones and casting curious glances in her direction. The man with the bread passed her by without a second glance. A man on his way home with bread, that was all. She was paranoid, that was all.

"*Buon giorno,*" she said to the boys.

They stared. She hauled out her Italian phrase book to ask directions. She was not only lost, she was late. If she didn't find the station soon, she'd miss the bus to the Amalfi Coast.

"*Dov'e il termini?*" she asked.

The boys burst into laughter at her accent, and she felt her face turn red. With a glance at her watch, she repeated the phrase, and they pointed back the way she'd come.

"*Grazie.*" With her suitcase clattering behind her, she turned around and headed down the hill.

Ten minutes later, she had a sinking feeling she was no closer to the bus station than before. She felt like giving up, like sitting down on her suitcase and giving in to tears of frustration. Instead, she kept going. Block after block, street after street.

Suddenly, there it was—the station! Swamped with relief, Anne Marie checked her watch. She'd missed the bus. When she went in to buy her ticket, she learned there would be another in an hour. Wonderful! She would still make it in time to meet Giovanni.

There was already a line outside, and she stood at the end of it. She didn't mind waiting; she was in Italy! If she could handle a ten-hour plane flight squished in a center seat between two Sumo wrestlers, followed by a second-class train ride from Rome to Sorrento, seated in the aisle on her suitcase while the train swayed and lurched, an hour in line under the sun was nothing.

She sniffed the air, laden with the scent of lemon blossoms. She had to remember everything to tell Evie, who'd insisted she make this trip, even when Anne Marie said she couldn't afford it.

"Borrow money against your retirement fund," she'd urged. "You must have at least six months of vacation accrued. Do you think the library will close without you? Do you think people will stop reading, stop dropping in to use the Internet, because you're not there?"

"No, but maybe I should just go to Oregon or Yosemite . . ."

"You've always wanted to go to Italy. Now go."

So she'd gone.

Though she wouldn't be here without her friend's encouragement, the person she had to thank most was Dan. Funny she could thank him for anything, after what he'd done to her, but she was no longer bitter about the divorce.

How could she be bitter about anything when she was in Sorrento, a gorgeous old town wedged between the mountains and the Mediterranean, where tourists had been coming for hundreds of years for the climate, the views, and the relaxed atmosphere of *dolce far niente*? The hills were dotted with lemon groves and olive trees. Her senses sang in the fragrant breeze that came up and cooled her face. She was here, she was really here. At last.

The guidebooks said to arrive early to land a seat on the right side of the bus, for one of the world's most spectacular drives along a winding road with views of the cliffs and the sea below. Looking at this line, she'd be lucky if she got a seat at all.

When the bus finally came, belching diesel fumes that clouded the air, Anne Marie wound up standing in the aisle, just as she feared. She stood between a solid German man with a mustache and a young Italian man who was listening to his Walkman. With her suitcase at her feet, her hand wrapped around the strap hanging from the ceiling, she felt the bus lurch, and they were on their way.

The bus rumbled onto the coast highway and hugged the first curve, only inches from the cliff that dropped five hundred feet straight down to the sapphire-blue sea that sparkled below. She gasped and gripped the strap so tightly her knuckles turned white. She told herself no bus had ever gone over the side and crashed on the rocks before. But there was a first time for everything. She could just see the front page of the *Oakville Times*:

ANNE MARIE JACKSON'S VACATION
ENDS IN DISASTER

"Just like her marriage," the gossips would say.

EX-HUSBAND ON HONEYMOON WITH NEW WIFE

The bus went around another bend. While others brought out their cameras and leaned out the windows taking pictures, Anne Marie was too terrified to look. Her heart pounded. She pictured the tires exploding; she imagined the expression on the driver's face changing from calm assurance to the terrified realization that the unthinkable had happened. Maybe it was his first trip on this road. Maybe he was still a trainee, unused to the curves and bends in the road.

Then the bus would go tumbling over and over until it crashed on the rocks below. She could almost hear the screams of her fellow passengers. Screams that would blend with the cries of the gulls, which would pick their bones clean as their bodies lay broken and bruised on the sand. Her own throat was too dry to scream, her palm was so sticky it stuck to the strap above her head.

Anne Marie turned her head, only to see that the bus was so close to an oncoming car they were certain to scrape sides. By some miracle, the driver avoided both going over the cliff and taking the paint off the Fiat. This kind of close call didn't happen just once but about twenty-five times during the next hour, always accompanied by honking horns and shaking fists. She resolutely stared straight ahead at the back of the bus driver's head, channeling her thoughts on something more pleasant. On Giovanni.

If he was surprised that she was finally coming to Italy to see him, he didn't say so in the brief note she'd received the day she was leaving. He'd just suggested they meet at a hotel in San Gervase today, which had caused her to change her plan of spending her first night in Rome.

If he was afraid she'd expect him to be her tour guide, the way he'd promised so long ago, he didn't have to worry. She had no such unrealistic expectations. She was a grown-up, divorced woman now, on her own. She'd gotten herself this far; she could get herself around Italy, too.

She didn't know if Giovanni remembered the way she'd clung to every word he said about Italy when he was an exchange student back in high school. He wouldn't know that she'd kept every postcard he'd sent afterward. Then his cards became fewer and farther between. And Anne Marie went off to college and got married.

But finally, she was here to do what he'd told her to do: let Italy soak into her skin like the sun. She wanted to see it all—the canals in Venice, the Colosseum in Rome, Michelangelo's statue of David in Florence. But first she had a date to meet him. After fantasizing about Giovanni off and on for some twenty years, it was time to put the dreams to rest and get on with her life. But if by chance dreams did come true . . . well, it couldn't happen at a better time.

As they approached San Gervase, Anne Marie craned her neck to the right for a quick look out the window. It was everything she'd imagined: a picture-perfect town squashed into a ravine with shops and whitewashed villas perched on the cliffs. Scarlet bougainvillea tumbled over balconies and climbed stone walls, and wild poppies covered the ground. There was a small sand beach below, and, best of all, there was the sea, sparkling in the sun, cool and inviting, impossibly blue.

Anne Marie stumbled off the bus, grateful to be on firm ground at last. She rolled her suitcase behind her down narrow, winding streets, delighting in the scent of jasmine and mint and lemons, of lemon candy and lemon granita.

On her way down the street, she accepted a free sample of *limoncello* in a small paper cup, the local lemon liqueur that was so strong it burned her throat. Her stomach was doing flip-flops at the thought of meeting Giovanni.

What if he didn't recognize her after all this time? What if she didn't recognize him? Maybe they'd just have coffee, and she'd give him the high school yearbook he'd left behind when he returned to Italy, and that would be it. She wasn't naive enough to think he'd throw his arms around her and confess he'd always been in love with her, that he'd never forgotten her and had been waiting for her all these years.

But if he *did* do that and say that, they'd go up to her hotel room overlooking the Mediterranean, and, with the air filled with the scents of wild herbs and flowering vines from the hillside below, and the sea breeze blowing in the window cooling their overheated bodies, he'd tell her that he'd never forgotten her, that he'd never been able to love anyone else.

He was so strong he'd literally sweep her off her feet. When they took their clothes off, she'd blush as he told her that for a forty-one-year-old woman she looked good—no, great. He'd fondle her breasts that were still firm, caress her still-flat stomach, admire her hips that were generous but not too wide. And he . . . he'd look like the statue of David on the postcard he'd sent her long ago. Her skin tingled just thinking about it.

Her skin tingled, and perspiration trickled annoyingly between her breasts. Her long hair lay heavy and damp on the back of her neck. She had to get it cut, she suddenly resolved. Right now, even if she was late for their meeting. See? She was already beginning to adopt an Italian attitude: if she was late, he'd wait for her.

Miraculously, she came to a cool, dark shop with a sign on the door—*Salone de Bellezza*. When she went inside, the smell of shampoo and hair spray hung in the air. A woman in a blue apron motioned for her to take a seat. Anne Marie nodded and, while she was waiting, thumbed through an old fashion magazine with a picture of a Sophia Loren look-alike. The model's hair was reddish brown, cut in layers that brushed her high cheekbones.

"Like that," she told the stylist, surrendering herself into the woman's hands.

And what hands they were. Anne Marie rested her head against the edge of the sink while those hands rubbed, massaged, sprayed hot water, then rinsed with cool water. She gave a shiver of pleasure as the hands worked in shampoo and conditioner and something else that exuded the essence of lavender and mint.

She forgot her worries about losing her husband and finding Giovanni. She forgot she was on a schedule and just let herself float away on a cloud of fragrance and sensual pleasure. She'd never known how sensitive her head was until this woman took charge, with her magic hands and potions.

Every bone in her body had turned to jelly; every remnant of the tension of the last twenty-four hours melted away. Anne Marie closed her eyes while the hands cut and shaped and blew her hair dry and then sprayed it.

"*Prego, signora.*" The stylist lifted the smock off, and Anne Marie opened her eyes at last.

She blinked at her reflection in the mirror. Her hair was no longer dull brown with streaks of gray. It was the color of the hair in the magazine. It brushed against her cheekbones, making them look higher, giving her an exotic look she'd never had before. They'd misunderstood; she'd only wanted it cut! But it did look wonderful. The entire staff of three women appeared behind her, beaming at her reflection with pride. They murmured things like "*bella,*" and "*graziosa.*" What could she say? She smiled and thanked them warmly.

She paid a ridiculously small amount for such a total transformation and walked out into the afternoon sunlight, feeling its heat on her bare neck. She felt naked; she'd had long hair forever. But she also felt lighter, and there was a bounce in her step as she headed for her hotel.

If only Evie could see her now! "You have the perfect excuse for skipping Dan's wedding," Evie had said. "You're no longer the pathetic ex-wife; you are a woman on a romantic tryst to meet her lover. Out of all the girls in our class who were in love with him, he chose you. He heard about the divorce. Now he wants you. He even sent you a ticket—first class."

"Who's going to believe that?" Anne Marie scoffed, shaking her head.

"Okay," Evie conceded. "Business class."

So she'd borrowed the money, packed, and left. Truthfully, she would have gone steerage class on the first boat; she would have mortgaged the house. Anything to escape the wedding of the year, when Dan married his dental hygienist with the perfect teeth and the perfect size eight figure. Since the divorce was so "amicable," the whole town expected good old Anne Marie to show up with a smile on her face and a gift under her arm. Hah!

Instead, she was on her way to a rendezvous.

But what if Giovanni had changed? What if he weighed three hundred pounds? What if he brought a wife and five children to meet her? Or what if he was single and wanted to marry her so he could get a green card? What if he wore his shirt unbuttoned to the navel and had four gold chains around his neck? She'd find out very soon; it was almost two-thirty.

Anne Marie found a taxi on the main street, across from the small sandy beach with bright blue and white beach umbrellas. As the well-aged Fiat with an equally well-aged driver made its way up into the hills above the town, her ears popped and she felt dizzy.

Finally, they pulled into the circular driveway of the four-star Hotel Athena on the edge of the cliff. When she got out of the taxi, Anne Marie's knees buckled. Nerves? Altitude? The driver set her bag at the hotel's open glass doors. She held out a handful

of euros, and he carefully picked out what she
hoped was the right amount.

For a long moment after the taxi had pulled away,
she stood alone in the quiet tiled driveway, taking
slow, deep breaths until the world finally stopped
spinning around.

There were no cars parked in the driveway.
Through the open doors she peered into the cool,
elegant lobby. There was no one there. No dashing
Italian with a sexy grin. She reminded herself he
was Italian and he'd be late.

Suddenly, she was aware she was *not* alone. The
sensitive skin on the back of her neck felt as if
someone had brushed it with a feather; she felt
someone's eyes on her. She whirled around.

There he was, leaning against the brick wall that
separated the street from the driveway. Tall, lean,
and muscular, he was wearing wrap-around sunglasses, black jeans, and a blue shirt. It was not
unbuttoned to the navel. He wore no gold chains.
He was taller than she remembered. Harder, older.
Well, what did she expect? She hadn't seen him in
more than twenty years.

She didn't realize she was holding her breath
until she exhaled.

"Giovanni?" she said, walking slowly toward him.

He took off his sunglasses. There was a long
silence. "No," he said.

His gaze locked with hers. Her bare arms were
covered with goose bumps. Though the air was
warm, a chill ran up her spine. Of course it wasn't

Giovanni. This man's eyes were not black, they were a light brown or . . . green or something. She couldn't tell without getting closer, and something warned her about getting closer, even as she felt an odd pull toward him. His face was all angles, with enough character lines to be interesting and squint marks at the corners of his eyes that showed how much time he'd spent in the Mediterranean sun. She stood rooted to the spot, while doves nesting in the cliffs above swooped and twittered.

She had to say something or move or walk away. Anything to break this spell he'd cast over her. What must he think of her, standing there staring? An American woman desperately looking for an Italian lover to make her vacation fantasies come true? How could he know how she'd been looking forward to this moment for the past twenty-three years but that he wasn't the one she'd been waiting for?

Too bad, a little voice inside her said.

"Welcome to San Gervase," he said in Italian-accented English that made every word sound like a caress.

"Thank you," she managed. "Are you . . . ?" He must be somebody, something. Chamber of Commerce? Bureau of Tourism?

"No," he said again.

Okay. It was time to stop staring. She gave him a brief smile, turned around, and tripped on a crack in the tile as she crossed the driveway. Flushed, she told herself she wasn't overly excited or nervous, just because a sexy Italian man had looked at her with interest and spoken to her. She'd been in this country for only a day and already knew Italian men were like that. It didn't mean anything.

She picked up her suitcase and looked over her shoulder before she carried it inside. Just one more look, to make sure he wasn't a figment of her over-active imagination.

The man was still standing there, draped against the brick wall as if he were part of the scenery. Like an extra in an Italian movie, the quintessential Italian stud, hired to give the place ambience or give tourists a photo opportunity.

Inside the lobby Anne Marie filled out the registration forms, handed over her passport, and asked the clerk if anyone had asked for her. He shook his head and summoned a boy to carry her bag up to her room for her. Before she followed to the elevator, she took one more peek out the front door. He was still there. She turned quickly, as if she hadn't seen him, but her heart was racing. He'd been staring at her.

At the door to her room, she gave the boy a tip. By the look on his face and his exuberant *"Grazie,"* she must have given him too much.

She kicked off her sandals and opened the doors to the balcony . . . and her mouth fell open. There it was. Everything she'd dreamed of, everything she'd imagined. The bougainvillea tumbling over the hillside, the red roofs of the houses that clung precariously to the cliffs, the sun glinting on the dazzling blue-green sea below.

She gripped the edge of the railing and looked down at the turquoise swimming pool three stories directly beneath her, surrounded by seminaked bronzed bodies. She breathed in the perfumed air, felt the sea breeze on her face, the cool tiles under her bare feet.

As pleasant as the room was, with its white-washed walls and spare, elegant furniture, she had to go downstairs. She had to be ready to greet Giovanni. She changed into a flowered cotton calf-length skirt and a black tank top Evie had assured her looked youthful but not desperately so and gave herself a critical look in the mirror. She was afraid Giovanni wouldn't recognize her, since she barely recognized herself.

There was no more time to dwell on her appearance. She went back to the lobby. He was an hour late, which was nothing by Giovanni time. He'd always been late for class, and the teachers just shook their heads. After all, he was Italian, he was Giovanni—charming, easy, lovable, and their star soccer player. She glanced out the front entrance. The man was still there. Same pose, sunglasses back in place. Damn. What was he waiting for? Who was he waiting for? Whoever it was, it wasn't her.

She chose a comfortable rattan chair in the corner of the lobby, where she could see the entrance but not the man outside. That didn't stop her from thinking about him, from wondering what he was doing there and what color his eyes really were.

She opened a guidebook called *Archeological Sites of Italy* and tried to read about the places she planned to go. An hour later, she had read only one page. Her eyelids were heavy, closing against her will. It must be about midnight, California time. Every time the phone rang at the desk, her eyes flew open, and she looked up expectantly, but the clerk never looked her way. Another hour after that, she closed her guidebook with a loud snap. It was one thing to operate on Italian time; it was quite another to make her come all this way and not show up at all.

She yawned and stood up as the man who was not Giovanni sauntered into the lobby. Was that a coincidence, or had he been waiting for her? She wiped her damp palms against her skirt.

"You are waiting for someone, for this Giovanni?" he asked. It was uncanny how much like Giovanni he sounded.

"Yes, why?"

He flipped his cell phone closed and put it in his pocket. "He won't be coming today."

She stepped back, startled and annoyed. "How do you know?"

"It's obvious: it's now too late. But I'm a tour guide. I can show you around, wherever you want to go. It will be my pleasure."

"Thank you, but . . . just because he's late doesn't mean he isn't coming at all." Even if Giovanni didn't show up, she would manage on her own. She hadn't come all this way to be taken in by a tour guide, if that's really what the man was. For all she knew, he was a gigolo. She blinked back tears of disappointment and fatigue.

His eyes widened at the sight of her tears. Automatically, he handed her a handkerchief from his pocket.

She took it automatically and wished she hadn't. "If Gio . . . my friend wasn't going to meet me, he would call me or leave a message. So, thank you for the offer, but I don't need a guide."

Giovanni would surely show up, at least to pick up his yearbook. In his note, he'd seemed pleased and touched that she was bringing it.

"What will you do now?" the man asked.

Anne Marie frowned. "Why do you want to know? What do you want?" Her voice rose, and she glanced pointedly at the clerk behind the desk, wondering if she should complain that she was being harassed. The desk clerk glanced up and then back down at his desk. He couldn't have been less interested. She took a deep breath and looked the stranger in the eye. "Who are you?" she asked.

"Marco," the man said. "Marco Moretti."

He glanced down at the book in her hand. "Are you interested in archeology?"

"Yes."

"Don't miss the Greek temples at Paestum."

"I won't." She didn't know how to end this awkward conversation. *Thank you* didn't seem quite appropriate. How about *good-bye? Arrivederci?* She understood *ciao* was too familiar unless an Italian said it first.

So she turned without saying anything and went to the desk to collect her key. The clerk handed it to her, along with a large, square white envelope. Where had that come from? No one had come through the lobby since she'd been there. She shot the clerk an inquisitive glance, but he gave her a blank look. She felt Marco Moretti's eyes on her back and slipped the envelope between the pages of her guidebook.

"Anna Maria?" Marco said.

She turned. The way he said her name sent shivers up her spine, reminding her of Italian lessons and the romantic sound of the overture to *La Bohème* she used to play over and over after Giovanni left and went back to Italy. But how did he know her name? Maybe from the hotel clerk?

"When you visit the ruins," he said, "you will surely need a guide. Someone who speaks English."

"I have a book," she said, and held it up. The envelope slipped out onto the polished marble floor. Before she could bend down, Marco had retrieved it and handed it to her with narrowed eyes. His fingers brushed hers, and she felt an electric shock zing through her body. She bit her lip to keep from gasping. He was so close she could see that his eyes were a light brown flecked with green.

She stepped back. She'd read somewhere that southern Europeans had a different concept of personal space, and this man surely did. He was too close. Much too close. Even in this cool lobby, she could feel the heat from his body. She stepped back again until she bumped into the front desk.

Marco was observing her as intently as she was him, and she felt like a rabbit cornered by a wolf. His gaze dropped to the envelope with her name scrawled on it, and she held it tightly, half afraid he might try to take it from her. But why? What an odd thought.

"The book is not enough," he said. "If you decide to go to Paestum, and you must go if you have come this far, you will need someone to explain the story behind the history, the art, and the architecture. I know things that are not in the book."

I'll bet you do. He was definitely the kind of man mothers warned their daughters about. How many women had he given personal tours to?

She had an uncontrollable desire to test him. "Such as?"

He stared at her.

"You said you know things that are not in the book." She held it up. "What are they?"

He hesitated only a moment, his eyes gleaming. "Such as which are the real Greek paintings in the museum and which are the Roman copies. Unless one is an expert, one can't tell."

"And you are an expert?"

"In some things. I am Italian." He shrugged, as if that explained everything.

She didn't want this very attractive man shadowing her around the museum, leaning over her shoulder, his sexy voice in her ear, explaining the paintings. That's what Giovanni was going to do. That's what he'd promised to do, so long ago back in California.

She gave Marco a brief, polite smile. "I'm sure you're a wonderful guide."

A hint of a smile touched his lips. "Are you?" he asked.

She blushed. She was just trying to be polite.

"If I decide to hire a guide, I'll keep you in mind."

How was she going to get him *out* of her mind? He was attractive in a rugged way, with a warm, deep voice that made her skin tingle all over. He had an air of mystery about him that was partly worrisome and partly intriguing. If only Giovanni would walk in now, it would solve all her problems. This guy could very well be some kind of con man. Giovanni would say a few choice words in Italian, the kind in the chapter on Elementary Cursing, and the man would disappear as fast as he'd appeared.

"I'm not talking about money," he said, looking offended. "I would take you because I love the temples. I want to share what I know, and you and I have much in common."

"What is that?" she asked skeptically.

"A love of the ancient world. An interest in antiquity."

"Yes, well, Giovanni loves them, too, and I can't make any plans until I see him. He's the one who told me about the temples and the statues and . . . and . . ." And the music and the paintings and so much more.

"A shame he hasn't shown up. Do you know him well?"

"Yes, but it was a long time ago. He was an exchange student at my high school, the star of our soccer team," Anne Marie said. "And he made the honor roll. Everyone admired him."

"And the girls, did they all fall in love with him there?" he asked with a slight smile.

Anne Marie felt heat rush to her face again. "I suppose some did. He made the other boys seem so young and so immature."

"Did he," Marco said, his voice flat.

She nodded, then realized she'd said far more than she intended. Maybe it was because she'd been traveling alone with no one to talk to; suddenly, her brain and her mouth were working overtime. "Well, thanks," she said, and turned and headed for the stairs.

Instead of fading away out the door, Marco was right behind her, his footsteps practically on her heels. Her heart pounded. What did he want with her? The letter? Her money? Her forty-something body? Not likely. Whatever it was, she was not giving it to him. Not without a struggle.

At the top of the landing she whirled around and faced him head-on. "What do you want?" she demanded.

Chapter 2

"To give you my card, in case you change your mind," he said calmly, handing her an official-looking business card. He paused. "What do *you* want?"

"I just want to find my friend, and I want to see Italy," she blurted. As if it was any of his business. He had no right to ask her any more questions, and she had no obligation to answer them. She'd done it out of habit; she was a librarian. It was her job to answer questions and to give out information, no matter who wanted it.

"I can help you," he offered again. "At least, the part about seeing Italy."

"Yes, I understand that, and I appreciate it. But I prefer to wait for my friend," she said firmly. How many times did she have to say it? "I'm sure he'll turn up sooner or later."

She didn't want a guide. She didn't need a guide. And if she got one, it would not be some sexy male who made her feel shaky and breathless just by looking at her. It would be a bilingual older lady or a white-haired gentleman with courtly manners who had no effect on her blood pressure.

"And if he doesn't come at all?" he asked.

"Then I'll see the rest of Italy by myself." Brave words, but she knew it would be so much better with Giovanni, who would translate, take her off the beaten path, introduce her to the natives.

"There are places that aren't safe, not for a woman alone," he said.

"I know. I'll be careful. You don't need to be concerned for me."

He shrugged. "Someone needs to, if not this Giovanni. He doesn't show up and leaves you alone, an American woman. It is unforgivable." He looked her over appreciatively, his gaze lingering on her breasts, her hips, and down her legs. Her skin felt singed where his gaze had lingered.

Ridiculous. She was being overly sensitive, and he was just being Italian. She was not the kind of woman men lusted after. After all, to him she looked totally wholesome, completely, boringly . . . American.

Compared with the Italian women, she looked hopelessly dowdy in her slightly baggy, wrinkle-proof travel clothes. She'd seen the dresses in the shops and the women on the street. She knew how much attention they paid to their appearance. She should have had a manicure, at least. She should have had a massage and a pedicure. She should have bought a dress at one of the boutiques. Then she wouldn't stand out like this.

Then he wouldn't look at her like . . . like . . . whatever he was looking at her like. Her skin was hot, then cold. She wished he'd go away. She knew what he must be thinking: no style, no panache, no flair. She gripped the guidebook in her hand.

"What will you do now?" he asked.

"I don't know exactly," she said. "Just enjoy Italy," she added quickly to sound more decisive and not like a woman who'd been stood up. She was beginning to doubt that Marco was a tour guide at all. A tour guide wouldn't ask personal questions. A tour guide worth his salt would have groups of tourists booked up to take around. He wouldn't have to hustle individuals in front of fancy hotels. Would he? "Good-bye," she said firmly.

This time, she ran up to the third floor, not caring if she looked like a scared rabbit. She jerked her door open and locked it behind her, then stood leaning against the door, panting, her heart pounding. She pressed her ear against the door, but there was no sound. He hadn't followed her.

Of course he hadn't. He meant no harm. It was just a misunderstanding, only a chance meeting. She'd just imagined his interest in the envelope.

Really, why should he care? Whoever it was from, it was none of his business.

Outside on her balcony, she ripped open the envelope and read the message inside.

Cara Anna Maria,

I am sorry to miss you today. So many things happen and I have much to tell you. First, trust no one, except me. This is Italy. Things are not what they seem. People are not who they say they are. Leave your hotel tomorrow and come to Paestum alone. I make a reservation for you at the agriturismo *estate there. Very comfortable. Very natural. Horses, buffalos, pool, and food. Come alone tomorrow night at 10:00 to the Temple of Ceres at the ruins. Not to fear— the moon is bright and the nights are long. Remember . . . alone.*

Giovanni

Alone. Alone with Giovanni for a tryst in the moonlight and the ruins. How romantic, and how Giovanni! Surely a married man wouldn't have sent such a message, would he? She sank into one of the lounge chairs on her balcony and reread the note. *Not to fear.* Then why all the mystery? Why stand her up?

Well, whatever problems Giovanni had were not her concern. She could only assume he was trying to make time for her, and for that she was grateful. She'd come to Italy for a change from the predictable existence she'd been living for the past twenty-odd years. What more could she want than a tryst with her first high school crush in the moonlight in the shadow of ancient ruins?

But this was Giovanni's last chance. If he didn't show, she was getting back on the bus to Sorrento, on the left-hand side of the bus, then taking the train back to Rome. There she'd see all the sites on her long list, visit Evie's cousin Misty, who was supposed to meet her at the airport if her flight hadn't been changed, deliver the box of Misty's favorite American candy from Evie, and just enjoy herself.

With a shiver of anticipation, she decided to go to the pool. Swimming was one sure way to stay awake, and her new black swimsuit was perfect for a forty-one-year-old woman in reasonably good shape. It was also practical, the way it dried quickly and folded up into a small plastic bag. Attractive, even, with the flattering deep V neck and a little skirt that covered her hips. But when she got to the pool, she realized it was far from sexy. Her suit looked like something somebody's grandmother would wear, compared with the skimpy suits worn by the other women at the pool, even those older and fatter than her.

But as she swam back and forth across the pool, the tension flowed out of Anne Marie's body the way the water in the pool sloshed over the sides. When she got out, she shook the water off her short hair, shocked all over again at how light-headed she felt. Then she lay down on a thick-cushioned chaise and let the afternoon sun warm her pale skin.

Marco used his pass key to get into her room. He wasn't surprised very often, but this Anna Maria wasn't at all what he'd expected. He wondered how she'd gotten recruited and what she was getting out of it. He had to give them credit for choosing her. She looked so innocent and unsuspecting; she would have fooled anybody. But he saw past the wide eyes and the tourist disguise. He'd almost missed her at first; the photo he got showed long hair. Very clever, cutting it before she arrived. But he'd recognized the big blue eyes.

Yes, he could spot an operative with no trouble. And this one had walked right up to him, unaware that he'd been fooled once and wouldn't be fooled again. His reputation was on the line. He'd promised to bring Giovanni in, and after two years and ten months of hunting the man down, he was close to the biggest victory of his career. He could feel it, smell it, taste it. It was the taste of vengeance, and it was sweet. Was he motivated to put the bastard away for a long time because of what he'd done to his sister or their long rivalry?

Of course not. It was a job. Giovanni was a crook. That's all there was to it. Just a job. A job that was the most important one of his career, because if he failed, the syndicate would lose faith in his agency. His aging boss might lose his job and his pension right before retirement.

He glanced down at the pool to make sure she was still there. Yes, that was her, the only pale body in sight, stretched out on a white chaise and covered with a modest black swimming suit that made him wonder what was beneath.

He didn't know why he'd thought she was innocent. Maybe it was her fair skin, like the alabaster statue of Venus in the museum. Maybe under that suit was a body that would tempt the saints. And he was no saint; the women in his past would testify to that.

He stood at the edge of the double doors to the balcony, forgetting he was in a hurry. The near-naked, surgically enhanced, overdone bodies in string bikinis didn't interest him. Just her. He frowned. Why was that? Because the more her suit covered up, the more he wanted to see?

No, it was because she was essential in tracking down Giovanni. Nothing more. Not because he felt so much as a twinge of conscience, knowing he was going to use her. And certainly not because he felt guilty. Marco Moretti, guilty? Not a chance.

Did it have anything to do with her long legs, the tears that had welled up in her big blue eyes, or the skin he wanted to touch, to see if it felt as soft as it looked? If it did, he was losing it, losing his cool just when he needed it the most.

He turned abruptly and found her purse hidden at the bottom of her suitcase. He found nothing of interest in it—just her airline tickets, her passport with a very unflattering picture of her, and her wallet with a photograph of her with her arm around a young man who looked very much like her. He studied it for a brief moment. It was probably her son, though she looked too young to have one that old. He went through the rest of the suitcase in seconds, sifting through her underclothes and finding nothing incriminating. And nothing remotely sexy, just the most sensible all-cotton panties and bras he'd ever seen—and he'd seen quite a few. No thongs or bikinis here, no lace or silk. All clean and wholesome, but, for some reason, her clothes came across as innocent and sexy at the same time. Just like her.

Other than clothes, there was a book with pictures of adolescents staring earnestly at the camera. *Cougars High School Yearbook*. Marco ran practiced fingers over the cover and the binding and detected nothing hidden there. Then he flipped through it and looked for her, but there was only one Jackson, a boy named Dan. He took more time than he should to go through the pages until he found an Anne Marie Rasmussen. She looked nothing like this woman, but who else could it be? Underneath the photograph, it said:

Honor Society, International Club, Volleyball.
Prediction: First woman to land on Mars.
Dream: To own her own bookstore.

He shook his head. She should have followed that dream. What had happened instead? He didn't pretend to understand the criminal mind, despite the training he'd received. He understood greed and hunger and revenge, all common motives. But this woman was not a common criminal. He knew women, and he knew there was nothing common about this one.

Next, he found Giovanni's picture, the face of his nemesis smiling from the page of the book, his dark eyes concealing secrets, his charm hiding the greed and ambition that were to be his downfall. That *must* be his downfall, if there was any justice in this world. Soccer star, artist, charming rogue. Yes, he was all of those. He could have been anything, but he'd chosen to follow in his family's tradition. And that was his mistake.

Marco would see to it that Giovanni would make one final mistake. Today, tomorrow, or next week, he now had the means to make it happen. The woman had what Giovanni wanted, and Marco had her—and he wasn't going to let her go until he'd caught Giovanni receiving one spectacular stolen diamond and put him behind bars.

Marco slammed the book shut, replaced it, and checked under the mattress and in the closet. The closet was empty, and so were the dresser drawers. It *had* to be there. Where was the dazzling gem that was so famous it was once displayed in a museum? He expertly tapped the suitcase with his knuckles to see if it had a false bottom. Nothing.

Next, he went through her tote bag. In it were two guidebooks on Italy, a diary, a paperback novel, and a box of elaborately decorated chocolates visible through the cellophane wrapper. The note taped to the box read: "For my homesick cousin Misty. Enjoy. Love, Evie." He had no idea why women got so homesick for a certain candy that they had to import it. His grandmother sent his sister boxes of marzipan from a certain candy shop in town. Surely, that was proof Isabella was not cut out for an ascetic life, eating bread and thin soup behind cloistered walls. But that was none of his business, he reminded himself.

In the bathroom, he went through Anna Maria's cosmetics, checking everything, even squeezing the American toothpaste and twisting her lipstick tube. Nothing.

The envelope was on the nightstand next to the bed. He read the note quickly and nodded to himself. Paestum was the perfect place for a handoff. Did Giovanni have any feelings for this woman? Or was he using her as he'd used so many other women for his own ends and to throw Marco off the track?

He heard footsteps in the hall, and he froze. They came closer, and the key turned in the lock. Four giant steps, and he reached the balcony seconds before the door opened and she came in. *Idiot!* Now his body was plastered against the outside wall on the balcony, where he could be seen easily from the pool. Marco forced himself to breathe slowly, praying she wouldn't come out there. If she did, what could he say? Marco was checking for termites, bringing extra towels, fixing the plumbing?

He could hear her inside the room, walking around on bare feet and opening drawers. His mind was racing, his body stiff. Then he heard water running in the bathroom. A shower—he was in luck! He peered around the corner of the doorway and saw her through the open bathroom door, bent over to pick something up from the floor. He had a great view of her bare backside and rounded hips. He paused and looked . . . and looked. *Idiot!* He made a silent run for it, slipping on the wet floor where she'd dripped water from her suit.

He cursed under his breath, opened the door, then went out into the hall and closed the door softly behind him. He was breathing hard. Whether from the close call or the view of the sweetest ass he'd seen in a long time, he didn't know. Maybe both—he hadn't seen many bare asses since he'd sworn off getting involved with women.

He walked down the stairs casually and confidently and stopped by the front desk.

"Where did the message for the American come from?" he asked.

The clerk shrugged.

Marco pulled out his ID card.

The clerk glared at him. Nobody wanted the government meddling in their business.

"I don't know. There was a call. They read the message. I wrote it down."

"A local call?" Marco asked.

The man didn't know.

"I want to know when she leaves the hotel and

where she's going," Marco said, handing the clerk his card with his cell phone number.

"How should I know where she's going?" the clerk asked sullenly.

"She's a tourist. You could suggest a restaurant, offer to give directions."

"What am I? The tourist information bureau?"

Marco sighed and went outside to smoke a cigarette, but before he could light up, his phone rang.

"*Pronto*, Marco. What about tonight? When do you pick me up?"

Damn. He'd forgotten all about Adrianna, but she hadn't forgotten about him. The minute she heard he was back in town, she'd been after him to spend time with her. He'd finally given in and told her he'd meet her for dinner. "I told you not to call me on my cell phone. It's for business."

"Business, *pfah*. Other policemen don't have such business."

"I do. I'm sorry, but I have to cancel our dinner tonight. I have work to do."

"What work? I don't believe you. What kind of a policeman has no days off, is always working?" He could picture her full lips in a pout. "Where are you?"

"Working." No one knew that he hadn't been a simple *agente di polizia* for years. Not since he was assigned to the Guardia Financia e Straniero, who were working with the South African diamond syndicate to put a stop to illegal diamond trading between the United States and Italy.

He couldn't even tell his grandmother, who would consider it her right to brag about him to her friends.

"My grandson is no longer directing traffic on the Coast Highway or arresting petty thieves," she'd tell them. "He's too good for that, too smart. He's chasing one of the country's biggest jewel thieves. When he cracks this case, he will be famous. His name will be in all the papers. And my granddaughter will finally understand why we broke her engagement."

Word would instantly spread through town, and he'd be useless in his job. It would be impossible to catch Giovanni. The bureaucrats who oversaw his agency would lose confidence in him and Silvestro, his boss. Their office would be closed, and they'd both be out of a job.

"You can't work tonight," Adrianna said. "You promised me dinner tonight. I'll meet you. Where?"

Marco shook his head. She reminded him of one of those lampreys that clung to the rocks at the sea, impossible to pry off. "All right, the Vista dei Mare at eight o'clock."

"Vista dei Mare? That's so far. Can't you come to town?"

"No." He hoped she'd decline. It would make his life easier, he had no time for women now. Maybe he would after he'd brought Giovanni in, but maybe not. Women had messed up his life more than once. Women distracted him, and he was prone to distractions anyway. This time, he would concentrate. This time, he would win.

"All *right*," she said. "I'll be there." If she could have slammed the phone down, she would have, but she was using her cell phone.

Marco went back into the hotel and spoke to the clerk again. This time, he gave him some money along with his instructions. He was barely out the front door to the patio when his phone rang again.

"Nonna, what is it? I told you not to call me on my cell phone." Why had he ever given anyone this number?

"I tried your other number, but you are never home, if you call your empty house a home. The shutters are closed, and the tomatoes in your garden are withering on the vine. Now, don't forget dinner tonight," his grandmother said. "I am cooking the *puttanesca* sauce right now, your favorite. With tomatoes from my garden."

"*Ai, dio mio,*" he said under his breath. "Sorry, Nonna, I can't make it tonight."

"But it's my birthday," she said.

He grinned. "No, it isn't. That's what you always say. Your birthday is in April."

"What kind of a grandson doesn't call his grandmother to wish her happy birthday?" she said as if he hadn't spoken.

"Happy birthday," he said.

"Antonio Ponti gave his grandmother a new TV for her birthday, with a remote control."

"Is that what you want?"

"I want my grandson to call me once in a while. Now that you're back in town, I want you to come

for dinner when I make your favorite dish. Is that
asking too much?"

"No, Nonna. I'll come. But I can't come tonight."

"You have a date, yes? You can bring her to meet
me."

"You wouldn't like her."

"How do you know? Did you hear Antonio is getting married next year to Bianca Camerata?"

"In bocca al lupo," he muttered. *Into the mouth
of the wolf. Good luck.*

"What?"

"I wish him the best."

"Better hurry, or all the good women will be
taken," she warned. "You're not getting any
younger."

Marco leaned against the brick wall of the patio
and closed his eyes. She didn't need to remind him
that he was getting too old to play games, to chase
thieves or women. After he caught Giovanni, he'd
retire from this kind of work and take a desk job
with the agency.

"I'm not getting married," he said. "It's too late.
I'm too old. And all the good women *are* taken."

"Non far niente," she said, dismissing this excuse.
"I'll find you someone, and you can settle down
here in town where you belong. Since when is forty
too old for a man? Think about me, do I die before
I become a great-grandmother?"

Neither mentioned his sister, Isabella, and the
reason she wouldn't be able to give Nonna the
much-wished-for great-grandchildren.

"I'll think about it," he said wearily.

"Don't think," she said. "Do."

He hung up with a wry smile. If she knew he was after Giovanni, she would have understood and wished him Godspeed. But he wasn't going to tell her or anyone until it was over. Until the bastard was behind bars and the diamond was back where it belonged.

Anne Marie woke up from her after-swim nap groggy and confused. Her inner clock said it was morning, but the sun was setting on the Amalfi Coast, casting a golden glow over the cliffs and turning the sea to the color of lapis lazuli. She splashed cold water on her face and got dressed in the flowered skirt and tank top she'd worn to meet Giovanni. She wasn't going to see anyone she knew tonight.

When she went downstairs to ask the desk clerk if she'd had any messages, he said no. Of course not. She had her message from Giovanni; she had her instructions. Then she consulted her phrase book and took a deep breath.

"*Conosce un buon ristorante?*" she asked, even though the man spoke perfect English. How was she going to get better if she didn't practice?

"There is the Vista dei Mare, signora," he said with an amused look. "Very good, very nice, very popular, very close. I will make a reservation. For eight."

She looked at her watch. It was only six. Of

course, Italians didn't eat until eight. "Yes. All right. Thank you."

He nodded and picked up the phone. She understood a few words, such as *ristorante, signora*. Why hadn't she studied more, studied harder? Because she never really thought she'd get to Italy. She knew Dan would never bring her here, and he never thought she'd ever get divorced. Never thought she'd have the nerve to come by herself.

But she had. She was here. The clerk caught her smiling to herself and gave her an odd look as he brought out a map.

"You are here," he said, putting one tapered finger on the map. "Restaurant is here."

It wasn't far; only about half an inch away. She folded the map and put it in her shoulder bag, thanked him, and started for the front door.

"Signora, where are you going?" he called.

She turned. "Out . . . just to look around," she said. "Why, is it dangerous?" It looked like a nice neighborhood, filled with villas on quiet streets. She'd taken all the precautions recommended by the guidebooks, such as wearing her money belt filled with traveler's checks and her passport hung around her neck under her shirt. This was hardly the slums of Naples—still, she was a stranger here; maybe he knew something she didn't.

"No, no, of course not. I was merely inquiring."

People were certainly not shy about inquiring. What were some of the questions Marco had asked? *What do you want? What will you do now? What if he doesn't come?*

"I'm going for a walk until dinner," she said.

He nodded as if that were the right answer. As she left, he was reaching for the phone again.

Her gaze swept the patio for signs of Marco. He wasn't there. She didn't know why she felt a twinge of disappointment; she certainly didn't want him harassing her anymore. He'd probably found some other American to hustle. Whatever the reason, he was gone. For good, she hoped.

There were plenty of people on the streets, none of whom tried to pick her pocket or pick her up. They were sauntering, just as she was, in the early evening dusk. At home, everyone rushed home at six o'clock. Nobody took time to sit at a café with friends, or strolled around admiring marzipan candies in the sweet shops, or bought a gelato cone and walked down the street eating it when they should be home making dinner.

She stood in front of a furniture store, wishing she could dump everything in her house, every memento of her previous life—from the Oriental carpet that had faded along with her marriage to the gold-plated mantel clock, a wedding present she'd always hated from his parents. When she got home, she'd do the whole house over Italian style, with bright Mediterranean-colored cushions, light wood and ceramics, and lots of blue and yellow tile.

Anne Marie left the shopping district, and suddenly she was in a neighborhood of older, smaller

houses, of gardens filled with flowers and rows of
beans and eggplant. She paused at a small stone
house where tomatoes grew on vines supported by
wire stands.

She could so easily imagine herself living in a
house like this. She'd be Italian, of course, and
she'd can these tomatoes for the winter ahead,
along with basil and garlic. When her husband,
who would look like Marco at the hotel this morning, came home from work, he'd call out, "Honey,
I'm home," which in Italian would be something
like *"Cara, sono a casa."* Then he'd come into the
kitchen, kiss her passionately, untie her apron, and
peel off the rest of her clothes. They'd make love
right there in the kitchen, on the warm tiled floor,
with the smell of red, ripe tomatoes in the air. He'd
confess he couldn't concentrate on his work, that
all he could think of was coming home to her.
When she reminded him of the simmering sauce on
the stove, he'd whisper in her ear that she should
live for the moment.

But she wasn't Italian, she had no husband, and
this wasn't her house.

After making sure no one was watching, she
reached over the fence to pluck a tiny red tomato,
still warm from the sun. The taste of summer itself
burst onto her tongue. So *this* was what tomatoes
were supposed to taste like. She stood for a long
moment, savoring the taste that lingered in her
mouth. That alone was worth the price of the plane
ticket. She reached for another.

Before she could pull her hand back, the front
door opened, and an old woman in a black dress
stepped out onto the porch. She had bright black
eyes and round, apple-red cheeks. She said something in Italian. She didn't sound angry. She
sounded curious.

"I . . . I'm sorry," Anne Marie said. "I just . . . your
tomatoes are delicious . . . *delizioso*." She had no
idea if that was really a word. It must have been,
because the old lady clapped her hands together
and repeated it.

"*Delizioso!*" she said. Then she waved her hand in
a sweeping gesture, as if she were royalty and Anne
Marie a peasant caught poaching. "*Prego.*" Anne
Marie thought she meant "Help yourself."

So she did. She smiled and put another tomato
in her mouth. It was wonderful. It was tart and
sweet at the same time. Along with her new Italian-
style house back home, she would have an Italian-
style garden filled with tomatoes and eggplant and
basil and lemons and olive trees. She could still can
tomatoes and make savory sauces.

"*Grazie*," Anne Marie said to the woman, who
continued to watch her with a kind of wide-eyed
amazement on her lined face.

The old woman inclined her head in a gesture
that meant "You're welcome" and "It's my pleasure"
all at once. Anne Marie left with a wave and a warm
feeling around her heart. That would never have
happened at home. It would never have happened if
she'd come to Italy with Dan. He would never have

approved of her stealing tomatoes from someone's garden.

She still had an hour before dinner. She heard church bells and decided to follow the sound. When she found the small church made of cream-colored travertine, with its twin spires and its old bell tower, there was a crowd out in front, the men in dark suits, the women in dresses and the kind of shoes Anne Marie had never worn in her life— butter-soft leather with lots of straps and impossibly high heels.

She looked down at her thick-soled Easy Spirits and vowed to buy herself a pair of Italian shoes. Even if she never wore them anywhere but in her own home, she'd remove them from their box and walk back and forth in front of the full-length mirror, admiring the way they looked, and she'd remember Italy. While she watched from across the street, a bridal couple came out the double doors of the church, and everyone clapped and oohed and aahed and threw rice at them.

The very pretty, very young bride wore a white lace dress and a veil that covered her long, dark hair. The groom was tall and thin. His black tie was askew, and he was smiling nervously. He reached for his bride's hand, and they looked at each other with such intense love Anne Marie had to turn away. It was too private a moment for an outsider to intrude on.

The church and the wedding and the bells and the organ music that flowed out the doors all combined to remind her of another wedding, across the ocean, in another time zone. With a glance at her watch, she realized that her ex-husband was getting married at that very moment to a woman a little more than half his age, who he thought would cure him of his midlife crisis. Anne Marie almost doubled up from the pain in her heart.

She hadn't thought it would bother her that much, but it did. It was not the loss of Dan; she'd come to realize that they'd grown apart years ago. Even if he changed his mind or if his fiancée walked out on him, she and her ex-husband were no longer soul mates, nor had they ever been. No, it was the loss of her marriage that hurt. Of an institution she believed in, of a dream she'd once had. It was a reminder that she'd failed at the most important thing in her life.

Did anyone in that church across the ocean wonder where she was? She hoped so. She hoped they found out, too, because she was having the time of her life. She absolutely was.

She forced her feet to move away from the church, away from the unhappy vision of another church in another town with another bride. She walked through the streets aimlessly for a while, then stopped at a small square and pulled out her map to locate the restaurant.

She soon arrived at the Vista dei Mare, pleased to see it was right where it was supposed to be, tucked away between two low-rise apartment buildings, with a small sign. When she opened the door, she smelled rich tomato sauce and olive oil simmering. She was fifteen minutes late, but they seated her right away at a small table with her back to the wall so she could look at the other customers, who were all Italian. She ordered minestrone and a pasta *arrabiata*, with no idea of what it was, and a glass of house wine. At least, that's what she hoped she'd ordered; the waiter spoke no English.

A young boy came out of the kitchen, poured her wine, and set a plate of toasted bread on her table. Then he rubbed fresh garlic on it.

This was the kind of place the guidebooks said to look for, she thought with satisfaction. Family restaurants where the locals ate. She nibbled at the bread, trying to get the image of the California wedding out of her mind. She knew how the church would look, with the plain wooden pews and the dark red carpet. She knew the flowers would smell sweet and cloying. She knew the organist would play the traditional march, and the music would float out the front doors open to the early autumn sunshine.

She knew, because that's exactly what happened when she was married there. How dare Dan have his second marriage there, too? Couldn't he have come up with something more original? All he was doing was repeating what he'd done twenty years ago. And he thought *she* was boring? He was the one who was boring! Funny she'd never seen that before. Anne Marie felt her throat clog with angry tears.

The waiter brought her a huge bowl of soup and sprinkled cheese on top of it. Steam rose from the bowl and brought the smell of broth and herbs, beans, and vegetables to her nose. She tried to concentrate on the food. On Italy, not California. She crumpled her napkin in her hand and looked around the room. She was the only one there alone. Everyone else had come with someone else. The couple in the corner, the family at the table by the door, the men at the bar. Everyone had someone. But it didn't matter. It did *not* matter.

She bit her lip to keep it from trembling. She thought about Giovanni, she thought about the Greek temples she was going to see, and she thought about her library and the patrons who would ask about her and miss her when she wasn't there. But none of those thoughts was strong enough to erase the image of the end of her marriage. It was one thing to divide the assets and sign the divorce papers. But to know that your husband was marrying someone else made it seem even more final and made her feel more alone than she ever had. Her sinuses hurt, her throat ached, and she could no longer hold back the tears. They rolled down her cheeks and into her minestrone. The waiter stopped abruptly on his way to another table with a platter of mussels in white wine sauce and stared at her.

"*Signora, cosa succede?*" he said.

She couldn't speak. She didn't know what he'd said, but even if she did, she couldn't answer. She could only shake her head. The tears continued to pour down her face and she sobbed aloud. Now other people were looking at her. The old couple who had just sat down at the next table both turned around to see what was wrong.

Oh, God, she didn't know what to do. She wanted to fall through a trapdoor and disappear. She could get up and leave, but she didn't think her legs would hold her.

The waiter disappeared into the kitchen, and the cook appeared at her table, his white apron smeared with sauce and a worried frown on his face.

"*Che cosa ha mangiato?*" he asked. He pointed to the soup. "*La minestra?*"

She looked up at him, but the concern on his face only made her cry harder. They were joined by a woman in an apron.

"*Indigestione?*" she asked.

Anne Marie shook her head.

The woman turned around and beckoned frantically. "Marco," she called to a man in the corner who was eating with a dark-haired, statuesque Italian woman in a red dress. "*Lei viene. La signora ave bisogno de traduzione en inglesi.*"

The next thing she knew, Marco and the woman who looked like an Italian movie star were standing at her table looking down at her.

"What's wrong?" he asked. "Is it the soup?"

"No, no," she said, blotting the tears on her face with her napkin. "It's fine. It's nothing."

"Nothing?" he asked, raising his eyebrows. "You have upset the whole restaurant with your crying. The cook thinks you don't like his soup. And he takes this very personally."

"I'm sorry," she said. She pushed her chair back and started to get up. "Maybe I'd better go."

"Go? You can't go now, unless you're sick."

"I'm not sick. I'm fine. I just don't want to cause any more trouble."

"Then sit down and eat your dinner. And stop crying." He handed her his handkerchief.

Anne Marie dabbed at her cheeks, then stuffed his handkerchief into her bag and looked from his stern face to the woman, who now had her arms crossed under her sizable breasts and was glaring at her.

"Thank you," she said stiffly. "I'll do that." She picked up her spoon and dipped it into the soup. She looked up. He was still standing there with the very attractive, very annoyed woman. "You can go now," she said. *Please go. Please, everyone, stop staring, and leave me alone.*

"Are you sure?" he asked.

Before Anne Marie could answer, the woman turned to Marco and began to speak loudly in Italian. Anne Marie didn't know what she was saying, she only knew the woman was angry about something. She just hoped it didn't have anything to do with her. But it must have, because the woman kept gesturing toward her and raising her voice. Marco said a few words that sounded hard and angry, and the woman slapped him across the face, spun around on the high heels of her open-toed sandals, and walked out of the restaurant, her head held high, her nose in the air.

For a moment, no one spoke. No one moved. The whole restaurant fell silent. If Anne Marie had thought such things happened often between volatile Italians, she must be mistaken. Everyone else seemed just as shocked as she was. Then, just as suddenly, the scene came to life again. The cooks returned to the kitchen, the waiter began serving food, and the customers resumed talking, laughing, and eating.

Only Marco stayed where he was, standing motionless beside her table. She looked up, her eyes dry, her self-pity forgotten. There was a red mark on his cheek, and she almost felt sorry for him, until he pulled out a chair and sat down across from her. He turned an empty wineglass right-side up and beckoned to the waiter. She put her spoon down and gazed into those green-brown eyes.

"Surely, even in Italy," she said as coolly as possible, "you are supposed to ask if you can join me."

"Would you have said yes?"

"No." How could she eat with this Italian exuding machismo across from her?

"Then why bother to ask?"

Chapter 3

The waiter brought a candle to the table, and the flickering light softened the hard planes of Marco's face. Next, he filled Marco's wineglass and set his plate of pasta in front of him. Everything was done so calmly, so smoothly, it was as if customers had shouting matches and then changed tables every night. Marco turned his attention from her to his food. He ate with such gusto he must have forgotten the violent incident with his date. Maybe they argued often, flew into rages, stormed out of restaurants, and got it out of their system.

Maybe that was a better way to deal with disagreements than years of silence, bottled-up resentments, and hard feelings until it was too late to salvage a relationship. Anne Marie stole a glance across the table, watching with admiration as he expertly twirled the pasta around his fork. But if Marco intended to eat in silence, why had he bothered to sit with her? Was it because it was improper for a woman to eat alone?

Whatever his reason, it was a relief to have the attention shift away from her, and she was almost able to forget the scene she'd made, which seemed minor compared with the one he'd made, and to eat her soup and the pasta that followed. After all, if he could do it, she could, too. But she wondered, who was the woman he was eating with? What was the argument about? Why did she leave?

Maybe Marco had broken up with her or she with him. Maybe she wanted him to give up his job and stop showing foreign women the sights of Italy and devote himself to her. With her looks, she could be a model or a movie star who needed him to be her permanent escort. Or maybe she was just an ordinary woman who was madly in love with him, and he'd cheated on her. She'd just found out tonight at dinner, which was why she'd slapped him and stormed out.

From time to time, Marco refilled Anne Marie's wineglass from the carafe on the table. From time to time, she glanced over at him. Once he caught her eye, and their glances held for a long moment. That was the time to ask the questions, but as she opened her mouth, the waiter came with some grated cheese for her pasta, and the brief moment was over.

When he finished eating, Marco leaned back in his chair and observed her carefully. "No more tears," he said with satisfaction. "No more sadness."

"No," she said, but the vision of her husband's wedding across the ocean pushed its way back into her mind, and her attempt at a smile failed miserably. He noticed.

"I know what will cheer you up," he said when she'd finished her dinner and he'd laid a pile of bills on the table. "Come with me." He took her arm, and before she could dig into her money belt and insist on paying for her own dinner, they were out on the street, his hand still wrapped tightly around her arm.

"You don't mind walking?" he asked with a glance at her low-heeled shoes. She knew what he must be thinking—so American, so sensible, so unflattering to the leg, compared with the high heels she'd been admiring on the local women. "It's not far."

"Of course not." The streets were full of people, strolling arm in arm. The *passeggiata* was the ritual evening stroll she could get used to. It was a time for Italians to see and be seen. Certainly, Marco was seen. Many people greeted him enthusiastically, hugging him, stopping to talk, and eyeing her with curiosity. But Marco didn't linger or introduce her to any of them. She didn't blame him. After all, she was just a tourist who'd be gone tomorrow. But she wondered about the several women who stopped to kiss him on the cheek and smile flirtatiously.

"We're going to the square, along with everyone else in San Gervase," he said, his hand on Anne Marie's elbow as he guided her down the narrow streets. "There's a concert tonight. You'll like it."

She liked it before they even got there. The sounds of a violin, an accordion, and the rich voice of an Italian tenor wafted through the warm night air. Anne Marie inhaled deeply, wishing she could capture the moment in her memory forever. It was just the way she'd imagined it. The only flaw in the picture was that Giovanni wasn't there to share it with her. Would he be upset when he learned a stranger was showing her his town instead of him, or would he be grateful someone else had relieved him of the obligation?

They went to a café that faced the small raised platform in the middle of the cobblestone square. Marco ordered a bottle of wine, though Anne Marie was sure she'd had plenty at dinner. He said this one was made from local grapes, and she must taste it. When it came, he filled their glasses and lifted his glass to hers.

"To your journey," he said, looking deep into her eyes. "Wherever it may lead."

She searched her mind for the appropriate response. "*Alla salute*," she said. "To your health. And to your country." She tapped her glass against his and drank some wine.

"You like it?" he asked.

"I love it. The flowers, the smells, the sights, the food, the wine . . ."

Obligingly, he refilled her glass. "What about the men?"

"The men? Well, they're fine, just a little . . . uh, over the top."

His forehead creased in a frown. "What does that mean? Is it a compliment?"

"It's just an expression," she said. "It means, oh, it means that the men are very friendly, *very* friendly. But then, I don't know any but you and Giovanni, and of course, I haven't seen him in a very long time."

"You keep in touch, you and your friend, yes?"

"Not really. Not until now. I wrote to say I was coming to Italy, and he . . . we arranged a meeting."

A small, dark-skinned woman in a long skirt and with a braid down the middle of her back came to their table, selling candy in a basket. Marco fished for some change in his pocket and gave it to her. She stood at the table, looking down at Anne Marie with her steady, black-eyed gaze, then took her hand in hers and spread her palm out flat. The woman frowned and said something in rapid Italian to Marco.

"She wants to tell your fortune," he said.

"All right, but I know what she's going to say. There's an ocean voyage in my future, I'll have a long life, and I'll meet a tall, dark stranger."

"What a cynic you are, Anna Maria," Marco said,

shaking his head sadly. "Shall I tell her to go away?"

"No, tell her to go ahead. Maybe Italian fortune-tellers are more original than the ones in my country." Besides, the woman didn't look as if she had any intention of going away, no matter what anyone said. She sat down and rubbed Anne Marie's palm with her finger, muttering to herself.

"What is it?" Anne Marie said, a little worried.

"She says you will have many surprises in your future," Marco said. "And a sea voyage, of course."

"What about the tall, dark stranger?"

"Is that what you're looking for?" Marco asked.

"No, but I'm sure that's what she's going to say."

"You're wrong," Marco said, after listening to the fortune-teller speak for a few moments. When the old woman paused, he continued his translation. "She says that the man you left behind has been deserted."

"That's not true. I didn't desert him, he deserted me. And he got married today. See? She doesn't know what she's talking about."

"I'm only repeating what she tells me," he said. "Do you want to hear it or not?"

"Go ahead, but I don't really want to hear about Dan."

"This is about you. You will find a greater love where you least expect it."

"I don't expect it at all." Anne Marie tugged at her hand, tired of the game, but the woman tightened her grasp. "I didn't come to Italy to find a

man or love. I came to see the country and
Giovanni. Why don't you ask her when I'll see him
and where he is? At least that would be useful
information."

Marco turned to the woman and said something.
Anne Marie wondered if he was really translating
her questions or the woman's answers correctly. For
all she knew, he was making the whole thing up.

"She says Giovanni will show up," he said.

"I know: 'where I least expect him.' Is that what
you were going to say?"

"Where do you expect him?" Marco asked.

Tell no one. Trust no one.

"I don't expect him until I see him."

The fortune-teller was still scowling at her hand.

"She says if you follow your heart, you will not be
lonely anymore."

"I'm not lonely now. And I intend to follow my
head, not my heart, this time."

The old woman let fly with a torrent of words,
her dark eyes focused on Anne Marie's palm.

Anne Marie sighed. In spite of herself, she was
curious. She turned her questioning gaze on Marco
and raised her eyebrows.

"She says the man you are seeking is in trouble,"
he said.

"He is?" she frowned. "What kind of trouble?"

"Big trouble."

"Then I have to find him. Maybe I can help him."

"Maybe, but you must not go alone. You must
take someone."

"Like you?" she asked dryly.

Marco shrugged. "If you like."

Anne Marie shook her head. "No," she said. She might be an innocent abroad for the first time. She might be a woman scorned and vulnerable. But she wasn't stupid. She didn't know Marco, but she knew Giovanni, and he'd told her to beware of strangers.

Why was he so anxious to take her to the ruins? He'd said it wasn't for the money. Did he know Giovanni? Did he know where he was? Did he know Giovanni wanted her to come alone? Giovanni, Marco; Marco, Giovanni. She tried to imagine how Giovanni would look now, but all she could see was Marco across the table, his handsome face impassive, his expression inscrutable.

The fortune-teller finally let her hand go and stood, then said something so distinct, in such an intense voice, Anne Marie felt the words were inscribed on her brain. Turning abruptly, the woman disappeared into the crowd.

"What did she say?" Anne Marie said.

"'*Camina chi pantofoli fino a quando non hai i scarpi*'" Marco said, scribbling the words on a napkin. "It's an old Sicilian saying. It means, walk in your . . . your . . . how do you say, slippers, until you find your boots."

Puzzled, Anne Marie looked down at her shoes. "I don't understand."

"It's hard to explain."

"Never mind. For once, I want to live in the

present, not the past or the future." She took a drink of wine. It really was very good. She'd have to buy some to take home. When she got home, she'd start giving small dinner parties for old friends, serving pasta with homemade sauce and Italian wines. Entertaining was something she hadn't done since Dan walked out, hating the thought of being a single woman surrounded by couples. But by the time she got home, she'd be a changed woman, single and proud of it, able to toss off dinner parties after work, able to sprinkle her conversation with Sicilian proverbs. She folded the napkin and tucked it in her pocket. Now she just had to find out what the proverb meant.

"Very wise," Marco said approvingly. "Italians say to live in the present is to eat the fruit when it is ripe."

"And the tomatoes," Anne Marie murmured. "I like that."

When the musicians returned to the stage after a break, the tenor's voice rose in the night air and filled her heart with such emotion Anne Marie forgot about Giovanni and her quest. She forgot to worry about tomorrow. But she didn't forget about Marco. How could she, when he was sitting in the shadows across from her, his shirt so white against his sun-darkened skin, looking so relaxed, so much at ease, like every woman's dream of an Italian lover.

"What does it mean?" she asked softly with a nod toward the singer.

"It's a love song," he said.

"But it sounds so sad," Anne Marie whispered.

"Because it is sad. He is singing of his lost love. It is spring, the saddest time of the year, when a wind has blown the blossoms from the trees just as his love has flown away. He remembers her hair, like dark clouds . . ." Marco leaned across the table and took a strand of Anne Marie's hair between his fingers. "Like yours."

She swallowed hard. It was just a song. Just a translation of a song. But Marco was real. The heat from his body, the sound of his voice, and the touch of his hand—they were real. She should stop him now, before she was lost in those dark eyes or got hypnotized by the sound of his voice, before she forgot she was following her head and not her heart. She sat there, lost in his gaze, good intentions all forgotten, while the music washed over her and filled her soul with its beauty.

"Her skin was as pale as marble," Marco said, so softly she had to lean forward to catch the words. He traced a line on the inside of her bare arm to her wrist. She shivered in the warm night air, and her heart thudded wildly. "As soft as velvet, and her lips were kissed by the morning dew."

Anne Marie knew it was pure schlock, probably invented on the spot for her benefit or used one hundred times on women more gullible than she, but she was helpless to stop reacting to it. Helpless to stop the tremors deep down inside and

the chills that went up and down her skin. She
knew what was coming next, and her lips trembled
in anticipation.

But he didn't kiss her. He merely traced the outline of her cheek with his hand. She ached with
longing for the kiss that didn't come. His knees
were pressed against hers under the table. She held
completely still, afraid to move, afraid to break the
spell.

"How does it end?" she asked in a whisper when
the last notes had faded and the listeners burst into
applause.

"I don't know," he said, staring into her eyes.
Then he shifted in his chair. "Oh, the song. It has a
happy ending. She comes back, and they ride off
into the sunset on his motorcycle. It's summer, and
the hot sun shines on them."

"Really?" Her eyes filled with tears again. For
someone who hadn't cried in months, not even
when Dan told her he was leaving, not even when
she heard about Dan's wedding, she was turning
into an emotional basket case.

He looked alarmed and stood up. "What's wrong
now? I told you it was a happy ending. Come, I'll
take you back to your hotel."

When she stood up, the whole square spun
around. She clutched the back of the wrought-iron
chair for support and looked at the empty wine bottle on the table. She must have had half of it, along
with the wine at dinner, and she wasn't used to
drinking so much. Marco's face was out of focus,

but she could tell he was worried by the lines on his face. He took her hand and drew her to his side.

"Don't worry," she said, feeling his hip press into hers. "I'm not going to cry. I'm fine." She was filled with love for everything Italian: the food, the weather, the wine and especially the men—the singer, the waiter, and Marco.

"Wait," she said, watching the crowd disperse and the musicians pack up their instruments. "I want to tell the tenor . . ." She leafed through her phrase book and headed unsteadily for the small stage with Marco following her.

The portly, dark-haired singer with the huge mustache was rolling up his sheet music.

"*Scusi, signor,*" she said. "*Lei canta molto bene.*"

He smiled and bent over to kiss her hand. His mustache tickled her sensitive skin, and she thought how romantic it all was, the song and the perfumed air and the full moon that hung over the square. If only Evie could see her now.

She felt Marco tug at her arm. She tried to shake him off but quickly realized she needed his support. She had no idea where the hotel was. She didn't remember any of the narrow dark streets they walked through. It occurred to her that Marco might be taking her somewhere else, maybe putting her aboard a ship and selling her into white slavery. After she passed out from all that wine, Marco would sling her over his shoulder and head for the docks, where he'd hustle her aboard a freighter bound for the West Indies. He'd get a few dollars for her from a stevedore, then he'd go to another fancy hotel, where he'd repeat the whole scenario. But surely they were looking for younger women for the slave trade?

Occasionally, she stumbled on a cobblestone, and she had to admit it was a good thing Marco was there to prop her up and steady her with his strong arm around her shoulders. She leaned against him and put her arm around his waist so she wouldn't fall.

A cat darted across their path, and she let out a shriek. Marco pressed her back against the cool limestone façade of a darkened apartment building and put his hand over her mouth.

"*Silenzio,*" he said. "You'll wake the neighbors."

Her eyes widened. Her heart was pounding. She was afraid. Not of waking the neighbors, not of being kissed by a stranger, but afraid he *wouldn't* kiss her. Afraid her heart would burst, it was so full, full of the night and the music and a dream come true.

When Marco took his hand away from her mouth, her lips felt cold. He braced his hands against the building, trapping her between his arms. Trusting her not to fall in a heap at his feet, trusting her to want the kiss she knew was coming. The kiss she'd somehow known was coming since she first saw him that afternoon.

He took his time about it. First, he said something like *in bocca al lupo,* and though she wanted to know what it meant, this was not the time to take out her phrase book. She didn't need a dictionary to know what the kiss would mean. It would mean nothing to him. Nothing but hello and good-bye. *Buona sera,* Ms. Jackson. *Arrivederci,* Ms. Jackson.

To her, it would mean more. Kissing a stranger would mean she was ready to take a chance, to live again, and to love again. Not him, of course. She might be a little drunk, she might be feeling jet lag and culture shock, but she wasn't crazy. Still, tonight . . . tonight she wanted him to kiss her.

When he did, she wasn't prepared for the shock waves that hit her like the waves on the Pacific shore. She wasn't prepared to feel as if the fires of Mount Etna were getting ready to explode inside her.

She kissed Marco as if she'd been waiting for this kiss for years instead of minutes. He groaned in the back of his throat and pressed his hard, hot body against hers. The fire inside her became a roaring bonfire, impossible to contain. She kissed him with passion that had been building for weeks, months, maybe years. And she blamed it all on Italy.

No one had ever told her she was any good at kissing, but she knew by the way Marco held her, by the words he muttered in her ear, that she was doing something right. So right she didn't want to stop. Somewhere, somehow, she was kissing and being kissed as she'd never been before. When she caught her breath, the whole world was spinning, and her past and the present were blending into one delirious dream.

"Giovanni," she murmured.

Marco pulled back, feeling as if someone had thrown a bucket of cold water on him from the balcony above. Anne Marie swayed against the façade of the building, her eyes closed, her swollen lips tilted in a dreamy smile. She was so beautiful in the pale moonlight it hurt to look at her. She'd just kissed him as if he was the man she'd been waiting for all her life, and then she'd called him Giovanni.

"Andiamo," he said brusquely. "Let's go."

Her eyes flew open. She looked surprised to see him. Of course she was; she thought he was Giovanni. That scum. That swine. When Marco found him, he'd drag her to the prison or to the gallows where Giovanni belonged, and he'd show her what Giovanni was, what he'd always been. A rat, as if she didn't know. And he was the fox who had devoted much of his life to chasing the rat. Was that what he wanted her to know?

Anne Marie looked at him for a long moment before she stepped forward and pointedly ignored his arm to walk by herself, though slowly and unsteadily. He kept his arms at his sides. Let her stumble, let her fall. It served her right. What was she thinking, to kiss a stranger on her first night in San Gervase? She was lucky he wasn't out to rob her or seduce her. Though she might think what he was really doing with her was worse, when she learned she was just a pawn to lure Giovanni out of hiding.

She made it to the hotel, staggering occasionally.

When she reached the open door to the lobby, her
eyes closed, and she leaned toward him and fell
into his arms like a stack of bricks. The night clerk
barely blinked an eye when Marco walked into the
lobby with Anne Marie in his arms and asked for
her key. For the third time that day, he climbed the
stairs to her room.

He set her on the huge bed with its smooth,
turned-down sheets, then took off her sturdy
American shoes and put them on the floor. He
admired her shapely bare feet and felt only a slight
pang of guilt when she moaned softly.

"You shouldn't have drunk so much, *cara mia*,"
he muttered, gazing down at her body, one arm
flung over the pillow, a strip of pale skin showing
between her tank top and her skirt. "The next man
you run into might not be as immune to your
charms as I am." Or less determined to let nothing
interfere with his goal, even a very sexy woman.

When the phone rang, Anne Marie didn't stir.
Marco hesitated only a moment before picking it up
and dragging the cord with him outside to the balcony.

"*Pronto,*" he said automatically.

"I'm calling for Anne Marie Jackson. Do I have
the right room?" a woman asked.

"Yes, but she's . . . not available to come to the
telephone." She wasn't available to do much of anything.

"Is this . . . is that you, Giovanni?" she asked.

"No," he said flatly. "It isn't."

"Oh. Well, I'll call back another time. What time is it there?"

"It's sometime after midnight," he said, wishing he'd never answered the phone.

"Oh, sorry," she said. "Could you tell her to call her friend Evie? Thank you."

He'd barely hung up when the phone rang again. Again, he answered it. This time, he was glad he did.

"Anna Maria?" a male voice said.

Giovanni! Marco gripped the receiver so tightly his knuckles turned white. "*Si,*" he said in a barely audible whisper.

"Did you get my message?" Giovanni asked.

"*Si,*" he repeated softly. He couldn't believe his luck. He was actually talking to the bastard.

"At last we will meet again," Giovanni said. "Tomorrow. I am so happy you have come to Italy."

I'll bet you are, Marco thought. *I'll bet you can hardly wait to get your "package."*

Giovanni said, "*Buona notte,*" and hung up.

A stroke of good luck, at last. The meeting was confirmed; he was so close to his goal he could taste it. What would happen to Anna Maria when he caught her and Giovanni in the act of giving and receiving the stolen spectacular yellow Bianchi diamond, missing for three months from a private collection in California? She'd be turned over to the American authorities, he imagined. It was up to them to determine whether she'd been the one to steal the gem or merely the conduit. He couldn't

imagine her breaking into a mansion in San
Francisco from the roof like a cat burglar, but anything was possible when so much money was at
stake.

All Marco wanted was to see Giovanni behind
bars, to make him pay for what he'd done. To have
his sister's betrayal avenged. Then and only then
could he relax.

He went back to the bedroom and took one last
look at the woman who was now lying on her side,
her face pressed into the pillow, her short hair
feathered against her cheek. Her skirt was twisted
around her hips, giving him a tantalizing glimpse of
her long bare legs.

No wonder Giovanni had fallen for her. The
combination of innocence, vulnerability, intelligence, and those long legs was irresistible. And
greed. No one would do what she'd done if she
weren't greedy. Or in love with Giovanni. Or both.
Maybe she needed the money to open that bookstore she wanted. He couldn't believe how clever
she was, how adept at concealing her true nature.
Not to mention concealing the stolen property.

But where in hell was it? The most obvious place
was on a piece of costume jewelry, but she didn't
wear any. It wasn't in her suitcase or her cosmetic
bag. Maybe she hadn't brought it with her. Maybe
someone else was going to give it to her, to give to
Giovanni.

Though she appeared naive and inexperienced,
she was obviously smart. As for her being in love

with Giovanni, maybe she'd be surprised to hear that Giovanni had already been married three times and probably still was. Her marriage was over, and she was on the rebound. He just hoped she didn't start crying again. He was running out of handkerchiefs.

He paused in the doorway before he let himself out. "*Ciao, bella,*" he said softly.

Chapter 4

The next day, Marco went to his office early to report to his superior. Silvestro, a gruff officer who'd known him since he was a boy, had taken Marco off the streets of San Gervase a few years back when he was only a local *agente di polizia* and chosen him to work for the Guardia. Silvestro had sent him to London for two years then to Rome for the past two years, where he'd worked on some difficult cases but none as hard as this one. None that meant as much to him personally.

The office was on the second floor of a building without any sign on the door, very different from the big government building in Rome. The Guardia did not care to advertise its presence in a small town like San Gervase. Silvestro was standing in the window, hands clasped behind his back, wearing a suit jacket and a shirt with no tie, waiting for him.

The place was quiet on Saturday mornings. Street crimes were easily handled by the *ufficio di polizia* in town. The atmosphere here was so different from the wild, chaotic, fume-laden streets of Rome. He was glad to be back in his hometown, but for how long? There were times, like last night, when he wished he could return to a more simple life. But right now, he didn't have the luxury of worrying about his future. Not until he caught Giovanni.

"Well, did you find it?" Silvestro Schiavenza asked.

Marco shook his head. "There's nothing in her room."

"Then she's wearing it."

"She's not wearing any jewelry."

"Not even a wedding ring?"

"No ring. She's divorced."

"That's right. I forgot. What about some cheap costume jewelry, necklace, bracelet? That's the way they often conceal it."

"I know. I checked. She's not the type to wear jewelry."

"Not the type? Every woman is the type. I thought you knew that; you know so much about women."

"Women, yes," Marco said. "Jewelry, no."

"Not even diamonds? Never bought one for one of your girlfriends?"

"They might get the wrong idea." Women got the wrong idea about him even without diamonds; he had no desire to contribute to any misunderstandings. "I understand they're making them in a Russian laboratory now that are almost impossible to tell from the real ones."

Silvestro sighed. "As if we needed a new wrinkle to our problems. So, what are you telling me? She hasn't got it? Are you sure? Did you strip her? Did you pat her down, at least? For you, that should be no problem."

"No problem," Marco assured him. He had no intention of losing his reputation. But he'd had the perfect chance to pat her down during that kiss on the way back to the hotel, and he hadn't. Why not? What was he thinking? He wasn't thinking—that was the problem. He'd gotten involved in that kiss, more than he'd intended, more than he'd wanted to.

"I checked her luggage. I checked the linings. I checked every place it could possibly be. Whether she's hidden it elsewhere or someone else hands it off to her to give Giovanni, I'll be there." He looked at his watch. "I must go. I'm taking her to Paestum this morning to meet him."

"If he shows up."

"He will, and I'll be ready."

Marco knew his boss was remembering the fiasco the last time they thought they'd gotten

Giovanni. The lights, the sirens, the backup forces. Marco had turned away for one minute to speak to a woman—one minute too many—and Giovanni was gone. Disappeared down a rat hole. Now he'd surfaced, and there would never be a better chance to trap him. All Marco needed was a little luck and this blue-eyed woman with an important package for Giovanni.

"You'll call for help if you need it. I can have a team there in minutes. Remember, he's a desperate man with great resources."

"But I have what he wants—the woman."

"You're sure about that? Why would Giovanni risk getting caught for an American woman when he can have any woman he wants?"

Marco knew he was thinking, *including your sister.* "She's . . . different."

The old man sighed. "Nobody's that different. Giovanni is interested in only one thing: money. If our information is correct, what the woman has is enough to set him up for the rest of his life. Don't let her out of your sight, and don't get involved with her. If we fail the syndicate again, they will lose confidence in us. My job, your job, everything is at stake."

"I understand. I have no intention of getting involved; I've learned my lesson," Marco said grimly.

"If we don't catch him actually receiving the jewel, the case won't stand up in court. There's pressure from every side. From the South Africans who control the diamond market, the insurance company in America, the Roman family who claims it belongs to them. This diamond has been stolen not just once but many times. The Bianchi diamond is nearly as valuable as the Hope diamond. Be careful, Marco. People will kill for a diamond, lie or die, or even cheat their best friend."

Marco nodded and went to the door. "Any word from the FBI?" he asked.

"They, too, are feeling pressure from the family the diamond was stolen from. But they have no more information for us, if that's what you mean. The Jackson woman has no record, no prior convictions—which doesn't mean much when it comes to a chance to make some big money."

"What about her family and friends—her son, her ex-husband, and a friend called Evie? Could the FBI do some checking on them? Discreetly, of course."

"I'll call and ask, if you think it would help."

"It might." He paused. "Not her son. He's just a kid; he wouldn't know anything. But check out her friend Evie and her ex-husband."

Silvestro scribbled a note on a piece of paper, then looked up.

"When are you getting married, Marco?" he asked.

Startled, Marco turned, the doorknob in his hand. Where had *that* come from? Was there a conspiracy against the unmarried? "Not you, too. Never. Why should I?"

"Because one day you'll be old, too old to chase women or thieves. My advice is to find someone now, before it's too late. Someone to spend your golden years with. Give her a diamond and settle down. Then, when you're sixty-three, like me, you'll have someone to sit in the square with in the evening, someone to share a grappa and watch the sunsets with."

"I can drink alone and watch the sunsets on my own. But thanks for the advice. I'll think about it."

"Do that, and when you think about it, think about me. Because I want to retire and plant roses and enjoy the sunsets with my wife, but if we don't get that diamond back—"

"We will. I promise you on the grave of my grandmother."

"Your grandmother is alive and well; I saw her yesterday. She's worried about you. She prays for you."

"I'm glad someone does." Before Silvestro could nag him further, Marco was out the door and on his way to the hotel.

He stopped only to buy coffee and rolls, which he thought might impress Anna Maria as a thoughtful gesture. But when he knocked at her door, there was no answer.

The cleaning woman called to him from the end of the hall. "*Troppo tardi,*" she said. "*E andata.*" She gestured with her hand. *You're too late. She's gone.*

"*Che cosa?*" he said, his teeth clenched. She was out cold when he'd left her. How could she be awake, on her unsteady feet, and out of the hotel so soon? He cursed her. He cursed himself. He cursed his superior for calling him in this morning and the whole agency he worked for.

Marco raced down the stairs and jumped into his car, spilling the coffee from the cardboard cup onto the leather seats and speeding down the hill, taking the curves much too fast on the way to the bus station. If she was going to Paestum, she'd have to go by bus, unless she'd hired a taxi to take her. But why so early?

He parked his car across from the beach. The sun, still low in the sky, slanted its rays on the calm blue water. The beach umbrellas were still packed away, the paddle boats were beached, and workers were sweeping the sand of debris. The air smelled of saltwater and fish.

He saw her right away at the first café along the strip. She had a cup of coffee in front of her, her tote bag over her arm and her suitcase at her feet. She was wearing sunglasses, and she was writing something on the small, round table in front of her.

"Do you mind if I join you?" he asked.

She looked up. If he thought she'd be pleased by his asking permission this time, he was wrong. There was a long silence. All he could see was his own face reflected in her sunglasses. "There are other tables," she said at last.

He straddled a wrought-iron chair and lighted a cigarette. "I prefer this one."

"Do you mind not smoking?" she said, wrinkling

her nose at the smell of smoke. "In California, it's illegal to smoke in a café."

"Even outside?" he asked incredulously.

She nodded.

"You're in Italy now," he reminded her.

"You're at my table," she reminded him.

He stubbed out his cigarette on the cement floor.

"What happened last night?" she asked.

"We had dinner, and I took you to a concert. There was a fortune-teller—"

"I mean later, at the hotel. I must have had too much wine, because my head hurts like hell this morning. And I can't remember how I got home."

He was relieved to learn she had no memory of their kiss. He wished he could forget as easily.

"You walked. Not very well, not very steadily, but you walked all the way back to the hotel."

"And then?"

"And then you went to bed."

She nodded slowly. "How do you know?"

"Because I carried you up the stairs and dumped you on your bed. When I left, you were sound asleep."

Her sunglasses slid down her nose, and she stared at him with bloodshot eyes. "I don't know what to say."

"What about 'grazie, molto gentile'?"

"Molto gentile?" she asked, "or molto suspicioso?"

"What do you mean?" he asked, smothering a smile. At least, she tried to speak Italian; most tourists didn't. But then, she wasn't most tourists.

"What I mean is that I don't know you. You follow me everywhere, and I don't know why. You say you're a tour guide, but why aren't you out guiding someone, then? What do you want with me?"

"Just to help you." He gave her a long, steady look. *Last night, I wanted to make love to you. Today, I want to catch you with one of the world's most spectacular diamonds and send you back to America in the custody of international agents.*

But a stab of guilt hit him between the ribs as he looked into her bleary eyes. What if she really was an innocent tourist? What if all the intelligence they'd gathered was incorrect? The agency had made mistakes before.

If she never met Giovanni, if she never handed over any stolen goods, he'd almost be sorry. This case was getting more and more interesting. Marco loved his job, and he loved a challenge. It was his personal life that was less than exciting. Women had left him feeling numb. But ever since he'd met Anna Maria yesterday, he'd felt anything but numb. His senses had come alive along with his libido. This woman, this case—they were both one hell of a challenge. He wouldn't jump to any conclusions, not yet.

"I might remind you," he continued, "that you don't speak Italian and you don't understand our customs. You are a stranger in a strange land. You cried three times, you drank a little too much wine, and you got lost on the way home. It has been my pleasure to help rescue you from these incidents, from embarrassment. And yet . . . and yet I have not asked you for one lira, nor have I heard one word of thanks from you, even after I took you to a concert, had your fortune told, and got you safely back to your hotel. What more do you want?" he demanded with an edge to his voice. It was time to put her on the defensive and see how tough she was.

"I don't want anything, except to be left alone," she said, standing tall and reaching for the handle of her suitcase. "I know you meant well, but I came to Italy to be on my own. Yes, maybe I caused a scene, and I got lost and had a little too much to drink, but I didn't break any laws, and I didn't need to be rescued. And I plan to return your handkerchiefs to you as soon as I wash them. No, I don't speak Italian yet, but I'm learning. The only way I can learn is to practice. And I will find my way around by myself. So, *molto grazie*, Marco, and *arrivederci*."

With her chin in the air, Anne Marie stalked off. She didn't dare look back, or it would spoil the effect altogether. She didn't hear footsteps behind her as she dragged her suitcase behind her out of the empty café and down the quiet street, so he'd probably gotten the message. Probably, he was still sitting at the café, watching her walk away, surprised and pissed off by her angry words and her ungrateful attitude. And wondering how on earth she planned to return his handkerchiefs if she was never going to see him again.

Probably, he thought he was irresistible and had

never been turned down before. Probably, he
thought of her as some helpless tourist eager to hop
into bed and have an affair—if not with Giovanni,
then with Marco. Or both.

Well, she wasn't. Yes, he made shivers go up her
spine when he touched her, and he made her knees
buckle and her head spin when he kissed her. Yes, he
made her feel shaky all over, empty and unfulfilled,
like a cat in heat, instead of a forty-something librarian whose recent sexual experiences had been all
vicarious.

Of course, there were logical explanations for
these strange reactions. Jet lag, culture shock,
and sensory overload. And all that wine. If only
she could remember what really happened last
night. Some parts were dreamlike, like the kiss,
and some were a blank. She resolved to stop
drinking wine in the company of strange men.
Now, Giovanni was a different story. He was not
a stranger; he was an old friend she could feel
safe with. She knew he wouldn't take advantage
of her.

But it wasn't Giovanni whose body had been
pressed against hers last night. It was Marco. What
if someone had seen them? Maybe someone had.
Her dreams had been filled with erotic longings,
disturbing sensations, and lust and passion right
out of an X-rated movie.

She'd been up at dawn, planning her escape to
Paestum. Unfortunately, nothing was open at dawn.
She'd sat at the beach on her suitcase for an hour,

waiting for a café to open. Then she'd barely gotten her coffee when he'd arrived.

Why? What did he want with her? This was the third time he'd shown up like this—in the hotel lobby, in the restaurant, and now here in the café. He never asked her for money, so that wasn't it. He hadn't ravished her last night, so it wasn't that. He was after something or someone, but what or who?

Enough about Marco. She had her coffee, and now she wanted to find an Internet café so she could check her messages. Despite her brave words back there at the café, she was experiencing a wave of homesickness that made her long for something familiar, a familiar voice or a kind word. She knew it was silly to be nostalgic when she'd only been away for a few days, but she was. She found a small shop with Internet access on a side street, paid the small fee for fifteen minutes, and settled herself and her suitcase in front of a computer.

Her pulse raced when she saw she had an e-mail message from her son. What if Tim was sick? What if he needed her? Yes, he was eighteen and a freshman in college and fiercely independent, but still . . .

Mom. Hope you're having a great trip. It is so cool you are getting a chance to do all those things you always wanted but never could. Live it up, Mom. La vida loca and all that. You won't believe what happened here. Or have you already heard? You know the wedding was yes-

*terday. Or it was supposed to be yesterday. There
we were in the church. I was standing next to
Dad at the altar. You remember he asked me to
be his best man, which I didn't want to do, but
you said it was okay, you understood. I was nervous, it being my first wedding and wearing my
first tux and feeling weird about my own dad
getting married to someone who, well, you
know, and then the music started, and she*

That was all there was. Anne Marie sat staring at
the screen. Where was the rest of the message? She
clicked the mouse. Nothing happened. She went
back to the counter and spoke to the woman in
charge, who shrugged. It wasn't her fault if there
was only half a message, was it?

"Why don't you ask the sender to repeat the message?" the clerk suggested in English.

Anne Marie went back to the computer and
wrote Tim a message asking him to resend the message, trying not to sound desperate for news of her
ex-husband. Still, she wondered, what could have
happened at the wedding? She scrolled down to a
message from Evie. Maybe she'd tell her what happened.

*Hi Anne Marie. I tried to call you last night
at your hotel. What happened in Rome? My
cousin went to meet you at the airport, but she
couldn't find you.*

Anne Marie felt a stab of guilt. They'd changed her flight at the last minute in San Francisco, and she'd forgotten to call Evie and tell her. She'd been in such a rush to see Giovanni she'd forgotten everything—the cousin, the chocolates, everything but Giovanni.

Misty can hardly wait to see you. I've told her all about you, and she wants to meet you when you get to Rome. I'll give you her number, and you can call her. Of course, she's dying to get her hands on the candy, too, but anyway, WHO was the man who answered the phone in your room last night? It wasn't Giovanni; at least, he said he wasn't. I can't believe you had a strange man in your room after midnight, and where were you, by the way? I want to tell you about the wedding, but I haven't got time to do it justice. Believe me, the whole town is talking. It's a good thing you weren't here. Call me. I have so much to tell you. Have you seen Giovanni? Have you met someone else? XOX, Evie

Anne Marie banged her forehead lightly against the screen in frustration. What had happened at the wedding? None of her other messages even mentioned it; they were all written before it happened. She signed off and continued to sit there staring at the screen, her mind in turmoil until the clerk came by and told her she owed another few euros, which reminded her she'd forgotten to settle

the check before she left the café, and now she
owed Marco for the dinner, the fortune-teller, the
wine, and also the coffee. If she thought he was
some kind of an opportunist, what must he think of
her?

It didn't matter. She'd figure out a way to repay
him without ever seeing him again, because she
sincerely hoped she'd seen the last of him.

He was waiting outside in his car, the top down
and the radio playing music. He tossed his cigarette
to the ground, got out, and opened the door, then
reached for her suitcase.

"Get in," he said.

She told herself to say good-bye to this oh-so-
charming and oh-so-full-of-himself Italian and be
on her way. "No thanks," she said. "I'm just going to
the bus station."

"Fine, I'll take you," he said. "It's too far to walk
with this suitcase." Before she could protest, he'd
picked up her bag and put it in the trunk of his
small sports car.

Feeling weak with apprehension and the lack of
breakfast, she didn't argue. What harm could it do
to accept a ride to the bus station?

"What's wrong?" he said, slanting a glance in her
direction. "Bad news from home on the Internet?"

"No," she said. "At least, I don't think so. I got a
message from my son, or rather half a message."

His forehead creased in a frown. "He's all right,
yes?"

"Oh, yes, it's just . . . nothing." She turned to

face him. "Did you answer the phone in my room last night?"

He shot her a swift look. "Why?" he said.

"Because my friend Evie back home in California wants to know who was in my room late last night. Why didn't you wake me up when she called?"

"You didn't tell me to, and neither did she. Besides, I didn't have the heart to do it," Marco said. "You looked so peaceful while you slept. Was it urgent?"

She shook her heard wearily. "It wasn't urgent, but now she wonders who you were. I don't know how to explain you."

"You aren't the only one," he muttered.

Marco's cell phone rang, and he spoke for a few minutes, taking his hand off the wheel to wave his arm in the air. When he hung up, he turned to Anne Marie.

"I hope you don't mind. I have to stop a moment at the house of my grandmother. It's on the way. She needs help moving something heavy to her garden. It should only take a moment."

What could she say, *Ignore your grandmother when she needs you?* What could she do, make a flying leap from the front seat onto the sidewalk? And what about her suitcase? It weighed a ton. Besides, her head hurt, her stomach lurched at every curve in the road, and she was beginning to notice that Marco had a habit of parrying her questions and never giving her a straight answer.

It didn't help her stomach to have him swerve

around the corners, so many corners it seemed they were driving in circles. Her body swayed into his, and her shoulder rubbed against the hard muscles of his upper arm. She pulled back and noticed Marco was staring into the rearview mirror. She turned her head to look behind them.

"Don't do that," he said, and put his hand firmly on her shoulder.

"What?" she said. "What is it?"

"Nothing," he said. "Just keep your head down."

"Why?" she asked, tugging at her skirt, which had ridden above her knees.

His impassive gaze drifted down to her legs. "Why do you ask so many questions?" he said. "Just do what I tell you." He pressed his foot on the gas pedal. She slid down in her seat, and the car leaped forward, throwing her backward into the tight-fitting bucket seat. She thought it must be the kind of sports car Tim talked about, that could go from zero to sixty in six point two seconds. She wished she could appreciate the performance, but all the breath was sucked out of her lungs.

They went around a few more corners on two wheels before coming to an abrupt stop, and this time, Anne Marie flew forward against the tightened seat belt. When the car stopped, Marco made no move to get out. He sat there without stirring, still staring into the mirror. The sun flickered down through the leaves of the olive tree on the side of the road. Anne Marie noticed how it made shadows on the hard planes of his face. She hadn't noticed before that his nose looked as if it had been broken and mended crookedly. She wanted to ask about it, but it was none of her business, so she just sat there staring at his profile and noticing how the tight lines around his mouth slowly relaxed. Slowly, he turned his head and looked behind them.

"What was that about?" she asked.

"I thought someone was following us," he said, taking a cigarette from his pocket.

"Who would want to follow you?" she asked.

"I might ask you the same question," he said. "Who would want to follow you?"

"Do you know you have a habit of answering a question with a question?" she asked.

"Do I?" He held up a match, glanced at her, read disapproval in her eyes, then put the cigarette back in his pocket.

"Where are we?" she said, looking to the right and the left. They were parked in front of a small stone house with a vegetable garden in front. Then she knew. It was the same house where she'd been caught pilfering tomatoes the night before and where she'd imagined herself living another life.

"Oh, no," she said.

"What?" he asked.

"Can I just stay in the car?" she asked.

"Of course. That's a good idea," he said, agreeing with her for the first time since she'd met him. "I'll only be a minute. If you notice anything suspicious, just lean on the horn."

"What do you mean, suspicious?"

He didn't answer. He was already halfway up the walk when the old woman in black came out to meet him. Anne Marie slid down in the leather seat as far as she could. She didn't want his grandmother to think he was consorting with a vegetable thief. Marco seemed equally determined to prevent the elderly woman from seeing Anne Marie. She sneaked a quick look to see him kiss his grandmother on both cheeks and turn toward the house.

But the old woman had other ideas. Anne Marie could hear her voice rise and get louder. A moment later, Marco came back to the car, his jaw locked in place, his mouth a straight line.

"She wants to meet you," he said through stiff lips. "Couldn't you hide?"

"I was hiding," she said. "What should I have done, get into the trunk?"

He opened the door. "It's too late. She's seen you. You have to come in."

The house was crowded with furniture and fabric and pictures on every wall and every shelf. The smell of bread baking and tomato sauce simmering made Anne Marie's stomach growl. The old woman's eyes widened in surprise and recognition when she saw Anne Marie.

"*Si accomoda, prego,*" she said politely. Then she smiled broadly and took both of Anne Marie's hands in hers.

"*Bella,*" the old woman said to Marco, nodding emphatically. "*Molto bella.*"

Anne Marie smiled at the compliment. No one

had ever called her beautiful before, not Dan, not even her parents. It didn't matter if Marco didn't agree; it was the old woman's opinion that counted.

"*Buon giorno, signora,*" Anne Marie said, happy to be able to practice her Italian. She then asked his grandmother how she was, and they exchanged pleasantries that were straight out of Lesson One in her beginning Italian textbook. It was very satisfying to have someone to practice with, someone who said all the right things and in the right order. By the end of the conversation, his grandmother had instructed Anne Marie to call her Nonna, and Marco was standing with his arms crossed, his expression pained. Maybe he'd think twice about bringing a stranger to his grandmother's house again. Not that he'd wanted to bring her in, but he should have let her go to the bus station on her own. But then she would have missed this opportunity to see the inside of a real Italian house.

When Nonna turned and spoke to him directly, he shook his head and pointed to his watch. His grandmother said something and disappeared into the kitchen.

"She wants us to eat lunch with her," he said. "I told her you have a bus to catch."

"That's right," Anne Marie said, but the sauce smelled so good, and she was so hungry. "Besides, it's much too early for lunch."

"It's never too early for lunch in this house. She thinks I don't eat enough. She says you like her tomatoes. How does she know that? For some reason, she thinks she knows you. She wants you to taste her *puttanesca* sauce."

"I'd love to. She's very kind," she said. Her mouth watered. If she could just have a piece of that fresh-baked bread before she left, to soothe her stomach and fill the void between her ribs. A taste of that tomato sauce wouldn't be bad, either.

"What time is your bus?"

"Uh, I'm not sure, but there will be another. I hate to hurt her feelings. I'd like to stay if you think it's all right."

"All right? You can't leave now, and neither can I. She's gone to cook the pasta."

Marco leaned against the wall and stared moodily out the window. He seemed more displeased about this delay than Anne Marie was, though he was the one who'd brought her there. She wasn't displeased at all. This was the kind of thing she wanted to do in Italy. Get off the beaten track, meet the real people, talk to them, eat their food. That was why she'd contacted Giovanni. She thought he'd be her ticket to seeing the real Italy. Whether Marco was real or not, she didn't know—but his Nonna sure was.

Chapter 5

Anne Marie went to the mantel above the tiled fireplace and looked at the framed photographs there. In a moment, Marco joined her.

There was a picture of a young woman with long dark hair and a dazzling smile.

"My sister," Marco said.

"She's beautiful," she said. "Where does she live?"

"In Rome. She has joined a convent."

"She's a nun?" Anne Marie asked.

"Not yet. We are hoping she will change her mind."

"Why? I thought it was an honor to have a priest or a nun in the family."

"Not for the wrong reasons."

"Is she doing it for the wrong reasons?"

"She's much younger than I. The baby of the family, loved and petted by everyone. When she fell in love, it was to someone we didn't approve of—for good reason. She wouldn't listen to us. She's as stubborn as she is beautiful. Then she found out he was married and that he was a thief. Her heart was broken, and she felt the shame. So she escaped to Rome and the Suore di Santa Teresa near the Palazzo Macino. They have opened the convent to a few tourists and pilgrims. Isabella is working there, washing the sheets, scrubbing the floors, to prove herself to the nuns or to herself. I don't know. I haven't seen her for a long time."

Anne Marie heard the bitterness in his voice. Did he refuse to see her, or did she refuse to see him?

She turned her attention to the next picture.

"My grandparents," Marco said. "This is Nonna and my grandfather, who died two years ago."

"Is that why she wears black?"

"It's the custom."

"He's very handsome." She glanced at Marco. The resemblance was unmistakable. The same eyes, the strong jaw and high cheekbones, and the wry half-smile. Even the same nose. Very dashing, very romantic, even as an old man. Would Marco look like that one day? "How long were they married?"

"Fifty-two years," he said.

Neither of them heard his grandmother come into the room. When they turned, she was standing behind them, wearing a white apron that covered her black dress. She pointed to the picture and said something to Marco. He smiled and shook his head. She shook her finger at him, then she held up ten fingers and went back to the kitchen.

"What did she say?" Anne Marie asked.

"She said the lunch will be ready in ten minutes."

"I got that. But what else?"

"She says I had better get going if I ever want to celebrate my fiftieth wedding anniversary the way they did."

"You've never been married?"

"That's right. I've had some narrow escapes, and I have no intention of getting married. She knows that, but she won't accept it. It's a running joke in the family. She loves babies, and she wants great-grandchildren. She wants to teach them cooking, to pass on her recipes. And show them how to grow tomatoes before it's too late. If we don't produce these great-grandchildren, she swears she'll have to go to her grave with her secrets."

Anne Marie was saddened to think of Nonna dying without passing on the family traditions.

"Don't worry," Marco said, smoothing a worry line from Anne Marie's forehead with his thumb. "She's not serious."

But his grandmother had looked very serious. She'd positively glared at him. Anne Marie turned back to the photograph. The touch of Marco's thumb across her forehead disturbed her. It was too familiar a gesture for a casual acquaintance. Unless . . . what had really happened last night?

"You look like your grandfather," she said.

"So, you think I'm handsome." He smiled. "Is that why you're following me around?"

"Me . . . me? Following you?" She was so upset she stumbled over her words.

"Didn't you follow me to the restaurant last night?" he asked.

"No, of course not! The hotel clerk told me about it. If I'd known you were there, I would never have gone there and interrupted your dinner with . . . whoever that was. You never told me who that woman was and what happened to make her mad enough to hit you."

"Her name is Adrianna, and she's always mad. She wants me to take her here and there. She doesn't understand that I have work to do."

"What kind of work?" she asked. She'd wondered about that.

"Helping tourists."

"Like me?"

"Most people are not like you. Most people cause me much more trouble than you."

"I thought I was outstanding at causing trouble, crying, making a scene. Which reminds me, I owe you some money, for the dinner and the wine and the fortune-teller."

"No, you don't."

"Was that all part of your job?"

"In a way."

"Even the fortune-teller?"

"All right, you can pay me for the fortune-teller. But only if she's right."

"That doesn't seem fair to you," she said, "since she can't possibly be right. I must say, whatever you really do, it seems like hazardous work. Just having dinner, you got slapped, then you had to escort me home and put me to bed."

"That was a tough job," he admitted. "But it was clear you weren't going to get there on your own."

"All in a day's work, I suppose," she said. "Or a night's work. Tell me more about what you do. Is it always so dangerous?"

"So dangerous I can't talk about it. And it would take too long."

"We have ten minutes," she said.

"That's not nearly long enough," he said. "And it's really not interesting enough."

"But you said it was dangerous."

"The most dangerous part is dying of boredom. Most of the time, I sit behind a desk and talk on the phone and do paperwork. Just the usual, planning trips for people, booking reservations, handling complaints and cancellations. That's the really dangerous part, dealing with disgruntled travelers. They can get very angry. It's an ordinary job with lots of headaches. There's so much, how do you say, bullshit in my business. People asking me questions I can't answer, making impossible demands.

"This is the good part—getting out of the office, helping people like yourself, making your visit more pleasant, if I can." He took a breath. "Now, tell me about your job in the bookstore. I mean . . . wherever it is that you work," he said.

"You're close; I work in a library. But I'd like to have a bookstore sometime in the future. How did you know?"

"I didn't. I'd better go see what heavy object Nonna wants moved." Marco headed for the kitchen before he blurted out something else he wasn't supposed to know. He had a feeling there was no heavy object to be moved, that Nonna just wanted to see him. He felt trapped between the proverbial rock and the hard place, and he didn't know how to get away.

Anne Marie was in the living room, and his grandmother was in the kitchen, and he was in between. Each woman had her own agenda, agendas that clashed with his. Anne Marie was trying to shake him and meet Giovanni without him. Nonna was trying to marry him off. It hardly mattered to whom anymore. It made him nervous to see the way she looked at Anne Marie. If Nonna only knew who she was, knew why she was there in San Gervase . . .

Steam filled the air, along with the fragrant aroma of the sauce his grandmother was now stirring on the stove. He had to admit he was hungry. She was right; he didn't get enough home cooking. He put his arms around her. She looked solid, all rounded curves and good high color in her skin, but she felt smaller and more fragile than before.

No matter how much she nagged him, she was his favorite relative. The one who'd taught him to play marbles on the kitchen floor when he'd spent the summers there as a child. When his father was given a post outside the country, he and Isabella had come to live with their grandparents for a few years. Nonna was the one who'd read folk tales to him and filled his head with dreams of love and adventure. How many of those dreams had come true?

He had a good job. He'd traveled as far as England. He'd been the star of the high school soccer team, at least when Giovanni wasn't there. He'd had his share of adventure and of love. But what about the future, what next?

"She's a nice girl, yes?" Nonna turned to face him, her black eyes sparkling.

"Yes, very nice. She's American. She's here on vacation." He stifled the urge to say, *She's Giovanni's girlfriend.* Wasn't it bad enough that she was from another country? Someone who was not going to be around in two weeks? Someone who, if he fell in love with her, might tempt him to follow her and never come back? What kind of a grandmother would want that for her grandson? Not that he would ever be tempted to fall in love again or follow anyone anywhere. He'd tried it once. It hadn't worked.

Nonna shrugged as if being American was no more of a drawback than having blue eyes. Which just went to show how desperate she was to find him a wife.

"I like her," she said.

"You like every woman I bring here."

"No," she said, waving her spoon in his face. "Not every woman."

"All right, only the ones with two ears and two eyes."

"Nice eyes," she remarked. "Blue like the Mediterranean."

"She can't speak Italian," he reminded her.

"She can learn."

"I don't know her. I only met her yesterday."

"Two days is enough. The first time I saw your grandfather, I knew. It was a Saturday night at the old dance hall at the beach. I was wearing a blue dress."

"I'll bet you were the prettiest girl in town, Nonna. And Grandfather couldn't take his eyes off you."

"Have I told you this story before?" she asked.

"If you have, I've forgotten. Tell me again."

"Well, your grandfather was standing on one side of the hall, and I was on the other with my mother and my aunt. I said to my mother, 'That is the man I'm going to marry.' She said, 'Who is he? Who is his family? I've never seen him before. He's not from here.' Of course, he wasn't from here; he was Sicilian. When she heard that, she hit the roof. She was afraid I'd go off with him to Sicily and never come back. After a while, he came up and introduced himself to us and kissed my mother's hand."

"I'll bet that got her attention."

"It got everyone's attention. A handsome stranger. Everyone was looking at him, wondering who he was."

"Then he asked you to dance."

"So, I have told you the story."

"I'm just guessing."

"Yes, he asked me to dance."

"He was a good dancer?"

"The best." She smiled dreamily, and he had a flash of how she'd looked then, her girlish figure dressed in blue, her dark eyes sparkling even as they did today, her long, dark hair piled high on her head. He knew exactly why his grandfather had crossed the room to ask her to dance. He felt a twinge of envy. She'd found true love at eighteen, she'd married at twenty, and she'd raised a family in her hometown where she was known and loved. It wasn't a bad way to live. But could he ever adjust to such a routine? Could he live a life without the excitement of the chase?

"Do young people dance today?" she asked.

"I don't know," he said.

"What do you mean, you don't know? What about you?"

"I'm not young." He didn't feel young. He felt old and cynical.

"But you know how to dance, don't you?"

He put his arms around her waist and twirled her up into the air. "Like this?" he said. "Am I dancing?"

Her laughter rang through the kitchen, just as young and girlish as it was sixty years ago.

Anne Marie heard the voices and the laughter that came from the kitchen. She went to the double kitchen doors and opened the top door just a crack, just far enough to see Marco lift his grandmother in the air and twirl her around. She didn't understand their words, but she understood the wealth of love and affection in that small room. She understood that Marco, however macho and tough he seemed, loved his grandmother very much, as much as she loved him. The sight of the small old woman, her eyes brimming with emotion, being lifted into the air by the big, strong man smiling broadly at her touched Anne Marie's heart with an aching sweetness. If she never saw Marco again, she'd never forget the sight of the two of them, enveloped in steam and tender affection, spinning around in that small, homey kitchen.

Hearing a knock at the front door, she started guiltily and closed the kitchen door. When she turned, she saw a strange man walk through the door. He looked as surprised to see her as she was to see him. He stood in the doorway for a long moment, staring at her. He was wearing skintight black pants, a white shirt unbuttoned halfway down his chest, and a whole set of gold chains around his neck.

"*Ciao, bella,*" he said at last. "*Da dove viene?*"

At last, some Italian she could understand. A phrase right out of the book.

"*Sono di Stati Uniti,*" she said carefully.

He laughed loudly. "You're American," he said. "I should have known."

The corners of her mouth drooped. Just when she'd found somebody to practice her Italian on, he started speaking English.

He held out his hand. "I am Rocco," he said, as if she should know.

She shook his hand. "How do you do? My name is Anne Marie."

"May I ask what you are doing in the house of my grandmother?" he asked.

"Your grandmother?" she asked. But of course, Marco wasn't her only grandson. There might be many others. This might be a family get-together at which she didn't belong. "I came with Marco, just stopping by for a moment on my way out of town."

He nodded, giving her a long, appraising look from head to toe. "Of course. So, you are one of Marco's girls."

"I'm not a girl, and I'm not Marco's," she said. "I'm a tourist, that's all. Just passing through."

He nodded, as if that was always the case with "Marco's girls." "Where are you from?"

"California."

"My cousin Giorgio lives in L.A."

"I live near San Francisco."

He put one hand over his heart. "I left my heart in San Francisco," he sang in a poor imitation of Tony Bennett. "Did you leave your heart there, too?"

"No," she said. "Where did you learn to speak English so well?"

"I'm just now returning from the States," he said. "I go every summer to work for my uncle in Maryland. Do you know Ocean City?"

She shook her head.

"He has a cannoli stand on the boardwalk. Ocean City is a fantastic place in the summer. You would love it."

"I'm sure I would. I love cannoli."

Rocco sniffed the air. "Mmm, it smells like *puttanesca* sauce." He sat in one of the overstuffed chairs and stretched his legs out in front of him. "So, Anna Maria," he said. "Sit down, and tell me more about yourself. If you are not one of my cousin's girls, who are you?"

She shifted uncomfortably from one foot to the other and finally perched on the edge of the sofa across the room from him.

"Just a tourist," she repeated. "Traveling on my own."

"On your own? No husband? No family?"

"I'm not married. And I'm old enough to be on my own, believe me. I have a son in college."

Rocco's eyes widened, and his mouth fell open in surprise, or at least in mock surprise. Anne Marie almost laughed at his response, it was so dramatic.

"I can't believe this," he said.

Inside her wallet was a recent picture of her with Tim at graduation. She crossed the room to show it to Rocco. "This is my son." She couldn't help the pride that crept into her voice.

"So, it is true," Rocco said, staring at the picture. "I see the resemblance. He's a handsome boy. He takes after you." He stood and handed back the photo but caught Anne Marie's wrist between his thumb and forefinger. "You say Marco is not your boyfriend."

"Of course not," she said. "I just met him yesterday."

"That means nothing to Marco. He's a fast worker."

Anne Marie sensed a certain amount of cousin rivalry in the air.

"Do you have a boyfriend?" Rocco asked.

"No."

"Marco doesn't bring just any girl to the house of our grandmother, so I am wondering . . ."

"There's nothing to wonder about. I'm here only by accident."

"By accident? There was an accident? Was that how you met? Did you break the law or lose your passport, or are you wanted by Interpol for some high crime?"

"No," she said with a laugh. "I don't think so. Why?"

"Why? Because my cousin Marco is working for the—"

The kitchen door flew open, and Marco and his grandmother came in carrying large, steaming bowls of pasta and sauce to the round oak table.

Anne Marie started guiltily and pulled her hand from Rocco's grasp.

"What in the hell is going on here?" Marco asked, glaring at his cousin.

"*Niente affatto*," Rocco said with a shrug. "Just getting acquainted with your friend Anna Maria. You can't have an exclusive on all the pretty women in town, Marco."

"No, I leave that to you," Marco said.

Their grandmother shook her finger at both of them. Then she kissed Rocco on the cheek and motioned him to sit at the table. A few minutes later, a young woman with a baby in her arms came in the front door.

Nonna waved her toward a seat at the table. Marco explained she was a next-door neighbor, and her name was Magdalenna, and her baby daughter was called Cecilia. They told her Anne Marie was a tourist, and Magdalenna asked where she was going next.

"A *Paestum*," Anne Marie said.

"*Per macchina?*"

"No, *per autobus*," Anne Marie said.

"*Santo cielo*," Magdalenna said, clapping her hand to her forehead. "*No lei sentire? El autobus e soppresso.*"

"What?" Anne Marie said.

"She says the buses aren't running. The drivers are on strike," Marco said.

"Oh, no." Now what? She had to get to Paestum tonight, or Giovanni would think she wasn't coming.

"Don't worry," Rocco said. "I'll drive you there."

"No, you won't," Marco declared. "She's going with me. It's already been decided."

"Is that true?" Rocco asked.

Anne Marie looked from one man to the other. She had to get to Paestum by ten. Giovanni had told her to come alone. Which man would she have the least trouble getting rid of?

"Nothing has been decided," she said. "Excuse me. I have to make a phone call. *Telefono.* Is that all right?"

Nonna waved her hand in the direction of the kitchen. Anne Marie went into the kitchen and closed the door behind her. She stood in the middle of the room, listening to the voices from the next room. She put her hand on the old-fashioned black telephone receiver that hung on the wall and stared at it. She could call the hotel at Paestum and make sure Giovanni had made a reservation for her. She could ask the desk clerk if anyone had asked for her.

Another idea: she could use her calling card to call home and find out what had happened at the wedding. Or she could slip quietly out the back door, take her suitcase from the trunk of Marco's car, and walk down the side streets until she found a taxi to take her to Paestum and leave Marco and his cousin Rocco behind. She stood there, wavering. She didn't really care what Marco or Rocco would think if she left. But Nonna was a different matter. She didn't want that dear old lady to think she didn't appreciate her offer of lunch. Then there was the lunch itself. Maybe she could eat first and sneak out afterward.

Before she could do any of these things, there was a loud crash in front of the house and the sounds of glass splintering and metal crunching.

Chapter 6

Anne Marie stood frozen in place on the rustic earth-tone tiles in the kitchen, listening to the shouts from the other room, then footsteps and the slamming of the front door. Finally, her feet propelled her through the kitchen door, past the empty dining-room table laden with bowls of pasta and sauce, and out the front door. There, a crowd of neighbors, including Marco, his grandmother, and his cousin, had gathered around Marco's car, with its rear end smashed and shards of glass and chrome in the street.

Anne Marie felt as if she'd stumbled into an Italian movie, with extras on the sidelines, gesturing and shouting. Marco, obviously the star of the movie, with his dark good looks, his narrowed eyes, his jaw like granite, stared at his damaged car in disbelief. In the distance, instead of a siren, the piercing sound of two-pitched horns indicated that at least one fire truck and certainly the police were on their way.

What if this were all part of the ongoing drama that had begun yesterday, starring Marco? What part would she play? The innocent tourist who was drawn unwittingly into a dark, dangerous intrigue? No one knew where she was. What if they really had been followed this morning, and now the police were coming to round them all up and take them to some dark, dank prison where no one spoke English? She'd be put in a cell with prostitutes who would laugh at her clothes and her innocence. She'd try to call the American embassy, but her calling card wouldn't work, and her passport would be taken away along with her purse. Her heart pounded.

"Marco is very upset," Rocco said, sidling up to Anne Marie and jostling her out of her reverie. "He loved his Alfa Romeo very much. More even perhaps than he's ever loved a woman."

By the look on Rocco's face, Anne Marie gathered this was saying quite a bit. "What happened?" she asked.

"Someone hit him from the rear," he said. "It looks serious. The trunk is crumpled, his gas tank ruptured, and maybe even his rear axle is damaged."

"The way Italians drive, I'm surprised there aren't more accidents," she said.

Rocco shook his head. "This was not an accident."

She frowned. "What do you mean? Why would anyone rear-end a parked car on purpose?"

"Marco has more than a few enemies," he said.

"Really? He seems so . . ." What could she say? *Seems so friendly, so solicitous, so generous . . .* On the other hand, there was a mysterious side to him. Among other things, there was that altercation in the restaurant last night. But it was one thing to slap your boyfriend and quite another to ram his car.

"Ah, yes, 'seems,'" Rocco said with a smirk. "Marco seems many different things to many different people. I've known him all my life, but only Marco knows who Marco really is."

Before she could get any more information from him, Marco walked over to them, his expression stern. "Go into the house now," he said to both of them. "The fire truck is going to spray some foam on the engine to keep it from catching on fire. Everyone must get off the street. My grandmother is anxious about the food getting cold. I will join you as soon as I fill out some forms and make a report to the police."

"How did it happen?" Anne Marie asked, still wondering if someone would really destroy his car on purpose.

Marco shrugged. "Just an accident. Nothing serious."

"Nothing serious? Your car is ruined, and Rocco said . . ."

Marco shifted his gaze to his cousin and raised his eyebrows. Immediately, Rocco changed his story.

"I only said you were lucky you weren't in it when the accident happened."

Anne Marie was amazed at how easily the lie rolled off his tongue and how easily Marco accepted it. There was an undercurrent here that she didn't understand. Maybe because she was a foreigner or because it was a guy thing. Whatever it was, soon they were back at the dining table, except for Marco, and Nonna was ladling sauce onto the pasta and urging everyone to eat. Rocco was pouring wine, and Magdalenna's baby had fallen asleep in her lap. As far as Anne Marie could tell, listening to the babble with Rocco translating from time to time, no one spoke of the accident, or the nonaccident, whatever it was.

When Marco came in, his grandmother passed him a plate of pasta, and he began to eat as if nothing had happened. Only the set of his jaw and a deepened line between his eyebrows hinted that anything was wrong.

"Is everything straightened out?" she asked him. "I mean, with the police and so forth."

"More or less. I don't know if the car is worth repairing or not. The tow truck is on its way. In the meantime, I must rent a car, but there isn't anything available. The tourists have cleaned out all the rental agencies."

He certainly didn't sound like a man devastated

by the loss of a beloved car. Perhaps Rocco exaggerated, or maybe Marco was good at hiding his true feelings.

"I still don't understand how someone could have hit a parked car from behind with such force," she said. "I was wondering if it had something to do with being followed when we were—"

Marco sharply nudged her with his knee under the table.

"Followed?" Rocco said, setting his fork down. "Who was following you?"

"No one," Marco said. "Americans have imaginations which are, how do you say, overbaked."

Rocco reached for Anne Marie's hand. "Don't worry. My car is here, and I'll drive you wherever you need to go."

"There must be another way besides the bus or car," she said, pulling her hand back. She did not want to get involved with another Moretti or be indebted to anyone. She looked around the table. "Train . . . boat . . . ?"

Magdalenna nodded. "*Si, barca per Salerno.*"

"That's right," Marco said. "There is a boat to Salerno. We can take you to the dock, and from Salerno you can take a train or bus to Paestum."

"Perfect," Anne Marie said with a surge of relief. She would be on her own at last, away from the man to whom unexpected violent things seemed to happen, and away from his eccentric but charming family, too. She would be on her way to meet Giovanni at last. And alone.

"What is not so perfect is that your suitcase has been damaged," Marco said. "I am afraid your clothes have been soiled by petrol when the gas tank ruptured. I'm sorry."

Her heart sank. How could she continue her vacation without the clothes she'd so carefully selected from catalogs for their easy wash-and-wear ability, their many pockets and sturdy zippers, their matching coordinates and wrinkle-proof fabrics?

No matter how anxious she was to survey the damaged suitcase, she soon realized that nothing could or should interrupt an Italian meal, no matter how casual the gathering. Not until everyone had eaten at least two helpings of pasta and several pieces of warm, crusty bread and drained their wineglasses could she go outside with Marco to look at her bag on the front porch.

She gasped at the sight of the smashed suitcase, which had a gash on one side and a huge, ragged hole on the other. The lock had sprung open, and she could see her clothes were indeed coated with thick, smelly gasoline.

"*Mamma mia,*" his grandmother said from the doorway. She pressed her hand to her heart. Magdalenna, who'd left her sleeping baby in the living room, wrinkled her nose when she got a whiff of the flammable liquid. Rocco hovered over Anne Marie's shoulder, surveying with undisguised interest her once-pristine new underwear, now gasoline drenched and reddish colored, and

Marco looked as if he wished he'd never seen her or her suitcase.

"It's all right," she said quickly. "I can get some new clothes. When I go home, I'll have these all cleaned. They'll be as good as new." Thank God she'd put the yearbook in her tote bag.

Marco repeated what she'd said to his grandmother, who replied in a torrent of excited words, which ended with her taking Anne Marie's hand and pulling her back inside the house.

"Nonna wants you to borrow my sister's clothes for your vacation," he said. "The ones she left behind when she joined the convent. In the meantime, she will have your clothes cleaned for you and have them ready when you return from Paestum."

"Oh, I couldn't let her . . ." Anne Marie said. She hated to impose, and she was sure the clothes of the young and lovely Isabella wouldn't fit. And even if they did, they wouldn't be at all suitable for a forty-something American librarian.

"But she insists," Marco said. "At least, have a look at the clothes. Take a few, and if you don't want to wear them, don't. But don't hurt her feelings," he said sternly.

Anne Marie flushed with annoyance. She didn't need to be lectured on manners by an Italian mystery man who was being pursued by someone who had destroyed his car and her suitcase.

She followed Nonna up the narrow staircase to a small bedroom that trapped the heat under a

slanted ceiling. Nonna raised the window and let a
gust of fresh air into the room. Then she opened
the closet and brought out dresses and shirts and
pants and even shoes, the kind Anne Marie had
seen on every stylish Italian woman. The old
woman held up a black sleeveless short dress with a
wide band of white across the neck. It was made of
some stretchy fabric and looked so small Anne
Marie was sure it would never fit her. Nonna had
no such reservations. She gestured for Anne Marie
to try it on.

What could Anne Marie say, what could she do
but take off her clothes? Then she had to remove
her money belt. If she hadn't, it would have made a
huge bulge under the dress. Isabella's dress felt
tight, tighter than Anne Marie ever wore her
clothes, but not uncomfortable. Nonna stepped
back, and her eyes widened as she looked Anne
Marie over.

Anne Marie knew what she was thinking: *It's not
you, dear. It's much too young for you. What was I
thinking? You are not the type to carry off these
clothes. We'll have to think of something else.*

This never would have happened if she hadn't
accepted that ride from Marco this morning.
Otherwise, she'd be on her way to Paestum right
now, alone with a full suitcase of her own clothes.
No, she'd never have met his grandmother or his
sketchy cousin or eaten a real, home-cooked Italian
meal, but her suitcase would still be intact, and her
carefully chosen travel clothes would still be new

and unworn and unwrinkled and ready for the meeting with Giovanni.

Suddenly, all she wanted was to take off the dress, get on the boat, wave good-bye to the disturbingly sexy Marco, and continue her trip by herself. Even loneliness would be better than this nervous feeling in the pit of her stomach that she was being sucked into the heart of the family of a man who had secrets and told lies and invited danger into his life.

Meanwhile, Nonna was still staring at her, no doubt planning what she was going to say about the dress so as not to hurt Anne Marie's feelings.

Isabella must be a size smaller than she was. The fabric hugged her breasts, her waist, and her hips. She had no shoes to wear with such a dress. Nonna tilted her head from side to side.

"*Bella,*" she said softly, "*molto bella.*" But she had a tear in her eye as she spoke.

Anne Marie was worried. Was she sad to see her granddaughter's dress on someone else? Was she sorry she'd offered it?

"*Grazie.*" Now Anne Marie didn't know if she was supposed to take the dress or not. She stood in the middle of the room, shifting from one foot to the other. She lifted the skirt up to her waist and was about to take the dress off when there was a knock at the door.

"*Avanti,*" Nonna said.

Marco stuck his head in the door. Anne Marie dropped the skirt that hit her mid-thigh, but not

before Marco had a good look at her cotton under-
pants. That must have been quite a thrill, she told
herself sarcastically.

Thrill or no thrill, he spoke in Italian to his
grandmother, but his eyes never left Anne Marie. It
was the dress, she told herself. He was only interested to see if his sister's dress fit her. Well, it didn't.
He could stop staring now. He could leave the room
and return to whatever it was he was doing. Surely,
there was more to be done about his car and the
accident.

"Very nice," he said at last, raising his eyes to
meet hers.

"What?" she asked.

"The dress. Nonna thinks you and Isabella are
about the same size. It makes her sad that Isabella
is wearing a gray novice habit now and not her own
clothes, but she is happy to know the clothes will be
worn by you. She will pack a suitcase for you, and
then—"

"A suitcase?" She could accept a dress or two
without feeling obligated, but a suitcase full of
clothes? She stopped when he shot her a warning
glance. "Then I must really be on my way," she said.
"Please thank your grandmother. For the clothes
and for the lunch."

He nodded but just stood in the doorway, hand
braced on the woodwork, looking at her with a
strange expression on his face.

While he did, his grandmother was carefully
packing clothes into an old-fashioned canvas

bag. She opened a dresser drawer that contained lacy underwear. Marco nodded to his grandmother, and that went into the bag, as well as dresses, pants, shirts, a nightgown, and even a swimsuit, all folded neatly and packed. Anne Marie should have stopped her, said that was enough, too much, but she didn't want to hurt her feelings.

She wanted to take off the dress and put her own clothes back on, but she couldn't undress with Marco in the room. So she just stood there, her arms wrapped around her waist, with the warm breeze from the open window bringing the scent of roses from the garden below. But it wasn't the breeze that made her skin prickle, it was the way Marco had stripped her bare with his hooded gaze.

She wondered if she'd ever met anyone before who exuded so much male magnetism. Maybe she had, but she hadn't reacted. She'd been a married woman, after all, and immune to the sexy glances of strange men, if there'd been any. Not any longer. She was only too aware of Marco, his remarkable eyes, the way he looked at her, his strong hands on the wheel, the way he drove. She had a feeling that the way he undressed women with his eyes was such a habit with him that he didn't even know he was doing it.

Her heart was beating so loudly she was sure he could hear it in the still room, even see it beneath the snug fabric of his sister's dress. She chastised herself for being so susceptible, for letting him affect her that way.

Then he was gone. Without a word, he closed the door behind him and went downstairs. She took the dress off, put on her money belt and her only remaining American clothes, which now felt bulky and baggy, and accepted the fact that she was leaving with a suitcase full of an Italian girl's clothes that would bind her to Marco's family until she returned them, even though she hoped she would never see him again after today. Not if she could help it.

Nonna kissed her good-bye, Magdalenna waved from the doorway, and she and Marco got into Rocco's car for the drive to the boat dock. It was a small car with no backseat, which meant she had to sit on Marco's lap while Rocco pulled away from the house with a squeal of his tires.

Uneasy with her body pressed against Marco's, she shifted her body forward until she was balanced on Marco's knees, her head brushing the roof, her own knees wedged against the dashboard.

"Is there a . . . a seat belt?" she asked, a hint of desperation in her voice. How was she going to endure a ride to town like this?

Marco put his arms around her and pulled her back against his chest.

"You don't need a seat belt," he said, his voice so close she could feel his warm breath against her ear. She stiffened.

"Relax," he said. "It's only a short ride."

But how could she relax with his arms around her and her body pressed against his, so tightly she could feel every muscle in his thighs and chest and arms?

He spoke to Rocco in Italian. Rocco answered, taking his hands off the steering wheel to gesture wildly. They were talking about her and her trip, she heard *"barco"* and "Salerno." They sounded angry, but she knew that Italians could sound and look angry and not mean it.

All she knew was that sitting on Marco's lap, feeling him beneath her as the car took the curves, suddenly aware of his very obvious erection beneath her and his low voice in her ear, was as close to torture as she wanted to get. It was that combination of pain and pleasure that could break the most hardened criminal. This was it; she'd had her adventure. Once aboard the boat, she would cease talking to strangers. Not even a smile or an innocent look.

When Rocco pulled up at the dock, she jumped off Marco's lap and planted her American shoes firmly on the pavement. She would have run toward the water and leaped aboard the boat if it weren't for her borrowed suitcase in the trunk and the necessity of saying good-bye and expressing her thanks.

She didn't want either of them to think she was an uncouth tourist, but she wanted to be rid of them. Now. Before she lost it. She'd been holding her breath, her nerves stretched as taut as a travel laundry line, the kind that was in her ruined suit-case along with packets of laundry soap. She'd been longing, waiting, for the moment when she'd be rid of Marco. That moment had finally come.

After thanking Rocco, after he'd kissed her on both cheeks and said good-bye, she turned to say good-bye to Marco. But he was already carrying a bag in each hand to the ticket booth. Two bags? Where had the second bag come from?

She hurried after him and tried to take them out of his hands. "Too heavy for you," he explained.

"But what . . ." She never finished her sentence, because he was now in the process of buying her ticket for her. That was going too far.

"No," she said loudly. "I'm buying my own ticket."

He held his hands up, his face a mask of inno-cence. "Of course. I was trying to help."

"I know," she said, feeling foolish for overreact-ing. "I appreciate it, but I don't need your help. I can manage. Thank you for everything. It was nice meeting you," she said shortly.

Though *nice* was hardly the right word to describe it. Disturbing, exciting, dangerous, intense, stimulating . . .

The ticket taker slapped her change on the counter along with her ticket, then spoke rapidly and pointed toward the boat.

"Let's go," Marco said. "It's leaving in ten min-utes."

"I can manage. Really."

"I want to be sure you get a good seat on top for the view."

He boarded the boat with her and carried the bags up the narrow stairway to the top deck, where he found her a seat up in front.

"This is good," he said, glancing around at the other passengers.

"Thank you," she said once again. *Now, go. Go back to your so-called boring desk job and your family and your damaged car and your problems, and let me go.*

She stood, shading her eyes from the sun with her hand, trapped by the look in his eyes.

"*Ciao,* Anna Maria," he murmured. Then he framed her face with his hands on her cheeks, leaned forward, and kissed her. Under a warm Italian sun, in the middle of the afternoon, with noisy tourists and travelers filing on board and taking their seats all around them, his lips met hers. With the smell of salt air and the deck moving gently underneath them, he kissed her good-bye.

He kissed her quickly, as if he, too, wanted to get it over with. Then he took a deep breath and kissed her again—this time taking his time, using his lips and his tongue and his teeth, leaving her knees weak and her head floating somewhere above her body.

Was this how Italians said good-bye in public? If so, how did anyone ever leave? And how did they kiss in private?

If he'd kissed her like this last night, she wished

she'd been sober enough to appreciate it. She'd never been kissed like this in her life and had no clue how to respond. All she could do was put her arms around him, cling to his lips, and hold on for the ride. It was wrong, it was crazy, but she didn't want to stop. She wanted to absorb the warmth of his body, the strength of his arms, and the magic of those amazing kisses.

Without breaking the kiss, without taking a breath, she felt Marco's cool hands slip under her shirt. She shuddered under his intimate touch, then gasped as his fingers found her money belt. Was that it? Was he just a common thief after her money?

"*Che cose questo?*" he muttered. "What is this?"

"It's . . . it's my money belt," she said breathlessly. "For safety. So no one steals my money."

She felt his lips curve against her cheek. "You Americans. You protect your money, but what about your heart?"

How could she answer, when he was kissing her temple and the corners of her mouth? The boat whistle split the air, but it seemed to come from another place and another time. He was holding her so tightly her breasts were pressed against his chest, and she could feel his heart racing. But why? From what Rocco had said, he had many notches in his belt, so what could it mean to him, kissing an American woman good-bye?

Her head was spinning. With a huge effort, she pulled back, put her hands on his shoulders, and took a deep breath. His eyes had lost the cynical look she was accustomed to seeing. He was studying her as if he were trying to decide who she was and why he was kissing her.

"Is this all part of your service?" she asked, trying for a light tone that said, *That meant nothing to me.* "See the ruins, learn the history, have an exciting ride through town and then a good-bye kiss? All for the same price? You must let me know how much I owe you."

His gaze hardened. He grabbed her by the shoulders and kissed her again. But this time, he devoured her. This time, his message was clear. *This is not about a job. This is about you and me. This is not good-bye. This is to show you it is something you couldn't pay for, because it's not for sale, and if it was, you couldn't afford it.*

Anne Marie was stunned. She was shocked. She clung helplessly to his shoulders, her hands wrapped around his neck, her fingers laced in his hair. She kissed him back without thinking, without caring that she lacked his technique and skill. If energy and enthusiasm and abandon counted, then they were even. But he didn't seem to care about her lack of technique; his hands were on her hips, pressing her against him.

Marco was breathing just as hard as she was. When she finally stopped and caught her breath, she saw that the boat was pulling away. The engines were chugging, and people on the dock were waving their handkerchiefs. And Marco was still on board.

122   CAROL GRACE

Had he deliberately distracted her so she
wouldn't notice he was once again following her to
where she was going to meet Giovanni? These coin-
cidences and accidents were happening a little too
often to ignore. This was awful. She had to get rid
of him, but how?

Chapter 7

"Marco," she said, her voice too loud in her ears. "Look."

If she expected him to panic, to run to the other side, leap into the water, and swim to shore, she was wrong. He merely glanced at the receding dock and shrugged.

She sat down with a thud on the wooden seat, stared out at the open sea, and tried to think. Had she prevented him from getting off in time? Or had he planned to stay aboard?

"What will you do when we get to Salerno?" she asked, smoothing her hair with her fingers. She couldn't believe she was having such a normal conversation with a man she'd been kissing as if there was no tomorrow just a few minutes ago. Of course displays of affection were commonplace in this country. His kisses may have meant good-bye, or maybe they were just a way of passing the time agreeably. To her, they were earth-shaking, unforgettable. But she'd die before she ever admitted it to him.

"Rent a car," he said, taking a seat and leaning back, his arms stretched out against the railing.

"And drive back to San Gervase?"

"Eventually," he said. "First, I may pick up a few tourists in Paestum who need a guide to the ruins. And, of course, I will be happy to take you on a tour, as well. Free of charge, naturally."

"Thank you, but I've studied the book, and I think I'm up on the history and the archeology."

She nudged the second bag with her toe. "What is this?" she asked, as if she didn't know. It was his bag, and no one packs a bag if he doesn't plan on taking a trip. But why? Did he know she was planning to meet Giovanni there? But why would he care? Another question was, why would someone follow a tour guide and smash his car? Because he clearly wasn't a tour guide—he was a threat to someone. And it was time she got rid of him.

"Just a few of my things," he said vaguely. "I like to be prepared. I'll get us some drinks."

Marco left his bag with her as a show of confidence. It was locked, after all, and he didn't think she'd try to pick the lock while he went to the snack bar one deck below. He hoped she had no reason to suspect he was other than some kind of stereotypical Italian playboy with a stereotypical warmhearted grandmother and the equally stereotypical cheesy cousin. Without any prompting from him, they'd all played their parts to perfection, because they were what they were.

And he was what he was. A man who'd had a few too many close calls, both with women and with the men he was chasing. It was time to settle down, which didn't mean getting married. It only meant it was time to stop flirting with strangers. He'd gotten carried away there on the deck. When she'd continued to make a big deal of the money, of his paying her way, he lost control for a moment. He had to show her it wasn't about money. He thought she'd gotten the message. But hadn't he gotten an even more important message?

Leave her alone. She's a wild card. She's your enemy. You're using her, and for all you know, she's using you. Her kisses scared the hell out of him. There was a sweetness in them he'd never experienced. She kissed as if she'd had no practice, but he knew she'd been married. After so many years, had she forgotten the passion? But didn't everyone? Wasn't that really why he didn't want to get married? Was he afraid the passion would die?

Settle down, they said. He was hearing that from all sides, and the voices were getting louder and more insistent, even the voice in his head. But where and how and with whom, he didn't know. Even more important, why? If he did, he could set-

tle down in his rented apartment in Rome, where
he'd be in the middle of the action. Or maybe in a
chalet in the Dolomite Mountains, where his parents had retired, though that might be a little boring. After he caught Giovanni, he'd give it some
more thought. In the meantime, he'd play the role
of the Italian lover. Why not? He'd run the tour
guide role into the ground with Anna Maria. It was
time to try something else.

He couldn't think about anything until he got his
car repaired. When he saw the damage, he felt
slightly sick, as if he'd been physically assaulted. He
knew who'd done it. If it wasn't Giovanni, it was
someone who worked for him. If they thought that
would prevent him from continuing to hunt him
down, they were wrong. It was a childish trick to
smash his car, but there was something of the boy
still left in Giovanni, the same boy who'd once
bashed Marco's toy cars in the schoolyard. Of
course, Marco had done his share of damage to
Giovanni's toys. Back then, it was just a game. Now
it was a warning, a signal.

*I know where you are. I know what you want.
Come and get me if you dare.*

Giovanni was too much a coward to engage
Marco in physical combat. Instead, he waited until
he was in the house to smash his car. For that and
for everything else, Marco would make him pay.

Flirting with Anna Maria took his mind off his car.
Kissing her was part of the game, an excuse to stay
on the boat, that was all. If he'd gotten a little too

involved in it for a moment, what was the harm? He was in no danger of losing his head. He needed Anna Maria to flush out Giovanni, and it would all be over soon, as soon as he caught Giovanni in the act.

He felt bad about Nonna. Of course, she'd jump to conclusions when he brought a woman to her house. She was fond of Anna Maria, and he didn't blame her. Hell, he was . . . fond? . . . of her himself. Though it was best he didn't feel anything at all. He was there to do a job, and she was going to help him do it, whether she wanted to or not.

He'd just paid for the drinks when he felt a tap on the shoulder.

"*Ciao,* Marco." Antonio Ponti, an old friend, would have shaken his hand if he hadn't been holding two full paper cups.

"I hear you've gotten engaged," Marco said. "Congratulations."

"Congratulations? For what? We haven't even said our vows, and I can see the future lying ahead of me. I feel like I've been sentenced to life in the catacombs. Everywhere you turn, there's a blank wall. Everywhere you look, there are the skeletons of those who've gone before you. There's no way out. No possibility of being released early for good behavior."

"Not that your behavior was ever that good," Marco joked.

"You should talk," Antonio said. "Somehow, you've managed to outlast us all. All I can say is, don't give in. Stand firm. Don't let any woman think you love her or you can't do without her or you're ready to get married. Have you seen those laboratory mice running around a maze trying to find a way out? That's me. Once you've said the words—those magic words 'Will you marry me?'—watch out."

"I will," Marco said. "But aren't you exaggerating? Bianca is a good woman, *non e vero?*"

"Yes, sure," Antonio said with a dismissive wave of his hand. "As good as any. Have you heard the latest about Giovanni?"

"I don't think so. I haven't seen him for a year or two. What is it?" Marco said, feigning nonchalance.

"He was in town the other day driving a new Maserati. Since his father went to prison, he's taken over the family business, and he must be doing well. He's bought a house on Ana Capri."

"Really." Marco tried not to show an inordinate amount of interest.

"And, as usual, he had a new woman with him, wearing a big diamond. Which only made Bianca jealous. Didn't Giovanni and your sister . . ."

"No," Marco said, wondering how big this diamond really was and where it had come from. "They didn't."

"Antonio," came a clear voice from the front of the boat. Bianca appeared and wrapped her arm around her fiancé's waist. *"Ciao,* Marco," she said, and leaned forward to bestow an air kiss on both cheeks. *"Cosa c'e ie nuovo?" What's new?*

"Niente affatto," Marco said.

"Nothing?" said Antonio. "Don't believe him. He's got a new girlfriend. An American, by the look of her clothes, and very pretty. That goes without saying. I saw him kissing her up on deck. So, who is she?"

"Just a tourist," Marco said, regretting his lack of propriety. It never occurred to him that anyone he knew would be on board. "I'm showing her around, that's all. Didn't you hear? I'm a one-man hospitality committee for the coast here. Making sure the tourists appreciate our national treasures."

"Have you convinced her you are one of them?" Antonio asked with a knowing grin.

"Not yet, but I'm working on it," Marco said.

"Well," Bianca said, tilting her head to look at Marco. "Maybe we'll be hearing wedding bells for you, too."

Marco shook his head. "Never."

"That's what Antonio said, but look what's happened," she said gaily.

Marco did see what had happened. His old friend claimed he'd lost his freedom and had been consigned to a life of misery, yet Antonio placed his hand around his fiancée's waist in a familiar, possessive gesture and gave her an intimate look that belied everything he'd said. He was not exactly the picture of a beaten, defeated man with no future. Marco didn't know whether to pity or envy him.

"I must get back upstairs with these drinks."

"*Va bene,*" Antonio said. "*Saluti a la famiglia.*"

Marco returned to the top deck with the drinks

to find Anna Maria was leaning back in her chair, her eyes closed, her head resting on the back of the chair. The two bags were on the deck next to her chair. He set the drinks down and went to stand at the railing, where he rested his arms and looked out across the blue water. It was better than watching her sleep in the sun, her fair skin turning golden, her lashes dark against her cheeks.

A few minutes later, he heard footsteps, and she joined him to lean against the railing, saying nothing but brushing her shoulder against his. He wanted to wrap his arm around her waist and draw her close and stand there looking out at the water. Not talking, not thinking, just standing and looking. He was so tired of thinking and analyzing and theorizing. When was it time just to live?

He stuffed his hands in his pockets and resisted the urge to reach for her. He was supposed to be on guard, alert and at attention. But seeing Antonio and Bianca had set him thinking, wondering . . .

That's what happened when you ran into old friends who, no matter how much they protested, seemed right together. It was not what he wanted. Not at all. Still, he couldn't get the image of Antonio and Bianca out of his mind.

"I've been thinking," she said.

"I thought you were sleeping," he said, keeping his eyes focused on the waves, trying to block out the warmth that radiated from her body and the scent of her skin.

"I was thinking about your family."

He was thinking about her. About taking off that ridiculous money belt, and everything else she was wearing, and making love to her. It was tempting, so tempting, to see if she made love the way she kissed, with a combination of naïveté and passion. He wanted to hear her call his name, to taste her skin, to watch her face when she climaxed.

This was insanity. It wasn't going to happen. The old Marco might have done it, but he was a new man. Mixing work and pleasure had gotten him in trouble in the past, and he wouldn't let that happen now. No matter how much he ached, he wouldn't give in to his instincts.

"My grandfather came from Sicily," he said, deliberately forcing himself to stop dreaming about something that wasn't going to happen. "You can't see it, but it's out there." He pointed to the south. "He came a long way to meet and marry Nonna."

"They must have had a good marriage," she said thoughtfully.

"They did. They had a love affair that lasted more than fifty years. If I had to get married, that's the way I hope it would turn out."

"Had to? No one has to get married, do they?"

"No, but I feel the pressure. From Nonna, and then I just ran into an old friend and his fiancée. He looked happy, but he warned me against getting married. Not that he needed to. Why should I?" he asked himself as well as her. "I don't need a wife. I have a house in San Gervase, an apartment in Rome. Friends, family . . . everything but a car."

"Or a girlfriend," she added. "Unless she's forgiven you for whatever you did."

"I don't think so. I haven't seen her since she walked out of the restaurant. God forbid she returns to bother me. She was more trouble than . . ." He almost said *more trouble than even you,* but she might have taken that the wrong way. "It *is* a good life, except for my car."

"Who did it? Your cousin said you have enemies. Why? What do you do to make such enemies?"

"I'm in the travel business, but I actually work for the government, for the department of tourism. I have various duties. Sometimes helping tourists like you, sometimes investigating hotels and attractions incognito to see if they are up to standard. If I give someone a bad report, they are angry with me." That sounded plausible, and for the life of him, he couldn't come up with anything else.

"Angry enough to wreck your car?" she asked.

"Evidently so," he said. "After all, one black mark from me, and their ratings go down in the official guidebook. They lose income, and some might even go out of business."

"You wield a lot of power," she said. "So, you think this was someone who was trying to get back at you."

"Perhaps." All those innocent questions. But were they really so innocent? Was she just as suspicious of him as he was of her?

"We're almost there," he said, gesturing toward the shore lined with villas and hotels.

"I just want to tell you how grateful I am for all you've done for me," she said.

He felt the heat creep up the back of his neck. It was not from the sun, but it couldn't be guilt. He had no reason to feel guilty. He was doing his job.

"There's no need to thank me," he said stiffly. *Not when I'm using you to further my career and to settle old quarrels. Not when you find out I'm on to you.*

"Yes, there is." She put her hand on his arm, and he turned to face her. "You gave me the chance to see Italy as an insider. You made me feel like part of your family. That's what I wanted. That's why I came. Not to be a tourist but to see how real Italians live."

She seemed so sincere, and he wanted to believe her. But he'd seen so many sincere crooks, so many con men and women, that he no longer trusted anyone. It was better that way. Assume the worst, and hope for the best. If her sincerity *was* an act, it was a good one.

"If you ever come to the States, I'd be glad to . . . well, to show you around Northern California, introduce you to the natives, so you can see how they live, or whatever you'd like to do," she said.

He stared at her. Would a jewel thief offer to show him around, take him past all the mansions where high society kept its expensive jewels, explain how easy it was to break in and take what you want?

"I'm not likely to visit America anytime soon," he said brusquely. He tried to imagine himself meeting her son, visiting her library, seeing where Giovanni had gone to high school, and being driven around by Anna Maria. "My work keeps me busy here in Italy."

"And your vacations?"

"My vacations?" How long had it been since he'd had a real vacation? What was the point? He'd vacation after Giovanni was behind bars. "This is my vacation."

"But you're showing me around. I thought it was part of your job."

"I enjoy it too much to call it work. Not when I have someone like you to show around."

A faint blush touched her cheeks. "I never know if you're serious."

"I'm always serious," he said. "Besides, I am the one who should thank you, for letting me see my country through your eyes. You have taught me to appreciate small things I took for granted." This much was true. He, too, could be sincere when he had to.

"Such as?"

His eyes drifted to her mouth, so soft, so sweet, so willing. He wanted to kiss her lips again and coax another response from her. He wanted to do more than that; he wanted to slide his hands under her shirt and cup her breasts in his palms. But they were on a boat in the middle of a crowd, so he could only think about it, fantasize about it. Nonetheless, he should have better control over his hormones. Otherwise, he wasn't going to make it through the next twenty-four hours. He hoped that was all it would take.

Her question still hung in the warm air, and he forced himself to think of an answer.

"Such as? Such as the music in the square, which I used to find sentimental. Such as the food in the restaurant I thought was ordinary. Such as kissing you while the boat rocked under my feet and the waves slapped against the bow." He brushed her mouth with his knuckles. A simple gesture that meant nothing at all, he was sure. Not to him. Not to her.

He felt her lower lip tremble, and a jolt of white-hot desire shot through him like a bolt of thunder. So much for controlling his hormones. He'd resisted many well-dressed, high-class women, nice local girls his grandmother would approve of, and many she wouldn't. He'd turned away from exotic dancers and highly paid models, all since the day he'd screwed up because of a woman—but since yesterday, his resistance had melted like a cup of gelato in the sun. There was something about this woman that affected him as he'd never been affected before. What in the hell was wrong with him?

She caught his hand and pulled it away, as if she felt it, too, and fought it.

"Anyway," she said, her voice not quite steady, "when we dock, we'll be going our separate ways. I can't impose on you any longer. I need to see the rest of Italy on my own."

"On your own?" he asked. "What about your friend Giovanni?"

"What about him?" she asked with a sharp glance.

"You said you were going to meet up with him."

"I don't know about that," she said. "I may see him, or I may not. He once promised to show me around Italy, but that was many years ago, and I wouldn't hold him to that. He doesn't owe me anything."

But what do you owe him? Marco wondered.

"In any case, I have my guidebooks."

"And your gift for Giovanni? You didn't leave it in your suitcase, did you?"

"No, I have it here." She pointed to her tote bag. "Plus a little present for the cousin of my friend who lives in Rome. Thank heavens I had the sense not to pack these things. Please tell your grandmother I will send back Isabella's clothes, and tell her how much I appreciate having them."

"Perhaps you can thank Isabella yourself," he said, "since you're going to Rome. You may want to stay at the convent. It's not expensive, and it's well located. Or maybe you've seen enough of our family."

"No, I'd love to meet her." She held out her hand to shake his.

Another excuse to kiss her? No.

"You have my card with my cell phone number. If you need help, any kind of help, give me a call."

She smiled, but he had the feeling she wouldn't

be calling him even if the leaning tower of Pisa fell over on her.

The boat docked, and he let her walk off ahead of him, her suitcase in one hand, her purse over her shoulder, and her tote bag in the other hand. A man in a uniform was holding a sign that said "Paestum." He saw her pause and speak to him. Then she nodded and got into a black limousine.

Marco shouted her name. He tried to run after her, but a crowd of tourists getting off a bus in the piazza blocked his way. He shoved his way through the crowd and stood watching helplessly while the limo disappeared down the dusty road. One more foul-up like this, and he'd have to go back to handing out speeding tickets on the Amalfi Drive. He couldn't lose Anna Maria. She was his lure, the bait to catch Giovanni. That was all.

Anne Marie congratulated herself on getting rid of Marco and finding a cheap and comfortable ride to the hotel in Paestum. It was blessedly cool inside the air-conditioned limo, and the driver was a wealth of information about the ruins and the sights along the way. She settled back against the backseat, proud that she was on her own at last.

Marco was just too *simpatico* for his own good. He should be kept away from vulnerable tourists like herself. He radiated heat that would have scorched the average female, and she was not at all average when it came to experience with men. She'd been in love with only two men in her life.

Giovanni, her high school crush, and her husband, Dan. Neither was anything like Marco. Giovanni was a romantic, but he was just a boy when she'd known him. Dan was not romantic at all, at least not in the past few years. But that was okay. She loved him because he was reliable and dependable. She thought they were too old for romance. Apparently, Dan thought otherwise.

No wonder Marco affected her as if he were a blast furnace and she were made of wax. She'd been in a different world these past years, without love and without passion, never knowing what she was missing.

When the driver turned off the highway toward the beach, they passed horses and buffalo grazing in the fields. Anne Marie knew at once she was going to love this place. It was so nontouristy, so rustic. How lucky she was to have Giovanni suggest it to her.

When she got there, she'd ask to ride one of the horses. Then she'd gallop across these fields, the wind in her hair, the power between her legs thrusting her forward. The horse would snort and breathe heavily as she raced toward the sea, at one with the animal. She'd hear the pounding of hooves behind her. She'd turn her head and see another horse and rider gaining on her, getting closer and closer still. Who would it be? Marco? Giovanni?

The driver said something, and she was suddenly back in a limo and not on a horse, which was probably better, since she'd never been on a horse in her life.

The road seemed to go on forever. No wonder there weren't many tourists here; it was way off the beaten path. The farther, the better, she thought. As long as she could be at the ruins by tonight to meet Giovanni, she didn't care how far away the hotel was.

When the driver finally stopped, she didn't see the hotel. She didn't see anything but vast fields of poppies and tall grass.

"Where is the estate, the *agriturismo?*" she asked, stepping out of the car and inhaling the warm, fragrant air.

"Not far," he said, waving his hand off in the distance. "They will come for you in a cart with horses. Very picturesque, no?"

"Yes, very. Could I have my bag, please?"

The driver opened the front door of the limo and pointed to her borrowed suitcase.

"This bag?" he asked with a smile on his thin lips.

She nodded.

He picked it up, then shook it and set it down again on the leather seat. He repeated the motion several times while she watched with a puzzled frown.

His smile disappeared. "This is not your bag, yes?"

"No," she said. "Not originally. How did you know?"

"This is Italian bag, not American."

"Oh, yes. You're right. I borrowed it."

"But where is yours, signora?"

"It is ruined, smashed. In an accident in San Gervase."

"An accident? Everything inside is ruined?"

She nodded. Why would he care?

He let fly a torrent of angry words and stamped his foot on the cracked pavement. Then he tossed her borrowed bag to the ground next to her feet and kicked it with his pointed leather boot. With an oath, he turned on his heel, got into his limousine, and drove away.

For a long moment, Anne Marie stood there, wondering what it all meant. Then she looked around. She was in the middle of nowhere. This was no estate. There was no hotel here or anywhere near here. Would someone really come for her in a horse-drawn cart? It didn't seem likely. More likely, she'd been dumped. But why? Why the interest in her suitcase?

She sat in the grass at the edge of the road and took out her guidebook. She read that the estate was open only in the summer. This was September, and it was closed. But Giovanni had said he'd made her a reservation. The place sounded so charming, so bucolic, so perfect. It probably was, but it wasn't here, and it wasn't open.

There was nothing to do but start back down the road. So far, she hadn't seen a single car, but sooner or later, someone would come by and give her a ride to town. The hot sun was beating down on her back, so she unzipped her bag and rifled through the beautiful, exotic clothes until she found a camisole top with thin straps. If she were back home, she'd never think of undressing in the middle of the road, but there was no one around— which was too bad in terms of hitching a ride but fine for changing clothes. In a minute, she'd exchanged her lycra and cotton shirt for the bare silky top and transferred the items from her bulky money belt into her purse, and she was ready to go.

When she got to her feet and picked up the bag, it seemed heavier than before. Or maybe she was just more tired than before. It had been a long day, starting at the crack of dawn with a hangover and a vague feeling of unease caused by her inability to recall the events of the preceding evening. Those events were still unclear and continued to recede. So much had happened since.

Anne Marie walked and walked, and still there was no sign or sound of a motor vehicle of any kind. The only sound was the buzz of the bees in the wildflowers on the side of the road. Her feet felt as if they were weighted with lead, and she was thirsty. Her bare skin prickled from the rays of the sun, and her arms ached from carrying the bag. Her old bag had wheels; this one didn't. All she could think about was getting to the ruins in time to meet Giovanni. If no one came by, she'd have to walk all the way there, sore feet or not.

She needed something, a shot of adrenaline in the arm, a cold drink, or a . . . a piece of chocolate to give her energy. No, she couldn't open the box of candy Evie had given her for her cousin in Rome. But she couldn't shake the thought of the rich, dark chocolates, hand-dipped, made from the finest chocolate beans, in her tote bag. Her steps slowed. What if she had just one, then shuffled the candy around so Evie's cousin never noticed one was missing? She'd have to reseal the package, but she had time to do that, she wasn't going to Rome for a few days. If she hadn't had this meeting set up with Giovanni, she would have stayed there, handed off the candy right away, and done the city before setting off for the Amalfi Coast.

She took the candy out of her bag and was dismayed to see how soft the chocolate was. The first chance she got, she'd refrigerate it, and it would be good as new. But, for now . . . she slit the seal with her fingernail and removed one round, delectable truffle with a swirl of dark chocolate on top. Anne Marie knew how expensive Nob Hill candy was. Each piece hand-made by ladies in white aprons in the pristine kitchens atop San Francisco's highest peak. Or so they said. Maybe those ladies in white were an advertising gimmick. Maybe it was made by a factory in Fremont across the Bay. In any case, each piece cost a small fortune, and they were well worth it.

She ate the piece slowly, carefully, while the rich, smooth chocolate slid down her throat. Her fingers and mouth were smeared with warm chocolate. She sighed and, with the box safely tucked back in her bag, vowed not to eat another one, no matter how hungry or how tired she was.

She had to admit eating the chocolate worked. She was infused with energy, at least for the next fifteen minutes, walking briskly and purposefully. Then she got thirsty. So thirsty she could think of nothing but water. And tired. More tired than before. She dragged her feet. The strap of her tote bag was wearing a ridge on her shoulder. If it weren't for the thought of Giovanni waiting for her, pacing back and forth at the Temple of Ceres in the moonlight, she would have sat down by the edge of the road, put her head on her knees, and cried.

But what good would that do? And she'd gone through three of Marco's handkerchiefs already. As soon as she got to a hotel room, she'd wash them out and send them back to him in care of his grandmother. She couldn't miss this appointment; it was the whole reason for her trip. Besides, she didn't want to meet Giovanni with red, swollen eyes. She wanted to look her best.

Far in the distance, she heard the faint buzz of a motor and saw a black spot on the horizon. Her steps slowed, but her heart beat faster. She set her bag down. Whoever it was, she would pay them anything to take her to a hotel near the ruins.

The black spot grew bigger, the buzz louder and louder, until she realized it was the throbbing of a twin-cylinder motorcycle. And it wasn't black, it was bright red, the kind her son pointed out every chance he got. The kind he wanted for graduation but didn't get.

Damn. Just her luck. How would a motorcyclist manage to take her anywhere?

If it had been an ordinary motorcycle rider, he wouldn't—but this was no ordinary rider, nor was he an ordinary man.

It was Marco, wearing a helmet, a leather jacket, and his wraparound sunglasses. She never been so glad to see anybody but decided to play it cool. His ego was already way too big.

He stopped, got off, took his helmet off, and stood there under the late-afternoon sun, looking at her as if she were a lost runaway.

"What are you doing here?" she asked.

"I came to find you."

"I'm not lost."

"What are you doing?" he asked.

"Walking back to town."

"It's a long way."

"I know that."

"What is this?" he asked, running a finger across her lips.

"Chocolate," she said, pressing her lips together so they wouldn't tremble at his touch. But it was no use. Her whole body was trembling. It was his touch and the shock of seeing him. She wrapped her arms around her waist, tore her gaze from his face, and focused on the candy.

"It isn't mine. I'm supposed to deliver it to someone, my friend's cousin."

"Misty?"

She frowned. Had she mentioned her name and not realized it? "I was so hungry I ate a piece, and now I feel terribly guilty, but even worse, I'm about to die of thirst."

He held out a bottle of water, and she almost snatched it out of his hand.

"Thank you," she said, her voice coming out as a dry croak.

She forced herself to drink it slowly. Nothing had ever felt or tasted so good as that water on her parched throat. After she'd drunk half the bottle and murmured her thanks once again, Marco ordered her to get on the motorcycle. This was the man who presumed to give her instructions in etiquette? She was beyond caring. Despite her bravado, she was glad he was there.

Instead of obeying instantly, she ran her hand over the smooth, satiny red surface of the motorcycle. "Where did you get this?"

"I borrowed it," he said.

"What is it, a Harley Davidson?"

His mouth curled in disgust. "A Harley? It's a Motoguzzi." He paused. "What did you think you were doing, going off with a stranger?"

"Everyone's a stranger," she pointed out spiritedly. "You're a stranger, too, for that matter. If I don't go off with strangers, I'll never go anywhere. How was I to know he'd dump me in the middle of the road?"

"How much did you pay him?" Marco asked.

"Nothing. He left before I could even open my purse."

"What did he want? What did he say?" Marco asked, his forehead creased with lines.

"First, he stopped to let me off back there in the middle of nowhere, even though he'd agreed to take me to the hotel. He picked up my bag, and when he noticed it was Italian and not American, he flew into a rage. What difference did that make? Obviously some, because you should have heard him. He was furious. He kicked the bag, and then he took off."

"Before you paid him," Marco said, looking doubtful.

"Yes. I was afraid I'd have to walk all the way to the ruins. It turns out the hotel where I was going, this wonderful agricultural estate I thought I had a reservation at, is closed for the season. I just hope I can find something else, because I . . . I really want to see those ruins."

"I'm sure you do." He strapped her suitcase onto the back fender and handed her his helmet.

Where she came from, it was the law that riders had to wear helmets, but in Italy? She'd have to trust Marco on that and hope he didn't get stopped and cited before they got back to the town. She fumbled with the chin strap so clumsily he had to buckle it for her, and his fingers grazed her chin. She looked into his eyes to see if he'd also felt the buzz she got from his touch, the buzz that reverberated through her body like an electric current, but all she could see was her own flushed face reflected in his sunglasses.

"*Andiamo*," he said, taking his seat and revving the motor. "Let's go."

She looked at the motorcycle and down at her skirt. He turned around, as if to ask what was the delay.

"You mount on the left side," he said, "as you would a horse."

She quickly went around to the other side.

"Now, swing your right leg over the seat and hang on."

He watched as her skirt ripped up the side when she threw her leg over the seat to settle behind him. The old Anne Marie would have blushed at that blatant, sexy look in his eyes. Now, she coolly met his gaze, and for one brief moment something passed between them, so swift and so fleeting she didn't know what it was. It might have been approval for her spunk, her cavalier attitude toward her clothes, and her willingness to climb on and go wherever he took her. But she feared it was more than that. Much more.

With a roar, the motorcycle leaped forward, and Anne Marie threw her arms around Marco's waist and buried her face in his jacket.

The Motoguzzi vibrated and throbbed. Her whole body vibrated and throbbed in time to the cylinders. Inside her helmet, a roar filled her whole head. Her cheek was crushed against the warm leather of Marco's jacket, and the rich, masculine smell intoxicated her as much as a large glass of Chianti. Her bare knees were pressed against the throbbing machine, her feet against the foot pedals, as the wind rushed by.

They were alone on the highway. Alone in the world, with the endless road stretching ahead of them. She was one with the man and the machine. The sun was low in the sky, the horizon limitless. She felt as if the ride would never end, and she almost wished it never would. The past had receded and the future with it, there was only the here and now.

In the small, dusty town near the ruins, Marco pulled up in the middle of a small commercial strip, in front of a shop that advertised souvenirs and tourist information and boasted Internet service. He got off and removed his sunglasses, then reached out to help her dismount. He made no secret of taking a long look at her legs and the torn skirt that revealed a stretch of her thigh.

Anne Marie's heart kicked into overdrive. She reminded herself not to take it personally, no more personally than the kisses or the touch of his hands. It was just the Italian way.

"Thank you again for rescuing me."

"Even though you didn't need to be rescued?" he said with a touch of irony.

"Right," she said.

"Just be careful. Don't trust anyone."

Didn't that also apply to him? Why should she trust him? Just because he kissed like the expert he was? Just because he kept rescuing her? Just because she'd met his family?

"Don't worry," she said. "I've learned my lesson. I'll find myself a hotel room and check my e-mail and buy a couple of things, like a toothbrush and a few souvenirs." Now, why did she go into mundane details? She was nervous, that was why, babbling, afraid to say good-bye again. Afraid to make a big deal of it. Afraid he wouldn't leave. She was getting close to her rendezvous, and she was afraid Marco would hang around, and then Giovanni wouldn't show up for some reason she didn't understand.

She raised her hand in a half wave, half salute, grabbed her replacement suitcase, and went into the store. *Be calm, be casual,* she told herself. *And whatever you do, don't look back to see if he's left.* That would show that she was too interested.

First, she went to the tourist information desk and asked for a room anywhere in the area. She wanted to be near the ruins, but she realized at this time of day, with so many tourists around, she couldn't afford to be choosy.

"For how many?" the clerk asked.

"Just one."

"You are alone?" he asked, raising his eyebrows.

Was it so strange for a woman to travel alone? She nodded.

He flipped through pages of paper, presumably lists of hotels and rooms. She held her breath.

"I'll try," he said. "But there are so many tourists in town tonight for the sound-and-light spectacle."

"What?"

"Yes, it's very special. A presentation of a Greek tragedy in the Temple of Neptune. Twice a year only. What about tomorrow? Tomorrow, I can put you in a very nice hotel."

"No, I have to see the ruins tonight. Please, I'll take anything, a hostel, a bed-and-breakfast, anything. I've come all the way from California to see the ruins."

He nodded. "If you can give me a few more minutes, *signora*. Perhaps you would like to buy some souvenirs while waiting . . ."

"Yes, yes, of course."

"You may leave your suitcase while shopping."

"Thank you. *Grazie*."

She'd be glad to buy some souvenirs. She would do whatever it took, if only the nice man would find her a place to stay. She would also check her e-mail.

She went to an Internet café, where she headed for one of the computer stations in the back of the store. There was another message from Tim, but this time the whole thing was there on the screen. She almost fell off her chair when she read what he had to say.

Chapter 8

Dan had been stood up at the altar. No one knew exactly why, but rumors abounded. Maybe his dental hygienist had found someone else—she'd been seen recently with her personal trainer. Or she might have run off with the dentist, whose marriage had been rocky for years. Maybe they'd both taken jobs with Dentists Without Borders, the international charitable group that treated poor people in foreign lands. Someone else said they'd seen Brandy at the airport on her way to her honeymoon alone.

Tim reported that Dan was overwhelmed with grief and shame. Anne Marie could imagine how mortifying it would be to be stood up in front of the whole town. Almost as mortifying as being dumped for a younger woman after a twenty-year marriage. Though she felt sorry for him, she also felt he had it coming to him.

Too overwhelmed by the news to check her messages from Evie and other friends, Anne Marie signed off and sat staring at the screen saver, trying to digest the news. She hoped that Dan hadn't dragged Tim into his personal misery. Tim should be off enjoying a carefree freshman year, not worried about his father's disastrous almost-wedding.

Suddenly, Anne Marie felt someone was standing behind her. The sunburned skin on her shoulders tingled with awareness; every nerve ending went on alert. She whirled around, remembering Marco's warning . . . and it was Marco. She should have known she hadn't seen the last of him.

"You frightened me," she said.

"I'm sorry," he said. "You look . . . disturbed."

"I am. I just found out my husband was left at the altar."

"Your husband?" He frowned. "I thought you were divorced."

"Oh, I am. I keep forgetting." She paused. "How did you know?"

He picked up her hand and matched it palm to palm with his slightly calloused and sun-browned larger hand. There on her ring finger was a pale band of white skin. For some reason, she'd left her ring on until the news of Dan's wedding. She knew now she'd been a fool to hope he'd beg her to take him back, that they'd reconcile and go back to being a normal couple, slightly bored with each other but familiar and comfortable, destined to spend the rest of their lives in Oakville, living adventures vicariously through Tim, who was now out in the world on his own. Waiting for their retirement. Waiting for grandchildren. Waiting . . .

Marco wove his fingers with hers. She held her breath for a moment, then let it out slowly. It was fortunate she was sitting down, because her legs were shaking so much she would have fallen down. And all he'd done was hold her hand. She licked her dry lips. He stared at her mouth. She'd better learn to deal with her runaway hormones, or she was going to have a very stressful vacation.

"You aren't wearing a ring, though you recently did," he said, moving his gaze from her mouth to her fingers. "You don't think I would have kissed a married woman, do you?"

"I think you'd kiss any woman around," she said dryly, snatching her hand back.

"That's not true." He looked surprised. "Why do you say that?"

"Your cousin said something."

"My cousin always says something. You can't believe him."

"Can I believe you?" she asked.

"Of course. You can believe the fortune-teller, too. You had a sea voyage, and the man you left behind was deserted."

"That's right. I owe you for that." She reached for her purse.

He raised his hands, palms forward. "Not now; I'll collect later. Right now, I have good news. The clerk sent me to find you. He's found you a room. In a small hotel quite near here, on the street that borders the ruins. And the price includes breakfast and dinner."

"That's exactly what I wanted! That's wonderful. Thank you."

"Don't thank me. I'm just the messenger."

"But how did you know? How did he know you knew me?"

He shrugged. She was getting accustomed to Marco's shrugs; he used them whenever he didn't want to answer her questions.

"Well, that solves all my problems," she said. "I hope your problems will be solved as well very soon."

"Oh, they will," he said. "Very soon." He gave her a brief smile and walked away.

That was it. For a moment, she was shocked by the suddenness of it. One moment he was there, the next minute he was gone. No good-bye, no handshake, and definitely no kiss. This time, it was final; she felt it in her bones. She felt relief and something else. Whatever it was, it couldn't have been disappointment. No, of course not. Yet she couldn't deny there was a hollow, empty feeling in the pit of her stomach. *What did you expect? Another soul-searching kiss? A farewell speech?*

When she came out of the tourism shop with the

brochure for the small, charming hotel in her hand, a bag of sundries in her tote bag, and her suitcase, she almost expected to see Marco there in the street, on his motorcycle. She almost expected to hear him order her to get on and insist on taking her to the hotel.

There was a motorcycle parked in the street, but it wasn't a red Motoguzzi; it was a gray Vespa. Which was fine with her. She was glad he wasn't there. She'd been trying to get away from him all day and all yesterday, too. She'd finally done it. He was gone. There were tourists on the narrow sidewalk, studying their guidebooks and speaking German and British English. There was no Marco and no transportation.

But there was a man selling jewelry on the street. When he saw her, he stepped in front of her and snapped open the black leather case that was strapped around his neck so she could see his display of silver rings, bracelets, and necklaces.

She meant to walk around him. She meant to turn him down with a few well-chosen words in Italian, but she couldn't think of them. Instead, she succumbed and let the persuasive salesman slide a silver ring with a large polished stone onto the third finger of her left hand.

"Le sta benissimo!" he said.

"Quanto costa?" she asked.

He mumbled some numbers. If she understood correctly, it wasn't expensive.

She held up her hand. It looked better with a

ring. Not so naked. Not so deserted. It wasn't a wedding ring or an engagement ring; it didn't announce to the world, "I'm attached to someone. I belong." It was simply a ring. A souvenir. And a cheap one. Maybe too cheap.

Anne Marie decided she didn't want it. She'd buy a nice ring somewhere else, in a shop. This one might turn her finger green, or he might be selling contraband goods. She noticed he kept looking over his shoulder, as if he were afraid of being caught doing something wrong. She took the ring off and held it out.

"No, grazie," she said. "Me dispiace. No me piace. E troppo caro."

"Signora," he said, backing away, refusing to take the ring. "Che buon'affare!"

"But I don't want it," she protested. "Please take it."

He shook his head. She realized they were blocking the sidewalk, and other tourists had stopped to watch and listen to their exchange. She felt her face turning red. She reached into her purse and pulled out a handful of euros. It was worth it to get away from this man and stop making a scene.

The peddler smiled so broadly she knew she should have bargained or insisted he take the ring back. Next time, she'd do a better job of it.

She turned and headed for the hotel, supposedly only an eight-minute walk.

As she trudged slowly past the ruins, she was able to appreciate the Temple of Neptune with its graceful Doric columns standing in the late-afternoon sunlight as it had been standing since 450 B.C. A car slowed, and a man stuck his head out the window and said something in Italian, which she interpreted as offering her a ride. As much as she longed to drag herself and her battered suitcase into the car, she firmly shook her head. He drove on. Italian men weren't so bad, she mused. You just had to be firm. Let them know what you want or what you don't want. As long as you knew what you wanted, that worked fine.

When she finally reached the hotel, footsore and out of breath, she was happy to see it was just the way she'd imagined, small and unpretentious, with eight rooms at most, a restaurant attached at one end. The man at the desk told her that her room wasn't ready. With a glance at her torn and dusty clothes, he suggested she take a seat in the courtyard around the pool, and he would have a cool drink sent to her.

"Thank you," she said. "I wonder, do you have a refrigerator here?"

"*Un frigo? Si, signora. Perche?* Why do you ask?"

"I have a box of candy that's melting in this heat. I wonder if I might leave it in your *frigo* just until tomorrow."

"*Certamente,*" he said with a small bow, and took the box from her hand. "It is my pleasure."

She smiled gratefully and left her luggage in the lobby, went to the courtyard, collapsed in a deck chair, and sipped a lemon granita.

Nothing had ever tasted quite so good as the
sweet-sour tang of lemon mixed with ice. She
stretched her legs, pulled out her guidebook to read
about the Greeks and the Romans at Paestum, and
let herself relax for the first time in two days. She
was there. Really there. And she was alone. Not
lonely—oh, no. Just alone.

The church across the ocean where her ex-
husband had been stood up seemed far away. The
image of it was fading as fast as the pale ring
around her finger. Would there be a time when
she'd scarcely remember she'd ever been married?
No, Dan would always be a part of her life in some
way, just as the memory of his betrayal would
always be a part of her. It would be a long time
before she'd trust any man.

She went to her room on the second floor, and
from her small balcony she could see the Greek
temples of Ceres and Hera and Neptune rising
from the red-brown earth in the dusk. It would be
beautiful tonight when it was floodlighted. But
she wouldn't be on the balcony tonight; she'd be
at the Temple of Ceres at ten o'clock. It was too
bad she couldn't also see the Greek tragedy in the
amphitheater, but she'd see the major attractions
later.

Anne Marie stripped off her dirty, torn skirt and
the rest of her clothes and ran the water in the large
bathtub. She rested her head against the curved
surface of the tub and closed her eyes. The cool
porcelain eased the pain of her sunburned skin, and

the warm water soothed her aching muscles. The soap had almonds in it, and the shampoo smelled like crushed rose petals. She wiggled her toes and stretched her legs. What bliss, to be dust-free and clean from head to toe.

As she soaked, she wondered where Marco had gone. If he really was a guide, he'd be out hustling tourists to make some money. Or maybe he'd gone back to San Gervase on his motorcycle. By this time, maybe he, too, had found a big bathtub, and he was soaking the dust off his broad-shouldered, narrow-hipped body. She imagined the water sloshing over his shoulders, down his chest . . . Marco would have a glass of Chianti in one hand. He'd step out of the tub to reach for a towel, but before he did, his cell phone would ring. He'd stand there dripping wet, completely naked, talking to someone. Anne Marie could picture it so clearly she had to force herself to take deep, steadying breaths to cool down.

She slid farther into the water and closed her eyes. The next time she opened them, the water had cooled. Her neck was stiff, and her skin was as wrinkled as a prune. She'd never fallen asleep in a bathtub before, but then, she'd never kissed a stranger before, either. Or gotten drunk on the local wine or had her luggage smashed or indulged in erotic fantasies about a man she scarcely knew. She could make a long list of the firsts in her life since she'd arrived, and she'd only been in Italy for three days. What next?

The hotel manager told her dinner was served between eight and ten, family style. She opened her suitcase to find something to wear to dinner and for her meeting with Giovanni.

Isabella had beautiful clothes. Anne Marie couldn't believe that a girl who'd wear silk bikini panties and a lacy half-bra would give them up for whatever nuns wore under their habits. All the clothes were snug but wearable. Unfortunately, the half-bra was so tight that the straps rubbed against her sunburned shoulders and the hooks dug into her sensitive skin, so Anne Marie took it off.

She tried on a short skirt and a bright purple hand-dyed silk T-shirt with an orange flower hand-painted in the middle. She never went without a bra, and she never wore purple, so with her sun-burned skin and short reddish hair and her nipples pressed against the silk fabric, she scarcely recognized the reflection in the bathroom mirror. If any-one from Oakville saw her tonight, they'd faint dead away at the sight of their very proper librarian dressed like a . . . a . . .

She'd lost her identity. Though it wasn't much of a loss, after all. Maybe she was in the market for a new one. At least for tonight. The only person she would see who mattered was Giovanni. In the pale moonlight, it was doubtful he'd notice she wasn't wearing a bra. And if he did? She gave a little shiver of apprehension. If he did, and he was as sophisti-cated as she imagined he would be, then he wouldn't be shocked.

She stood in the bathroom staring at herself, wondering if she'd gone off the deep end. She never wore clothes this tight. She might not be able to eat a bite of food, for fear of bursting the seams. Never mind. She had no choice.

Isabella's shoes were the kind Anne Marie had been admiring on all the Italian women she saw. They were a little tight, like the skirt and the shirt, but she was determined to wear them until she had a chance to buy some of her own.

When she entered the small dining room, teetering just slightly in those beautiful shoes, she slipped into a seat at the long table with a dozen or so other guests. Some were English, one couple was German, and there were four American women, and everyone was speaking English. Italian food and English conversation. What could be better? She helped herself to marinated eggplant and roasted green beans from a tray of assorted *antipasto* and was having a fine time talking about where to go and what to see in Italy, when Marco walked in and took a seat across the table from her.

Suddenly, the *antipasto* platter she was holding was too heavy, and she set it down with a thump. Suddenly, her throat closed, and she couldn't speak or eat another bite. Suddenly, she was aware of his eyes on her, on her breasts and her nipples that puckered and pressed against her shirt in reaction to his unexpected presence. She thought about tucking her napkin into her shirt and covering herself. She thought about jumping up and leaving the

table, but that wouldn't do. She wouldn't give him
the satisfaction of knowing he'd chased her away.
She shouldn't be ashamed of her body. For a forty-
one-year-old, her breasts were firm and even tilted
upward. Why shouldn't she be proud of her body?
Why shouldn't she stay there, eat her food, and look
him straight in the eye? She had a date tonight. An
assignation.

She'd obviously been naive to think she wouldn't
see him again. For some reason, maybe because of
his mysterious job or because of Giovanni, he was
following her. She knotted her fingers together in
her lap and forced a smile as he smoothly introduced himself to everybody, including her.

As the only Italian at the table, and the only
attractive man, he was instantly the center of attention. It didn't hurt that he was also the Italian man
of every woman's dreams. Or that the four
American women were part of a book club from
Ohio who had recently read *Dante*. Anne Marie
noticed the looks the women gave him, some blatant, some discreet, but all admiring. She listened
to the conversation around her, watched the looks
the women sent his way, and gritted her teeth.

What was wrong with her? Surely, she didn't
begrudge Marco a chance to show off his knowledge of the area. Since she'd turned down his offer,
why shouldn't he look around for other clients?
She'd studied the guidebook; now she'd see how
much he really knew.

"Tell me," she said pleasantly when there was a

break in the conversation. "What's the difference between the Roman sculpture and the Greek?"

"That's a good question," he said, and turned his gaze on her. "The answer is in the museum. I'll take you tomorrow and show you the examples. Then you'll see the difference for yourself."

She nodded. Just as she expected, he'd given a safe, meaningless answer.

He turned and asked the women if they still had cowboys and Indians in their part of America. They laughed merrily and happily filled him in on life in the U.S.A.

He laughed with them at his own seeming lack of knowledge and said he was thinking of taking a vacation in the States one day. He asked them where he should go and what he should see, while Anne Marie seethed. When she'd asked him about coming to the States, he'd dismissed her offer summarily. But what really bothered her was watching him flirt with these women, because it made her realize she was nothing special to him. Not that she'd really thought she was. But still . . .

As the women chattered, he appeared to listen intently. She recognized the look, the way he leaned his elbows on the table and concentrated on whoever was speaking. He'd done that to her. He'd given her his undivided attention at the restaurant, at the concert, and on the boat. She knew what it felt like to have a handsome, sexy Italian look into your eyes and give you the full force of his personality. Not that she was jealous of the American women, all well dressed, all younger than she was. It was just interesting to realize this was his modus operandi and that she'd been right to mistrust him. Tour operator? Hardly. Smooth operator? Definitely.

"I hope you bought a ticket for the performance," he said to her.

"No. If it's in Italian, I wouldn't be able to understand it."

"I'll be happy to translate for you." He turned to the four American women in their cute, youthful outfits, more stylish than the kind she used to have in her suitcase. The kind she'd planned to wear tonight. How dowdy she would have looked—not that she cared. "For you, too," he told the women.

They beamed at him and said that would be great, and they made plans to meet at the entrance to the temple.

The memory of his last translation for her, of the love song in the square, came flooding back. Was it only last night? She couldn't repeat a scene like that: soft words in the moonlight, music, and too much wine. After the hangover this morning, she knew enough to avoid any further evenings with Marco. Especially this evening, when she had more important things to do.

"I may not make it," she said with an elaborate yawn. "I've had a long day."

"What, miss the performance?" he said.

"I'll see," she said vaguely. "I don't feel that well. I think I got too much sun today."

"You do look a little sunburned," he said, regarding her with one of those intent looks that were guaranteed to singe her already exposed skin. "Have some minestrone. Hot soup on the inside cools the warm skin on the outside."

"What about the soccer match?" she asked hopefully. "I hear Italy is playing Germany tonight." If Marco were safe in a bar tonight watching the match, she'd feel better about meeting Giovanni alone.

"That's right," he said. "But I'll be at the play."

The women looked at her as if she were crazy. What woman in her right mind would decline the offer of a bona fide Italian hunk to accompany her to an event? Well, compared with Giovanni, Marco was nobody, just a page in her travel journal. Not even a page, just a paragraph.

"Excuse me," she murmured, and left the table when the coffee was served. Her plan was to skip the play altogether, go to the temple early with the yearbook, take a seat at the base of a column, and just wait. Thanks to the women, Marco was now obliged to go with them to the performance in the Temple of Neptune and would never suspect she'd be in the Temple of Ceres—the one most likely to be ignored, a bit off the beaten path.

"Where are you going?" he called just as she reached the doorway.

She didn't turn around. "To my room." She kept walking as quickly as she could in her heals, much higher than she usually wore. He couldn't follow her. It would have been rude and obvious to bolt from the table in the middle of his conversation with the others. She smiled to herself as she reached the door to her room. She'd made it.

Inside, she knotted a lavender silk sweater over her shoulders, brushed her hair, applied fresh lipstick, and surveyed herself critically in the small mirror. She had a brief moment of uncertainty. Too late to have plastic surgery or Botox injections to eliminate the wrinkles. She was what she was. It was now or never. She looked around the room, at the pale gray walls and the cool tiled floor and the king-size bed, and wondered if she'd be alone when she returned. Would she and Giovanni make love in that bed, the way she'd dreamed about it?

The air wasn't filled with the scent of lemon blossoms, and there wasn't a sea breeze wafting in through the open window, but maybe fate had meant for her to meet her destiny here. Here, with a full moon shining on their heated bodies, she and Giovanni would finally make love. Not as hormone-driven teenagers but as mature adults who knew what they were doing. Not as the beginning of an affair but as the culmination of a long-lasting friendship.

She chided herself for getting carried away. This was just a meeting of old friends, nothing more. If she had any other romantic expectations, she was setting herself up to be disappointed. But there was no denying the butterflies in her stomach or her icy fingers. She grabbed her tote bag with the yearbook inside. With a careful look in each direction, she left the hotel and crossed the street to the ruins. She paid the admission and, inside the main entrance, took a sharp right turn and followed the path that led to the Temple of Ceres.

Though it was an hour before the performance, already people were headed in the other direction to get a good seat in the amphiteater. Fortunately, she didn't see Marco or the American tourists. She hoped she'd sounded convincing about going back to her room to rest and recuperate.

Why would anyone doubt her word? She looked sunburned. If anyone knew the kind of day she'd had, as Marco did, they wouldn't blame her for collapsing in her bed. If she hadn't dozed off in the bathtub, if she weren't looking forward to the most exciting meeting of her life, if the adrenaline weren't coursing through her veins, she'd probably be comatose by now. The old Anne Marie would have been in bed reading a guidebook, resting and getting ready for tomorrow. But the old Anne Marie read dry journals for fun, wore sensible shoes, and never stayed up past ten-thirty.

Neither fatigue nor sunburn, not even dengue fever or malaria, could keep her from this meeting tonight. She'd been looking forward to it for weeks, years, maybe forever. Maybe she was making too much of it, but she couldn't stop her heart from racing as she approached the front of the temple. No floodlights for the Temple of Ceres. Just a full moon lit up the temple. It was better that way.

She tilted her head back, looked up at the temple, and let herself drift backward in time. She imagined the pale stone walls decorated with gleaming marble and statues of the gods and goddesses. She imagined she was a Greek woman who believed in the power of Zeus, Hera, Ceres, and Neptune. If she were, she'd be wearing yards of hand-spun white fabric draped at an angle over her body and criss-crossed between her breasts with hemp. She might ask her favorite goddess for a favor. She might beg her to let her love again. To turn her life around for good. She might offer a sacrifice.

But that was then. This was now. There was only one person who could turn her life around, and that was herself. She'd taken the first step by coming here. Now she had to be bold and take the next step. But where, in which direction?

She closed her eyes for a moment and thanked whatever gods there were for bringing her here. When she opened her eyes, he was there: Giovanni. Looking like the ultimate gift of the gods, standing only a few feet away, leaning against a pale marble pillar, smiling at her.

Chapter 9

"Giovanni," she said, her voice unsteady, her hands shaking. She took a step forward. So did he.

"Anna Maria. It is you, at last. *Benvenuto a Italia.*" His voice was deeper, so deep it struck a chord in her heart. He put his arms around her and kissed her on the mouth. She closed her eyes and wondered why she didn't feel anything. No thrills, no chills, no accelerated heartbeat. Just a vague feeling of disappointment.

What did she expect? That her knees would buckle, she'd faint dead away and have to be given mouth-to-mouth? He'd always been handsome; he still was. He'd always been charming; he still oozed charm. He'd always been the most charismatic male she'd ever known. So what was the problem?

He stepped back to look at her, and she was afraid he'd be as disappointed as she was. She thought she'd improved over the years, but maybe he didn't think so. Evie told her she was the epitome of a late bloomer. But had she bloomed enough? Or too much? She held her breath, wondering.

For a long moment, they stared at each other. He'd changed so much. There were lines in his face, but they only added character. He was wearing an unlined Armani jacket, the kind Don Johnson wore as Nash Bridges, with an expensive T-shirt underneath. His hair was cut stylishly short, almost spiked. In the moonlight, he looked smooth and hip. He had money and confidence. He must have done well, whatever he did.

"You look beautiful," Giovanni said.

"Thank you." It must be the moonlight. Or Isabella's clothes. The way he said it made her feel beautiful. He could always do that. He'd made her feel beautiful when she was a shy, awkward teenager. "So do you. I mean, you look great. How are you?"

"Fine, now that I see you. I am so sorry about the *agriturismo*. I didn't know it was closed. I hope you found another place. You came alone, yes?"

She glanced around. There was no one there. Thank God she'd ditched Marco. "Yes," she said.

"And you brought my yearbook?"

She reached into her tote bag and handed it to him. He thumbed through the pages and nodded to himself.

"So many memories," he said. "Of the happiest time of my life."

"Really? High school was the happiest time in your life?" It certainly hadn't been for her. She'd suffered from not being in the in crowd, from not being popular with boys, from being tall and gawky and a nerd.

"I was away from home, away from all the problems that one has in one's own country," he said. "It was a chance for me to be not my father's son but a person in my own right."

"You were quite a person in your own right. Everyone admired you. You were the most exciting boy we'd ever known."

Giovanni caressed her cheek with his warm hand, his Rolex watch shining in the moonlight. "And now," he said. "Am I still the most exciting man you know?"

"Well . . ." He couldn't know about Marco, about her mild flirtation with him, could he? Even if he did, so what?

"Never mind," he said dismissively. "Tell me where else will you go in Italy?"

Here it was. He was going to offer to show her around.

"I . . . I'm not sure. I want to see it all, but, of course, I don't have time to do that. I thought Rome, of course, and Venice and Florence . . ."

"Yes, you must not miss Rome or Venice or Florence."

She waited, but he didn't say anything about

accompanying her. He clearly had better things to do than play guide to someone he barely knew anymore. It was only her runaway fantasies that made her think that he'd be overjoyed to see her.

"I cannot tell you how often I have thought of you, and now that I see you looking so very beautiful, I am even sorrier I must leave you." He certainly looked sorry, but if he was, then why did he have to leave after such a brief visit?

"Now?" she asked, teetering backward on Isabella's high heels.

"Yes, I must go. My life is not my own anymore."

"Are you . . . you must be married." It was none of her business, but she had to know.

"Yes." His lips curved at one corner in what she imagined was a sad smile. Of course, he was married. No one who looked like that and who had money to dress as he did would have remained single.

"I . . . I don't know what to say." There was a hard lump in Anne Marie's throat. She'd expected something more than a five-minute meeting.

"Say *ciao* and *buona fortuna*," he said softly, taking her hand and kissing it. "Good-bye and good luck."

Before she could say anything, he was gone. He'd disappeared into the shadow of the temple with his yearbook under his arm, as fast as he'd appeared.

Anne Marie stood staring into the darkness, hearing no footsteps, nothing but the faraway sound of the audience applauding. She shivered and thrust her arms into the sleeves of Isabella's sweater, unable to believe it was over.

She'd come thousands of miles across the ocean, spent thousands of dollars, to see Giovanni, and now it was over. She'd given him his yearbook, and now she might as well go home. The adrenaline that had kept her going during this long day was gone; she felt empty, like a deflated balloon.

She turned and walked slowly back down the path to the exit, her head down, fighting off tears of disappointment and fatigue. She was an idiot for expecting more from a man she really didn't know.

She literally ran into Marco, her head hitting his chest. He grabbed her by the arms, and she met his gaze. Even in the moonlight, she could see he was angry. He obviously didn't like being ditched.

"What happened?" he demanded. "Where were you?"

"I went to see one of the temples. I told you I wasn't going to the play."

"You told me you were going to your room."

"I changed my mind. Is that a crime?"

"I was worried about you."

"There was no need to worry. Now, if you'll let me go . . ."

He dropped his hands. They walked side by side in silence. Her feet hurt. Her shoulders ached.

"How was the performance?" she asked.

"Excellent. You still have time to see the second act."

"No, thanks. I'm tired."

"I'll see you back to the hotel."

Before she could protest, Marco had taken her elbow and was guiding her down the path. She was too tired to make conversation; all she could think of was Giovanni. How suave he was, how different from twenty years ago, and yet how much the same. He was always sure of himself; now he was even more so. He always said the right thing at the right time; now his charm had been polished to a fine patina, just like his physical appearance. There were no more rough edges, or, if there were, they weren't visible to the naked eye.

She tripped on a stone in the dark, and Marco caught her arm. She'd never admit it, but she was grateful he'd come along. The shoes were tight and uncomfortable and made walking painfully slow. She was even more grateful he hadn't come along sooner and interrupted her brief and precious meeting with Giovanni. If she never saw him again, she wanted to keep the memory of how he looked and how he'd kissed her hand and told her she was beautiful. She'd have to remember everything to tell Evie.

"How did you like the play?" she asked to break the silence.

"You already asked me that."

"Oh."

"Your mind is elsewhere."

"Yes. It must be the magic of the temples in the moonlight. It's very atmospheric, very romantic. I'm glad I came out."

"Yes, it must be the temples," he said. She slanted a glance in his direction, but it was too dark to see if he looked as caustic as he sounded.

"You should have been there," he continued.

"I'm on vacation. 'Should have' no longer applies to me. I've been doing what I 'should have' for too long. From now on, I'm going to do what I want to do."

"All right," he said, a hint of amusement in his voice. "What do you want to do?"

"I don't know," she said airily. "Maybe dance barefoot in the streets." It was a safe thing to say. It sounded wild and daring, but there was no chance of it happening. The streets were deserted, her feet hurt, and she'd never been much of a dancer. Dan said she had no sense of rhythm. "Isn't that what Italians do?"

"Some do," he admitted. "My grandmother did. She thinks our generation doesn't dance enough. But then, she has no idea what kind of dancing is done these days. I'm sure she'd be shocked to see the gyrations and hear the music. There is a place I know where there's traditional dancing, the kind even my grandmother would like. It's just a short ride away."

"On your Motoguzzi?" she asked.

"What else?" he said. "If you really want to go."

Before she knew it, they were in the parking lot of the ruins. He was holding his leather jacket for her to put on. She slipped her arms into the sleeves as if it was the most natural thing in the world to go for a motorcycle ride in the moonlight with a man who wasn't the man she'd come to Italy to see. Who wasn't the man she'd been dreaming about for twenty years.

If it weren't for the fact that Giovanni had blown her off, as Tim would say, she might have thought twice about taking off on a motorcycle in the middle of the night. Maybe that was why she was behaving like a woman who'd just escaped from prison, who was taking her first breath of fresh air, who was tasting freedom for the first time. She'd met Giovanni, he'd kissed her, and the highlight of her trip to Italy was over. She might embellish it a little when she told Evie, but in her heart she knew that Giovanni had no room or time for her in his life. It was time she got a life, too. As for her vacation, anything else that happened was gravy.

So she threw caution to the winds and jumped on the motorcycle for the second time that day. She knew why she was behaving like an irresponsible, braless twenty-something, taking off with a man who was definitely not her type and whom she hardly knew, to a place that probably wasn't in the guidebooks. She was rebounding from Giovanni's cavalier treatment of her. Once she'd admitted it to herself, she felt better. She felt liberated. Why shouldn't she dance in the streets or whatever popped into her mind?

Once again, she buried her face in Marco's back as the machine sped forward into the dark night. This time there was only his cotton shirt between her cheek and his back. With the jacket flung wide open, only her thin, body-hugging shirt was between her breasts and his back. This time, he wore the helmet, and the wind tore through her hair. Her skirt was scrunched up high on her thighs, her silk panties exposed.

Who cared? It was dark. The road stretched ahead like a ribbon in the moonlight. She could have gone on forever, clinging to a man she scarcely knew, inhaling the wildly masculine scent of his body and trusting him to take her away and bring her back, going with her emotions and not her brain.

Was it wrong? She didn't know or care. All she knew was that the ride was over too soon. The lights of a small town ahead drew close. Marco cut the motor, and she could hear the music wafting through the summer air. He pulled up behind a brightly lighted bar, got off, and held out a hand to help her get down. Her whole body was trembling from the ride, the vibrations, and the smell and the feel of Marco's warm body. She wrapped her arms around her waist and shivered. Despite the leather jacket, without Marco's body welded to hers, she felt cold and alone.

Marco gave Anna Maria a brief glance, but not too brief to notice her breasts outlined against the fabric of her thin shirt. He smoothed her windblown hair with his hand, when he really wanted to cover her breasts with his palms and stroke her taut nipples. His whole body was hard. He shouldn't be here. He should be chasing Giovanni. But what for? He'd been behind the temple when Anna Maria gave Giovanni the yearbook. He'd hoped to see them exchange money or the diamond—something more valuable than an old book he'd already examined in her room—but it hadn't happened.

What had happened afterward had surprised him. He'd watched while Giovanni slit open the book's binding, shook the book, and pulled out a scrap of paper. Giovanni read the message, swore loudly, tossed the paper onto the ground, and stalked off in obvious disgust.

Marco left the shadows, picked up the crumpled paper, and read the note. It said simply, "Gotcha."

Marco didn't know much American slang, but he got the message. There was nothing of value in the book, and Anna Maria or whoever sent the book had the upper hand. But why? Was it a double-cross?

Marco congratulated himself for not jumping the gun and arresting the man for receiving a twenty-year-old souvenir. Unless she'd slipped Giovanni something else in the dark, but he didn't think she had; the crook wouldn't have been so upset.

What would Giovanni do now, knowing that Anna Maria hadn't delivered the goods and had even rubbed it in his face? Marco assumed it was he who'd sent the limo driver to pick her up. The idea was to get the diamond, which he thought was in her suitcase. When the driver saw it wasn't really her suitcase, he dumped her. Giovanni must be back out there looking for the jewel, mad as hell. Marco tried to think like him, to plan like him. But he wasn't in the mood to think like anybody, not even himself tonight. He'd done what he could. Now he wanted to let the rest of the evening unroll by itself, to sit back and watch what would happen.

Mostly, he wanted to watch Anna Maria. He wasn't prepared for her. He didn't know she'd affect him like this. He didn't know what she'd do next. She was flushed and windblown. Flushed with triumph or something else? He preferred to think she was just an American tourist with no other agenda than to see the country. Just another American in Italian clothes with her hand in his, so warm, so vulnerable, so ripe, and yet so unconscious of her sexuality at the same time.

Just when he thought he had her figured out, she did something to surprise him. But was she working with Giovanni or against him? Was she working for someone else or for herself? He was tired of wondering, of worrying, and of thinking.

If he was tired of this game, Anna Maria was, too. He saw the irritation on her face when he found her on the road, encountered her in the dining room, and then on the path tonight. Even on the road, she could have walked back to town if he hadn't shown up. So, from now on, he'd no longer be the white knight. He'd be the classic, sweet-talking, seductive Italian lover.

He leaned down to brush his lips against her ear

as they walked into the noisy bar, and a whiff of flowers and spice hit him where he was most vulnerable.

"There is dancing, but it's not in the street. I'm sorry."

She nodded and looked around. He couldn't tear his gaze from her face. For a jewel thief, she ought to be able to hide her feelings better. Her eyes were lit up, and her lips curved in a smile at the sound of the keyboard and the singer in his white dress shirt with the gold chains around his neck. He was actually singing in English, an Enrique Iglesias song called "I Will Survive." So much for tradition.

"Do you like it?" he asked. He didn't only mean the song, he meant the whole place: the patrons, the peeling paint on the walls, the blue-collar ambience.

"I love it," she said. "It's so . . . so . . . cheesy."

"I know that word," he said. "Rocco told me it means . . . not good, right?"

"Usually. But tonight, it's good. Very good. Just what I needed." She smiled at him, her eyes shining. "Thank you for bringing me here."

He smiled back, and a hard knot in his chest he didn't even know was there dissolved. This was not good. Not good at all. Not when another part of his body was hard when it shouldn't be. He was not going to make love to this woman or *any* woman until Giovanni was out of the way.

He stood there in the middle of the bar, the music blaring, patrons laughing and talking, yet he didn't hear a sound. His gaze held hers for a long, long minute while he forgot about the past and the future. *Live for the moment. Eat the fruit when it's ripe. Make love, not war.*

Everything she was thinking was mirrored in her eyes. There was longing there, indecision, and fear of the unknown. There was sexual awareness, too. She knew he wanted her. But he knew she'd been let down tonight and was looking for something she'd missed. Something she'd been waiting for for a long time. She looked incredibly sexy tonight, and he knew why. She had dressed for Giovanni. And he'd never played second best to Giovanni.

He was marginally aware that the song had ended and an old man with an accordion was playing a tarantella. He'd been around women all his life; he'd had numerous affairs. He recognized the look in Anna Maria's luminous blue eyes. She wanted to make love tonight. But his job description said nothing about taking her to bed, even though he wanted her so badly at this moment that he ached. She eased herself onto a bar stool and swung her long, lovely legs back and forth restlessly.

"You said you wanted to dance," he said gruffly.

She looked down at her high heels and made a face. He reached down and took her shoes off, running his hand under her bare arch, lightly caressing her toes. If they were alone, he'd do more than that. He'd run his hands up the insides of her legs, behind her knees, and all the way along her thighs. Then he'd slide his hands under her shirt and cup

her breasts. He could not keep his eyes from her
form-hugging shirt, from her nipples that teased
and tantalized him. When he touched them, he
wanted to watch her face. He wanted to hear her
sigh and moan. He wanted to be the one to show
her what it was all about. Maybe she knew. Maybe
she didn't. She had an innocent look about her that
told him there were things she didn't know.

But it wasn't going to happen—unless, of course,
it brought him closer to catching Giovanni. Unless
it caused her to divulge something he didn't know.
Like why Giovanni was there. What did she really
have for him? When would she give it to him, and
where was it? He couldn't let her out of his sight
again. When he did, disaster struck. A stranger took
her for a ride and dumped her on the road. Even
when Marco was a few yards away, Giovanni
showed up and took his yearbook, and there wasn't
a damn thing he could do.

He shoved these thoughts to the side, stood, and
held out his hand.

She slid off the stool into his arms, and electric-
ity crackled as he pulled her close. Every curve,
every bone, every muscle in her body seemed a perfect match. Her head fit between his shoulder and
his chin. Her hair brushed his cheek and sent
waves of her elusive fragrance to blanket his senses.
Despite the accordion music, the clapping in time
to the syncopation, he could hear her heart beating.
Or maybe he just wanted to hear it so badly he
thought he did. It took him a few minutes to realize

this wasn't a slow song. Everyone else was dancing in a circle.

She hooked her arm in his, and they got pulled into the circle of dancers. A lone dancer went into the circle and danced by himself. Not professionally, not even very gracefully, but with verve and enthusiasm, egged on by the shouts and applause of the others. Unexpectedly, Marco found himself smiling and shouting encouragement. He'd always avoided this type of place, but tonight, with Anna Maria's hand in his, her face beaming, her eyes glowing, he fell into it as if he'd been going to bars like this all his life.

On the sidelines were people eating a late dinner. Now and then, they would leave their tables and join the dancing, then go back to their food and wine.

Two old men went to the center of the circle and did a kind of a Russian dance, facing each other and kicking their legs out straight ahead of them, trying to see who could outlast the other. Anna Maria was clapping and laughing, and he smiled.

When it was over, he found a small table for them. She propped her elbows on the table and leaned forward.

"I'm having such a good time," she said.

"I know."

"Thank you for bringing me here."

"My pleasure," he said. Too much pleasure. He shouldn't be enjoying himself so much; this was work.

"How did you know about this place?"

"It's well known among the locals, but I haven't been here for years."

"Did you bring her here, your girlfriend?"

"Adrianna? Oh, no. It's not her kind of place. She prefers something more . . . how do you say . . ."

"Classy, sophisticated?"

"Yes. Less cheesy, as you say. This is not a place to bring your girlfriend, unless . . ."

She waited, her eyes wide, her gaze unwavering, for him to finish the sentence and say . . . *unless you're planning to seduce her. Unless she's American and you hope the music and the atmosphere will put her in the mood for the kind of sex you've been thinking about, fantasizing about, part earthy, part sublime. Sex with an Italian man she's never going to see again.* Was she already halfway there? Three-quarters?

Whatever was in her past, a bad marriage, bad sex, or no sex, he wanted to give her something wonderful to remember about Italy. When she found out who he was and whom he worked for, she'd want to forget him as quickly as possible, whether she was guilty or not. As soon as she learned he was after her old boyfriend, she'd never want to see him again.

"Unless . . ." she prompted.

"Unless she is like you."

"Like me? What am I like?" she asked, her gaze a little anxious.

"Ah, Anna Maria," he said. "You are like no one I've ever known."

"Is that good?"

"No, it's very bad." He stood and held out his hands and pulled her to her feet. Someone was playing a slow song on an electronic keyboard, and he seized the excuse to take her again in his arms and hold her tight against him. This time, the musicians cooperated.

They swayed to the music, which happened to be, for some reason, the Italian wedding song. The thin fabric of her shirt teased and tantalized him, leaving just enough to his imagination to drive him crazy. As if he needed any more reason to lose his mind and his cool. He couldn't get enough of the scent of her hair and her skin, and he wondered how long he could hold out. How long before he could suggest they get back on the motorcycle and go to the hotel and up the stairs to her room.

He stopped asking himself what was wrong with him and just gave in to the sensations. Maybe nothing was wrong. Maybe it simply had been so long since something was right he didn't recognize it.

He kissed the tender spot behind her ear, and he felt her shudder. She tilted her head to one side, and he kissed her temple; then his tongue traced the outline of her lips. She closed her eyes and parted her lips, inviting him to join with her in yet another dance. When her tongue met his, everything—the music, the bar, the patrons—was forgotten. It was just the two of them, alone, locked in space. He let one hand drift down to the small of her back, and he pressed her closer against his erection. If there'd been any doubt before, there was no way she couldn't know how much he wanted her. He could feel her heart thudding wildly against his chest. She pulled back and caught her breath.

"Have you had enough?" he murmured in her ear.

She shook her head. Her eyes were still closed. She rested her chin on his shoulder and murmured in his ear. "Not yet."

"I mean enough of the bar."

She opened her eyes, and he saw the answer he was looking for in her heated gaze.

The ride back in the moonlight seemed to take twice as long as it should have. Her bare legs were wrapped around him, her skirt riding up so high it was as if she wasn't wearing one, her breasts pasted against his back, her face pressed into his shirt. His jaw was clenched in frustration as he pushed the engine to its limit until he saw the lights of Paestum. When he pulled up to the hotel, all was quiet. There was a light in the office, and the night clerk waved to them. He was holding an envelope in his hand. Marco got off the bike, opened the door, and took it. It was addressed to Anna Maria, and his gut wrenched when he recognized the handwriting. With his back to her, he stuffed it in his pocket.

He went back outside and hung his helmet from his handlebars. Then he put his arm around her. She winced.

"It's my sunburn," she said. He kissed the hot skin under the hollow of her throat.

"I've got something that will fix that." He carried her shoes in one hand as they walked unsteadily, hip to hip, shoulder to shoulder, up the stairs to her room, weaving slightly as though they'd had too much to drink.

She fished the key from her tote bag, opened the door, and flipped the light switch. Then she screamed.

Chapter 10

As Marco shoved her back against the wall, she gasped. He swore.

The bed was destroyed. The mattress was split open, and there were bare coils and tufts of cotton batting everywhere. The valise Nonna had given Anna Maria was sliced in half. Her clothes were in a heap on the floor.

Marco strode across the room and flung the closet door open. No one. Nothing. Then he went into the bathroom. There was no one there. Anna Maria's cosmetics were scattered, lipstick smeared, lotion bottle emptied. Her tube of toothpaste hadn't been touched, and he picked it up. Why hadn't it been squeezed dry? Because it was Italian. Brand new. Whatever they were looking for had to come from the United States.

He went back to find her sitting in a chair, staring straight ahead. Kneeling on the floor, he put his arms around her. She was not a small woman, almost as tall as he was, but she fit into his arms for the second time tonight as if she was meant to be there. Nothing could be further from the truth. She was meant to be across the ocean in the arms of someone else. Anyone else, but not Giovanni, and definitely not him.

"Who could have done this?" she whispered, her soft cheek against his. "Why?"

"Someone thinks you have something they want," he said. "What is it?"

"I don't know." She shivered.

"Okay," he said. "Get your clothes. We're getting out of here."

"Where will we go?"

"To my room."

She drew her eyebrows together in a puzzled frown. "Next door," he said.

"I thought the hotel was full."

"It is. I pulled some strings. Now, come on. Let's go."

There was nothing Anne Marie would rather do than get out of the room. It made her feel sick to think of some demented stranger pawing through Marco's sister's beautiful things. Marco filled his arms with most of the clothes, and she picked up what was left, then went into the bathroom for her toothbrush and toothpaste.

She felt as if she'd been hit by a cyclone, knocked down and blown away into a different place. A dangerous place. Like a barefoot robot, she followed Marco to his room, which was a cool, clean, and untouched mirror image of hers. The only sign that it was his was his small valise on the luggage stand. The bedside lamps made small circles of light on the walls. The air was clean and fresh, the faint scent of his soap and shaving lotion only noticeable if she thought about it. If she thought about him. Which she did.

Once inside with the door locked, she shuddered, then heaved a sigh of relief. Marco put his jacket around her shoulders, poured some dark red liquid from a bottle on the bedside table into a glass, and gave it to her.

"Drink this, and I'll be right back."

It tasted like dark purple grapes, but it was twice as strong as wine, and it burned her throat as it went down. By the time Marco got back, she had her bare legs tucked under her, and she'd stopped shaking.

"Where did you go? What did you do?" she asked.

"I told the management what happened, and I made a few calls."

"I don't understand. Why would anyone . . ."

"That's what we have to find out. Are you sure you don't have anything anyone would want?"

"Positive. You've seen everything I have, and that's not even mine; it's Isabella's. I'm glad her clothes are all right." The thought of her first ruined suitcase triggered something in her mind. "You don't think this had anything to do with the accident in San Gervase, do you?" The accident that might not have been an accident.

"The only thing I know is that it has something to do with you," he said.

"Me? It was your car they smashed."

"No one smashed my car before you came."

"I suppose no one followed you, either, no one slapped you in a restaurant or . . ." She shook her head. "I don't believe it. Do you really expect me to believe your life was uneventful and dull before I came? Are you saying that you sit in an office all day and shuffle papers for the bureau of tourism? That all this excitement happened because of me?"

"Don't you believe me?"

His gaze was steady; he looked so sincere. She wanted to believe him. She wanted to trust him. Even more, and until the moment she walked into that room next door, she'd wanted most of all to make love to him. He made her feel beautiful, sexy, and exotic. The sight of her room had ruined what might have been the most romantic night of her life.

He wasn't the man she'd been dreaming about for twenty years, but in a way, that would have been better. When it was over, it would be over. No regrets. This man probably didn't know the meaning of the word.

He was experienced, no doubt about that. His

touch was incendiary; just the sound of his voice in her ear on a crowded dance floor turned her knees to rubber and caused an ache in the center of her body. An ache that got more intense as the evening went on. There was only one cure, one way to stop it, she'd thought: to give in to her wildest dreams and make love all night long.

But she was wrong. There were two possibilities. Having someone ransack her room had also sent her libido crashing.

Marco went back to the bathroom, and she heard the water running. She sat in the chair by the small table in his room and stared off into space. Starting with that wild ride to the dock on his lap, he'd made it blatantly obvious he was just as turned on as she was. How did he feel now? Was he just as revolted, sick and angry, and, even worse, baffled as she was? Marco came out of the bathroom and stood in the middle of the room. His shirt was unbuttoned. She tore her gaze away from his chest.

He took a cigarette from his pocket.

"Smoking isn't good for you," she said.

He put it back in his pocket. "Neither is playing dangerous games."

"What does that mean?" she asked, wide-eyed. Did he know she'd sneaked off to see Giovanni? Even if he did, what was dangerous about meeting an old friend and giving him his yearbook?

He answered her question with one of his own. "How do you feel?"

What could she say? Nervous? Disappointed?

Disgusted? Worried? All those, and yet it was worse. She shivered. Her skin burned hot, but she was cold inside.

"I've got something for your sunburn," he said, holding a tube of ointment in his hand. "Lie down on the bed."

The king-sized bed was turned down for the night, and the sheets smelled like sunshine and fresh air. She lay on her stomach, closed her eyes, and waited. Inside her head, a voice was saying, *Watch out. Be careful.*

He lifted the hem of her shirt, lightly spread a cool lavender lotion over the prickly skin on her back, and gently massaged her shoulders with his large hands. She let out a long sigh of bliss.

"I'm not wearing a bra," she said, her voice muffled against the pillow.

"I noticed," he said.

He'd noticed? Had everyone noticed? Was she dressed like a slut? Acting like one? At the moment, she didn't care. All she cared about was Marco's hands, those strong fingers, and what havoc they were playing with her nerve endings. Alternately soothing and exciting, and she wanted him to go on forever.

"You like that?" he said, his voice as rough as the rocky shore of the Amalfi Coast.

"Oh, yes," she murmured. But her shirt was bunched uncomfortably around her shoulders. She yanked it off over her head.

His hands returned to move in lazy circles from

her shoulders to the back of her neck. It was
smooth, it was stimulating, and it was thrilling. She
didn't want him to stop. Not now, not ever. The
image of the ransacked room receded. The only
thing that mattered was the way he continued to
stroke her skin.

"Feel better?" he asked.

"Yes." *Better, and more alive than ever before.*

Marco shifted to the center of the bed, straddling
her with his knees pressed into the mattress. He let
his hands skim over her soft skin, from her neck
across her shoulders, long strokes down her spine
to the curve of her hips. He slipped his hands under
her skirt and caressed the swell of her round bottom. He stilled his hands and waited for her to
protest. If she did, he wouldn't blame her. She'd
had one hell of a night. If it weren't for the damned
bastards who had ransacked her room . . .

"If you want me to stop, say so," he said.

She didn't say so. Instead, she made little sounds
of pleasure, sounds of desire that made his whole
body feel as if he might spontaneously combust.
With his hands cupping her bottom, he flashed on
the day he'd seen her in the bathroom of the hotel,
bending over, giving him a tantalizing glimpse of
her sweet ass. If he'd known then what he knew
now, what would he have done? Turned in his resig-
nation? Told Silvestro he couldn't handle the case,
that he'd gotten emotionally involved? No, he was
physically involved, and that was all.

"No," she breathed. Her voice was no more than a sigh, but he could hear the yearning in it. "Don't stop."

He moved his hands to the backs of her knees. She moaned. He kneaded the taut muscles of her calves. She murmured something unintelligible.

He traced kisses where his hands had been, moving up her spine, across her shoulders, behind her ears, feeling her skin heat beneath his lips. His body was on the brink of exploding.

A few more strokes, a few more kisses, and he'd gently roll her over, look into her eyes, and watch her while he kissed her breasts, her belly, and then . . . It was what they both wanted; he knew it. She'd told him with her eyes, her body, and her voice. She wanted him. He wanted her. It was inevitable. He'd known it the first moment he'd set eyes on her in the hotel courtyard. It was just a matter of time. And now was the time.

The purring sounds she made made him ache with desire. She was ready, and, God knew, he was more than ready.

But was she ready in spite of what had happened tonight or because of it? Was she still in a state of shock at seeing her room vandalized? If so, he couldn't seduce her. He was no saint, but he didn't take advantage of women in shock.

He moved his hands back to her shoulders, touching her lightly with the tips of his fingers. He rested his cheek against her shoulder. He could feel her breathing slow down. He heard her sigh and felt her muscles relax. He kissed her flushed cheek. Her mouth curved in a half-smile. Her eyelashes fanned in a smudge against her cheekbone. She was asleep.

Marco felt all the air leave his lungs. It was over before it had begun. He was filled with a sense of regret so sharp it pierced his chest.

The first thing Anne Marie remembered when she woke that morning was the touch of his hands on her skin—his callused fingers tracing the outline of her muscles, leaving imprints she could still feel. She buried her face in the pillow and tried to remember what had happened next. She was still wearing her skirt, but her shirt was gone, and she was covered with a sheet. Her mouth was dry and tasted like grapes. She turned over and blinked at the sunlight that filtered through the half-closed blinds.

Of course, she was in her room at the hotel. But it *wasn't* her room. This was his room. She saw Marco sprawled in a chair, his legs stretched out in front of him, looking miserably uncomfortable. His hair was angled across his forehead, his wrinkled shirt hanging loose and unbuttoned. She spent a long moment contemplating his bare chest lined with dark hair.

His bare feet made him look vulnerable for the first time since she'd first laid eyes on him. She swallowed hard and sat up in bed as it all came back. The meeting with Giovanni, the motorcycle ride through the dark streets, the dancing, the music. And then the ransacked room. And now she was in Marco's room, in his bed, while he slept on a chair. And she was half naked. She found her shirt stuffed under the pillow and tugged it on over her head.

The last thing she remembered was his smoothing lotion on her back. It was all a blur, except for the sensations that lingered. The way her whole body had thrummed like a guitar until his strokes became so gentle she'd fallen asleep and slept as if she'd been drugged—soundly, deeply, profoundly.

A less pleasant memory was her ransacked room and the knowledge that someone was looking for her or for something she had—and they weren't doing it in a very nice way.

She swung her legs over the edge of the bed. She had to get out of there, away from whoever it was who'd done this to her. She had to find a safe haven.

"Are you all right?"

Anne Marie's pulse jumped. A second ago, he'd been asleep; now, Marco was sitting up in his chair, wide awake, his dark eyes alert.

"Yes, thank you," she said, trying to avoid staring at his chest again, at the expanse of muscle and bronzed skin visible. "I . . . I'm sorry about taking over your bed. You should have made me sleep in the chair. This is your room."

"I didn't mind," he said.

"If it's all right with you, I'll use your shower."

"Be my guest," he said with a wave of his hand.

"Then I'll be on my way."

"On your way," he repeated. "To where?"

"I don't know. Somewhere else. Somewhere where I won't stand out, where I can disappear into the crowd, where I feel safe. There's got to be a hotel somewhere where this doesn't happen." She gestured toward her former room next door.

"You wouldn't leave on an empty stomach, would you?" he asked. "Breakfast is included, you know."

"That's right." Once she had some coffee, she'd be able to think more clearly, be able to make plans calmly and rationally. She'd be able to put the events of yesterday in proportion, if not out of her mind, and concentrate on her future travel plans.

"And we'll buy you a new bag for your clothes before you go."

Her gaze fell on the stack of clothes on the table. Instead of the tangle they were in last night, they were now neatly piled. One more thing to thank him for. She wrapped her arms around her waist and headed for the bathroom.

"Anna Maria?"

She turned. Marco was standing at the door, so impossibly sexy, in a rumpled way, it hurt her eyes to look at him. "I'll go out for a while, to give you a chance to get ready."

She nodded. What more was there to say except thank you, again and again?

"Lock the door behind me," he said.

After she'd dutifully locked the door, she noticed his leather jacket on the back of the chair he'd slept in. She picked it up to inhale the intoxicating smell of the leather and the smell of Marco, and an envelope fell out of the pocket.

It was addressed to her and had been slit open. Where had it had come from, and why was it in Marco's pocket? She read the brief message written in Giovanni's fine handwriting. Memories of his postcards written in that same slanted script came rushing back. How excited she'd been, how she'd saved them all in her scrapbook.

"It was so good to see you, my dear Anna Maria. I am sorry I could not spend more time with you there. You mentioned going to Rome. Please call me at the number below when you arrive. *Ciao* and *buon viaggio.*"

Another chance to see him, to wrap up a chapter in her life with a little more satisfaction than she had last night. But should she call him? Did he really want to see her, or was he just being polite, trying to make up for last night?

Marco sat at a small table on the patio with a cup of strong black coffee in front of him, smoking a cigarette. He was going to quit, but not now, not today. He reached for his cell phone, and the minute he switched it on, it rang.

"Where are you?" his grandmother asked. "Rocco said you went on the boat with the American girl."

"That's right," he said. "We're in Paestum."

"We" she said. He could hear the surprise and almost glee in her voice.

What good would it do to deny any personal interest in Anna Maria? To proclaim that this was all in the line of duty or that he'd accidentally been prevented from getting off the boat in time? His grandmother would believe what she wanted to believe. He could picture Nonna now, sitting in her kitchen, something simmering on the stove, a *torta* in the oven and a smile on her face, her eyes bright and hopeful. But she didn't start in on her usual harangue; she had other matters on her mind.

"Marco, I'm worried," she said. "I have had a call from your sister in Rome."

"With good news, I hope," he said. They kept expecting Isabella to say she'd had enough of convent life, that she was returning home to take up a job and find a husband.

"Some. She has put off indefinitely taking her vows."

"Good."

"But here is the bad news. She says she has heard from Giovanni. He's going to Rome to see her next week."

"What?" Marco gripped his cup so tightly he was afraid it might break.

"I don't know what it means," Nonna said. He could tell she was worried. "If she's putting off the vows because of Giovanni, or . . ."

"It doesn't mean anything good," Marco muttered.

"I thought perhaps you—"

"She doesn't want me interfering in her life. She made that very clear. Does she know that you were going to tell me?" Marco asked.

"Well . . ."

"In fact, she told you not to tell me, didn't she?"

"Marco, I can't let her ruin her life. Hasn't that man done enough to her already?" Nonna asked.

He couldn't agree more, but the last time he'd tried to save her from Giovanni had been a disaster.

"What can I do, really? What can anyone do? She's an adult. She makes her own decisions," he said.

"You can go there. You don't need to make a scene or make any demands; just a friendly visit from brother to sister."

"She doesn't want to see me." They'd parted on acrimonious terms, arguing and yelling, just as they'd done over trivial things over the years.

"Of course she does. She's just too stubborn to admit it. Don't tell me you're too stubborn to try?"

"Call it what you will, I won't go to the convent and play the role of the big brother anymore. I gave her my advice once. She didn't take it then. She won't take it now."

"Please. Just think about it."

"Nonna, I'm working. I know I don't appear to be, but I am."

"Working? With a beautiful woman and the wild-flowers and the temples and . . ."

"How does Isabella sound?" he interrupted. "Do

you think she really plans to see him, after all he's done to her?"

"She sounded unsure. She sounded happy and sad at the same time. I'm worried. I don't want her to become a nun, but on the other hand, there are worse things."

And the worst of the worse things was Giovanni. Marco caught sight of Anna Maria just then, walking gracefully toward him in Isabella's shoes, tight-fitting designer blue jeans, and a black shirt stretched snugly over her breasts. The enticing mixture of her American body in Italian clothes caused him to lose his train of thought.

"I must go now, Nonna. I'll call you later." He stuffed the phone in his pocket and smashed his cigarette into the ground with his heel.

"Sit down," he invited, and poured her a cup of coffee from the pot on the table. He pushed a plate of pastries toward her and was pleased to see her take one and bite into it hungrily. He was afraid the events of the night before might have affected her appetite. She'd slept well, though, better than he had. But why shouldn't she? She had the bed; he had the chair.

The fragrance of the coffee mingled with the faint scent of her skin and hair. The sun picked up red highlights in her short hair. A feeling of well-being washed over him. It was purely irrational. Everything possible was going wrong. If Giovanni hadn't ransacked her room, then it was either one of his men or a rival. He doubted they'd found what they were looking for. If they'd found something he hadn't, he'd better give up undercover work. Marco shoved those thoughts aside, leaned back in his chair, put his sunglasses on, and watched Anna Maria while she ate.

If only life could be this simple. Having breakfast in the company of an attractive, intelligent woman, warm sunshine, birds twittering in the trees above, and a good cup of coffee. What more could a person want?

Suddenly, he realized she was wearing a ring. Not her wedding ring but a ring with a large stone. The kind of ring that could be used to conceal a diamond if one wanted to. He felt as if he'd been hit over the head with a piece of granite from the San Gervase quarry. Where had the ring come from? Why hadn't he noticed it before? He bit his tongue to keep from exclaiming or accusing her.

After a long moment, when she realized he was staring at her behind his glasses, Anna Maria stopped chewing and set her cup down.

"What?"

"Nothing. I'm just trying to follow my own advice and live for the moment, eat the fruit when it's ripe, and not worry about tomorrow." But he had to ask. "By the way, where did you get that ring?"

She brushed the crumbs from her mouth. "On the street."

"On the street? You found it lying on the street?" he asked.

"No, I bought it yesterday from a street seller in Paestum. Do you like it?"

He reached across the table and took her hand in his. He rubbed her palm with his thumb, then studied the large amber stone. "How much did you pay for it?"

"I don't remember. Not much. Why, does it look cheap?"

She sounded so innocent. Too innocent. Though he'd seen many photos of concealed stones, he couldn't be sure this was one of them. Maybe she had bought it from a street seller, or maybe it had been handed off to her by someone.

"Cheap? No, it's fine." He stared at it, as if by concentrating he could see if there was a diamond hidden under the amber stone. He imagined its fiery brilliance. He pictured the many facets, the smoldering fire of its intense yellow color. He stared at it so long his vision blurred.

"It doesn't matter," she said a little too casually. "I liked it, so I bought it. It covers that white ring around my finger that you noticed. I prefer not to announce to the world that I'm divorced."

"That bothers you, doesn't it?" he said.

"Yes, it does. It means that I failed at the most important thing I've ever done."

"I don't believe that," Marco said.

"I don't expect you to. You've never been married. If you had . . ."

"If I'd been married to you—"

"Then you would have left me for a younger, prettier, more exciting woman."

"Not every man is looking for a younger woman."

"What are you looking for?" Anna Maria asked.

"I'm not looking."

"But if you were?"

"An honest woman," he said. "Someone with integrity. Someone I can trust. Someone who doesn't play games or carry a lot of baggage."

"Baggage?" she said, and laughed. It was the sound of a bubbling brook, and it struck him like a fresh breeze on a warm summer morning.

"With you, I don't see how any woman could carry much baggage. Since I met you, my baggage has been smashed and dumped until I'm reduced to a pile of clothing that, while beautiful, isn't my own. As for honesty, I think you get what you deserve. If you're honest with a woman, she'll be honest with you; and if you don't play games . . ."

"Yes, I understand. But, fortunately, I am not looking for a woman at all."

"Well, good," she said. She drained her coffee cup, reached into her bag, and pulled out the letter from Giovanni. "Speaking of honesty, where did this letter come from, and why didn't you tell me about it?" she said.

"Oh, I'm sorry, I forgot. The night clerk gave it to me. I meant to give it to you, but when we found your room had been ransacked, I forgot."

"You opened it."

"Just to see if it was urgent, after you fell asleep." Damn, why had he forgotten to tell her? Or simply disposed of it?

"It's important to me, if I want to see Giovanni again."

"Again?" he asked.

"I saw him last night."

"I see."

"He's an old friend. We only had a few minutes together last night, which you probably guessed. It would be good to see him again."

Marco sighed. What was it with Giovanni and women? They didn't seem able to resist him. But in this case, it was Giovanni who had obviously not gotten what he wanted from Anna Maria. Unless he really just wanted to see her again. Marco could understand that. She was a special woman. She might not be honest, she might have baggage of the emotional kind, she might not be as young as her husband wanted, but she was different from any woman he'd ever known. She was warm and open and so incredibly desirable that he forgot everything he was supposed to remember about her when he touched her or when she looked at him with those incredibly expressive blue eyes. Maybe Giovanni felt the same way. Though why would he contact Isabella, then?

"Then I suppose you will be going to Rome," he said.

"I was always going to Rome."

"What a coincidence—I'm going there, too. I'm going to rent a car. Then we'll buy you some new baggage for your clothes, so you can pack up."

"And some shoes. I can't walk in these another

day," she said, removing his sister's high heels. "Maybe that's what the fortune-teller meant about walking in my slippers. If I only had a pair of slippers, I'd wear them."

"I'll go get the car. Don't talk to strangers, and don't get into any cars, no matter what the driver says. Is that clear?"

Without waiting for an answer, he left her at the table and went to exchange his borrowed motorcycle for a car. He also had to call his office and give them an update on Giovanni and the missing stone. Maybe Silvestro would have some news for him.

Barefoot, with shoes in hand, Anne Marie went to find a phone booth and call Evie. She had to tell her about Giovanni, what little there was to tell, and find out more about Dan's aborted wedding.

Squeezed into the booth on the street in front of the hotel, she inserted the PIN card she'd bought in Rome and dialed Evie's number.

"Anne Marie, how are you? What's happened? Did you call my cousin yet?"

"I haven't had a chance."

"Why, what are you doing?"

"Just . . . traveling around, seeing things. I'm visiting a very interesting archeological site right now."

"Have you seen Giovanni yet?"

"Yes, last night."

"Did you give him the yearbook?"

"Yes."

"What did he say?"

"He just said thank-you."

"How did he look?"

"He looks great, almost like a movie star, suave and well dressed. He's obviously doing very well."

"Uh-huh. When will you be in Rome?"

"We're heading there today."

"We? Who's we?"

"Just someone who's giving me a ride."

"Anne Marie, don't accept rides from strangers. Especially Italian strangers. It's not safe."

Good Lord, Evie was as bad as Marco. But it was easier to agree with her than to argue with her, because she always won. "Okay, so tell me more about Dan. Did Brandy really stand him up?"

"Not only that . . ."

While Evie was in the middle of the details of the break-up, there was a knock on the glass door of the booth. Still listening to her friend, Anne Marie turned around to see who it was.

Chapter 11

Marco was on the other side of the glass door. He was holding a pair of women's sandals in his hand at eye level. His mouth was moving, but she couldn't hear what he was saying.

"Got to go, Evie," she interrupted. "I'll call you later."

"Wait, where are you staying in Rome? I want to get your number. I'm going to call my cousin and tell her you're on your way. She'll help you find a place to stay, introduce you to her friends, and—"

Anne Marie hung up as Marco's knocking on the door became louder and his expression more intense. She didn't really want to hear any more about Dan, and she didn't want Evie's cousin to take her under her wing.

The contrast between her old life and her new life, however temporary, was never clearer. Here she was, standing barefoot in a phone booth, with the sexiest man she'd ever known waiting for her with a pair of leather sandals in his hand. While thousands of miles away, life continued as it had for decades. It was getting harder and harder to remember who she was back there.

She wished Evie could see her in her Italian jeans and snug-fitting shirt, clothes a forty-something librarian would never be caught dead in in that other world. She'd probably be fired for wearing Isabella's clothes to work in Oakville. Or at least cause a few stares at the Friends of the Library book sale.

She opened the door to the phone booth and wished even more that Evie could see Marco. If she'd thought Giovanni was handsome, what would she think of Marco, his narrow hips in black jeans, his broad shoulders in a dark blue shirt, and his soulful eyes regarding her intently? No one had ever looked at her that way before. No one had ever given her a sensual massage like the one he gave her last night. No one had ever danced with her the way he had or kissed the way he did. He was so good at it. Maybe too good. She hadn't known a man could be so tender and so tough at the same time. Butterflies swarmed in her stomach. What was she doing, reliving every minute of last night like that?

Suddenly, there was no glass between them,

nothing between them but the sweet, warm air. She wanted to throw her arms around him and breathe in the clean, male scent of him. Instead, she sat on the edge of a low stone wall, slipped the new sandals on, and told him they fit perfectly.

"Where did you get them?"

"At a shop in town," Marco said.

"How did you know what size I was?" she asked.

"I observed your feet last night," he said with a gleam in his eye.

She wondered what else he'd observed when he'd been applying lotion to her bare back and loosening her clothes for her the night she drank too much wine back in San Gervase.

"Did you find a car?" she asked, trying to wipe away the erotic images.

He pointed to an ivory-colored touring car at the curb with the top down. "It was all they had."

"It's beautiful," she said. "What is it?"

"An old Lancia. A classic. They didn't want to rent it, but I said I'd take good care of it and return it in good condition. It should get us to Rome, even taking the scenic route."

"Are we taking the scenic route?"

"It's the only way to see Italy. Of course, it will take longer, but I strongly recommend it. If that's what you want."

"Of course I do, that's why I'm here. To see the country and meet the people." On the other hand, touring the country in a gorgeous classic car with a man she scarcely knew was not very cautious. He could pull off the road and rob her blind and dump her body in an old catacomb, and no one would ever find her. There'd be enough air for her to last a few days, during which she'd draw on the walls with a sharp stone—beautiful, primitive images of animals. When tourists visited the site years from now, they'd be told the etchings were from prehistoric times. Her bones would be piled in a corner for the tourists to gawk at, and archeologists would use them to carbon-date her life. How surprised they'd be if they knew she was a literate, educated woman who just had a talent for crude, simple artwork.

Coming back to reality, why would Marco rob her when she had nothing left to take? If he was going to do it, he'd had many opportunities already, yet he was still taking care of her. Still bothering her, still mystifying her . . .

Something had happened in the last few days. Marco, not Giovanni, was the epitome of the man she'd hoped she'd find here. Could she trust him? Maybe not. Did she know him? Not very well. Was she going to Rome with him? Absolutely. She'd be crazy to turn down the opportunity.

She paid him a ridiculously small amount for the sandals and for a leather valise he'd also bought her. When she protested, he explained that leather was a good buy in Italy.

Now she was on her way to Rome with a man any red-blooded woman would give her right arm for, a man who was sometimes mysterious, always sexy and exciting, and often downright disturbing. With the wind in her hair, the sun on her bare arms, and the disturbing events of the night before becoming a dim memory in the bright sunshine, she was so happy she laughed out loud.

Marco turned his head and smiled at her. Her heart raced right along with the Lancia's engine, and when he reached over and put his hand on her thigh, she felt as if the wind had sucked the breath right out of her lungs.

"Who were you talking to on the phone?" he asked, putting his hand back on the wheel.

"My friend Evie. The one you talked to that night in San Gervase."

"You are old friends?"

"We went to high school together, but I didn't really know her then. She was in a different crowd from mine. The popular crowd, from the ritzy side of town. I've just gotten to know her recently."

"I see. Was she in love with Giovanni, too?"

"Too? Did I say I was in love with him?"

"You didn't have to. I could tell by the look on your face."

Her eyes widened in surprise. "You're wrong. I had a crush on him in high school, but I'm much too old for that kind of thing now."

"Too old to fall in love?" He sounded surprised.

"Wait a minute, I thought you didn't believe in love."

"I don't, but you do."

"Once was enough. Oh, it's exciting at first. It's what comes afterward that's so hard. I don't believe in forever after now; I've learned my lesson. You sounded so surprised. Are you suddenly some kind of romantic?" she asked.

He shook his head. "Not me. I could have told you love was an illusion. But you, being a woman, wouldn't have listened. You had to find out for yourself. You've been disappointed, and I'm sorry." He did look sincerely sorry for her.

"Disappointed?" Her voice rose. She didn't want his pity, and she felt compelled to set the record straight. "Yes, you could say I was disappointed. I told you I felt like a failure."

"Felt," he repeated. "Does that mean you don't feel like that anymore?"

She hesitated. "I don't know. I do know I thought I had a happy marriage. I thought we would grow old together, watch our grandchildren grow up, learn to play golf together, plant some rosebushes, have time to remodel the house . . . whatever."

"And now?"

"Now I'm in Italy. I'm in a beautiful car I've never been in before, passing scenery I've never seen before, wearing clothes that aren't mine." *Sitting next to the sexiest man I've ever met, a man I never dreamed could exist.*

Anna Marie looked down at her snug-fitting jeans pulled tight against her thighs, wondering who she was fooling. Inside, she was still the same straitlaced librarian, the same dumped, divorced, disappointed woman she was when she'd left

California—wasn't she? Or were those feelings of failure receding with every passing day? With every touch, every look, every kiss from this man she didn't know?

She sneaked another look at Marco's profile, at his high cheekbones, at his hair windblown across his forehead. When he turned and their eyes locked and held for a brief moment, her pulse quickened, and she knew she was not the same woman who'd left California only days ago.

That woman never looked at men the way she was looking at Marco. That woman never felt sexy or wildly feminine, the way Marco made her feel. Somewhere between there and here, she'd left that woman behind, standing on a corner somewhere wearing clothes that were practical and sensible but could never be called provocative or glamorous or even stylish.

"Then I was wrong," he said. "You're not in love with Giovanni."

"Of course not; we're just friends. At least, I hope we are. You read the note he sent me."

"I'm sorry about not giving it to you."

"But not about reading it?"

She wished she didn't sound so prim, but he seemed to bring out that side in her. Except when he was bringing out the wild, wanton side of her. No wonder she was having an identity crisis. It wasn't just the clothes or the hair; it was him. It was the way he made her feel.

He slanted a provocative glance in her direction.

"Haven't you ever given in to temptation? Or are you too old for that kind of thing, too?"

"I don't think we know each other well enough to be having this conversation."

"Then let's talk about your friend Giovanni."

"Why are you so interested in him?"

"I have a few questions I'd like to ask him."

"Write them down. I'll ask him for you when I see him."

"I have an idea. I'll go with you. We'll have a get-together, the three of us."

"He might not like that."

"I'm sure he wouldn't." He paused. "So, Giovanni was a big hit in America?"

"Oh, yes. Everyone at my high school was in love with him."

"Even your friend Evie?"

"Evie? Oh, no!"

"What's the matter?"

"The candy. Evie's cousin's candy! I left it at the hotel."

"We'll buy her some along the way."

"No, it's a special kind. It's Nob Hill candy, made by hand on Nob Hill in San Francisco. They've been making it there for more than a hundred years. We have to go back."

He put his foot on the brake, and the car screeched to a stop. He turned around and headed back to Paestum.

"Thank you," she said. "I'm sorry."

He didn't speak for a long time. She felt terrible

making him turn around, and she tried to think of something to say to break the silence.

"Don't you know anyone who's happily married?" she asked at last.

He shook his head.

"I do. I have several friends who are."

"How do you know?" he asked curiously.

"I guess . . . I guess no one really does know. Why do you ask?"

"I ran into an old friend on the boat who's gotten engaged. He said he was dreading marriage. He was feeling trapped."

"Then why marry?"

"I don't know. Maybe he thinks he's in love."

"What about your grandparents? I thought you said—"

"I said they were married for fifty years. For them, it worked. For Antonio and Bianca, it might work. But you have to believe. I don't, so for me, it wouldn't work. I know myself."

"I admit I don't know you very well, Marco, but I saw you with your grandmother at her house, in her kitchen, and I know that you love her very much. So, don't tell me love doesn't exist."

"That's different," he said shortly.

She shook her head. It wasn't different. He was a tough man, but he was capable of love, whether he believed in it or not. "Tell me, don't you ever get lonely?"

"No," he said a little too quickly, keeping his eyes on the road.

She studied his face once again, knowing he wasn't likely to acknowledge love or being lonely, not to her.

"Do you?" he asked.

"Yes. Ever since Dan left, I've been the odd man out. I liked being part of a couple. I liked being married. I liked knowing someone was waiting for me to come home, that someone thought about me and brought me little presents, flowers, or candy sometimes. That I came first in his life. Of course, I was wrong." Her lower lip quivered for a moment as she thought of just how wrong she'd been. How duped, how betrayed, how stupid.

"You're not going to cry again, are you?" he asked, sounding alarmed.

"No." She clamped her back teeth together.

"Let's change the subject," he said. "What else did you like about marriage? Did you like sex?"

She sucked in a sharp breath, her tears forgotten. He had a way of shocking her, of making her see things from a different perspective. A male perspective. A very macho male perspective.

"I'm not going to answer that," she said, her lips stiff.

"By not answering it, you are answering it," he said.

"All right, then," she said, feeling her cheeks grow warm, staring at the road ahead. "We didn't have sex that often. In retrospect, maybe that's something I should have done something about. Only, I didn't know what to do. I thought that's the way it was after twenty years of marriage. No surprises, just . . . just comfortable sex. Predictable sex. Once-a-week or maybe once-a-month sex." When he didn't say anything, she swiveled her head in his direction. "Is there something wrong with that?" She shook her head. "Never mind, I know the answer. There was something wrong, or I'd still be married."

"Maybe you didn't want to still be married."

"Of course I did. I told you, I loved being married."

"Maybe you didn't want to be married to him."

"We'd been together for more than twenty years. You don't just throw over something like that because your sex life is predictable or boring."

"So, you found it boring."

"I found it comfortable. That's different."

"If you say so," he said.

"I do say so." She looked out the window. She'd never discussed her lackluster sex life with anyone, and she had no intention of discussing it with some Italian man who probably had sex every day and twice on Sunday, with a woman like his girlfriend from the restaurant. Why had she let him drag her into this discussion?

"What about you?" she asked boldly. Why should she be the only one put on the spot? "How do you like sex?"

He flicked an amused glance in her direction. If he was shocked by her frankness, he didn't let it show.

"Of course," she continued, "you're an Italian male. I don't know why I should even ask."

His fingers tightened on the steering wheel. "That's right, we're all alike: amoral, sexually obsessed, shallow, and after only one thing—the conquest." He sounded annoyed and disappointed. "I thought you were too smart to put people into niches."

"We have a saying: 'If the shoe fits, wear it.' Maybe I'm not as smart as you think, not about men. But I'm learning. There's a good reason for stereotypes; they're often based on fact. What's your stereotype of an American?"

"Open, frank, happy, trusting, naive," he said. "There, I've just proved your point for you. Because that's you."

She shrugged. It wasn't such a bad description.

"You're wrong if you think I'm only interested in sex and the conquest," he asked. "If I were, I would have made love to you last night."

She slid a glance in his direction. She wanted to ask why he hadn't, but she was afraid to hear the answer. Was she that unattractive? That old? Of course, she'd fallen asleep. But she would rather have . . . no, she wouldn't even go there.

It was a relief to pull up in front of the hotel, run in, and retrieve her chocolates. By the time she got back to the car, she hoped he'd forgotten what they were talking about.

Why did he care about her personal life, anyway? Was she a challenge to him? Did he want to see how repressed she'd been? Did he think he was going to take her to bed and give her a thrill? If he did, why *hadn't* he done it last night? The thought of his toying with her infuriated her and made her heart race at the same time.

She straightened her shoulders and turned her head to look out the window as they wound their way into the countryside once again.

"Those cows grazing are special to this area, which is famous for its cheese. We'll have to stop and get some," Marco said.

Her lips curved in a reluctant smile as she realized he was trying to change the subject to something neutral and safe.

"Do you see what I mean?" she said, waving her hand at the cattle standing in the shade of the spreading oak trees. "The whole world is made up of couples, including cows. Not one is by itself. It's natural to want company. Surely, you must agree with me."

"I never thought of cows being lonely," he said.

"Because they're not. They're never alone."

"I'm sorry I brought up the cows," he said with a loud sigh. "Now, it's your turn to change the subject."

"Maybe it's because of your job that you're never lonely," she suggested. Maybe he'd drop a clue about the real nature of his job.

"Yes," he said. "At the end of the day, I'm always glad to get away from it."

"From the tourists, you mean?" He was no more

a tour guide than she was a belly dancer. "Then why aren't you trying to get away from me? At the end of the day, there I am, still around, a pesky tourist who wants to see everything and do everything and asks too many questions. Yet you've offered to drive me to Rome. And I haven't paid a cent for your services. In fact, I owe you money. So, why are you doing this? How can you afford it? You must have a very generous nature."

His mouth curled in a half-smile. "Then that's your answer," he said.

As usual, his answer really wasn't an answer at all.

Marco had no idea where he was going. Giovanni would be in Rome in five days. He could drive to Rome in a matter of hours and wait there, but he wasn't in the mood for Rome. Rome was too noisy, too frantic, too busy, and when he got there, he'd have to face problems he didn't want to face.

He'd have to come to grips with the very real probability that Anna Maria was going to give Giovanni the gigantic diamond he was expecting. It might be under that new ring she'd acquired, or it might be somewhere else. Maybe she didn't even have it yet.

If she gave it to Giovanni, he'd have to arrest them both. The idea of her in cuffs and behind bars was disturbing. It shouldn't be; he'd arrested women in the past; he'd seen justice done and closed the door on the case. It might not be that easy this time.

But why else would Giovanni want to see her again, if he didn't think she had something for him? Marco turned his head to look at her in the stretch jeans that hugged her hips and the shirt that rippled across her breasts every time she moved, and he knew the answer to that one. She was a sexy woman, and Giovanni liked sexy women. Was that all there was to their relationship? Was she simply a tourist with nothing to hide? Or was she a criminal who was smart enough to double-cross Giovanni and deal with one of his rivals? Giovanni wasn't the only diamond dealer in Italy, not by any means. But if it wasn't a double-cross, then what did that "Gotcha" note in the yearbook mean?

He was definitely not in the mood to go to Rome or to think about Giovanni and jewels or to analyze the woman next to him. He was in the mood to drive through the countryside in a classic touring car with her at his side. He was in the mood to watch her out of the corner of his eye. To see the sunshine on her hair, to watch her cheeks turn pink when she got upset about his views on love and marriage.

Was he really the loner he pretended to be? He never thought about it. He never thought about love or marriage much, brushing off his grandmother's nagging.

Sex was another matter. That was one of his favorite subjects to think about, especially when he fantasized about making love to Anna Maria. He couldn't imagine her husband not wanting to take her to bed every day. If he had a woman like that at home, he'd come home for lunch every day. He'd make love to her on the terrace, in the garden, under the olive tree, and in bed at night. Her ex-husband must be an idiot.

For some reason, he was being forced into the question of marriage on all sides. First his grand-mother, then Silvestro, then Antonio, and now Anna Maria. Everything he saw and everything he heard only underscored his belief that he was not cut out for marriage. If he had been once, it was too late now.

A voice inside asked if this trip would be the same if he were by himself. No. Would it be better or worse? He refused to answer that. It would be different, that was all.

The road was climbing into the mountains, where the wind was cooler. The trees were deep green on both sides of the road. There was no more grass, no more cows grazing.

Anna Maria hadn't spoken for a long time. She'd described herself as pesky. He thought that meant annoying, and, if so, it didn't describe her. She was easy to be with, even easier to look at. His gaze wandered her way once again, and he wondered idly if she was getting sunburned again.

Even now, he could feel her skin beneath his fingers, smell the lotion he'd rubbed into her ten-der skin, and hear her sighs. He wanted to let his fingers awaken the passion he knew was just beneath the surface. He wanted to make love to her, to show her what she'd been missing in her comfortable, boring marriage, to give her something to remember. He'd spent an entire evening watching the outline of her breasts under that silk shirt, and he still hadn't seen them. Still hadn't touched them or kissed them. Though he could have turned her over last night on his bed, she was asleep by then, and there were rules about that.

"Where are we?" she asked.

"I don't know," he said.

"Is this what you do for fun when you're not working? Drive around on back roads with a stranger?"

"I don't think of you as a stranger anymore. Not after last night."

She stared at him for a long moment, and her cheeks flushed. He gave her a knowing smile, then turned his attention back to the road.

"Last night," she repeated. "I thought you said . . ."

"Nothing happened," he said. "Not yet."

She slid down in her seat and closed her eyes. Mesmerized by the sight of her long legs in tight pants, imagining how he'd feel when they were bare and wrapped around him, he pictured stopping by the side of the road, walking off into a copse of trees, and making love in the tall grass, her hair a halo around her head, her voice catching as she called his name when she climaxed.

He'd stroke her face, kiss the valley between her

breasts. And she . . . she'd use her mouth, and she'd . . .

He swerved back over the dividing line of the road, forcing himself to stop looking at her and keep his eyes on the road. His fantasy was *not* going to happen. Not now, not with her, despite the erection he now had. It was those months of celibacy—it must be. After all, she was just another tourist. She wasn't really beautiful. She wasn't young. She wasn't voluptuous. She wasn't Italian, and she wasn't his type.

Not only that, but she was here today and gone tomorrow. Which was a good thing; he wasn't looking for anything permanent. It was *not* a good thing that she might be in jail tomorrow or next week. That sobering thought ought to help him control his hormones.

Anna Maria didn't open her eyes until he'd stopped in a small town. She sat up straight, blinked, and looked around.

"Where are we?"

"The sign says 'Benvenuto a Racalmuto.' It's just a small town where people live. It's not on the map of things to do and see."

She smiled. "I'm glad. Thank you for bringing me to Racalmuto; it's just the kind of place I wanted to come to." She sniffed the air. "What smells so good?" She looked around and saw they'd stopped in front of a bakery. "Why don't we buy some bread and cheese and wine and have a picnic?"

She looked so absurdly happy about such a simple idea. He smiled. He tried to imagine Adrianna getting excited about a picnic. She and every other woman he knew would have insisted on a four-course lunch at a restaurant. They would not like to sit on the ground, get their clothes dirty, and subject themselves to crawling creatures.

"There may be ants," he warned.

"What is a picnic without ants?"

For a moment, he forgot all his problems, forgot to wonder who she was and what she was doing there. He only wanted to hold on to the moment, hold on to that smile and the look in her eyes. Put them away for another day when the sun wasn't shining on her hair and he had other things to do but have a picnic in the country with a woman who didn't care about dirt and ants and who did things to his heart rate and his attention span.

After a long moment, she exhaled slowly.

"Well," she said, and blinked again as if waking from a dream. She opened the car door, took her purse, and walked away.

He stood on the curb, leaning against the car door to watch her walk into the bakery, her hips swaying slightly in her tight jeans. He wasn't the only one looking. He noticed a painter on a ladder across the street put his brush down and give her an appreciative leer. Since the man was at work and on a ladder, Marco felt sure she was safe, and he strolled down the street to an open-air fruit market to buy cherries and plums. On the way back, he bought a bottle of wine, then paused in front of a small jewelry store.

He stared at the gold rings in the window, at the emeralds and the diamonds. He was studying the jewelry so intently he didn't know she was standing next to him until she spoke.

"You say you don't believe in love," she said. "But they say diamonds are forever. Do you believe that?"

Chapter 12

"I don't believe in forever," he said, which was exactly what Anne Marie expected him to say. "The wedding ring you had. Was it like that one?" He pointed to a diamond ring in the window.

"I never had a diamond, just a gold band. When we got married, we were young, and Dan couldn't afford one. Then, when an anniversary came around and I might have gotten one, I decided I'd rather have an appliance or a new car, so I kept wearing my gold wedding band. Until I came to Italy. Maybe you're right; maybe there is no such thing as forever. There wasn't for me. No diamond and no forever." A month ago, the thought would have made her cry. Now, it just made her mad that she'd been betrayed. She put her hand on Marco's arm. "Don't worry, I'm not going to cry."

"Why not?" he asked.

"I don't know. Everything that happened back in Oakville seems so far away from here. I have so much else to think about. New people, new things to see like the temples, my ruined suitcase, my clothes . . ."

"And Giovanni."

"Yes, of course." She dropped her hand from his arm. "Giovanni has a way of taking your mind off other problems. He's one of a kind—charming, good-looking. You're from the same town and about the same age. I can't believe you've never met him."

"Maybe in Rome," he suggested.

"I doubt it. With him, you never know. He shows up when he wants to or when he can. He's married, did I tell you?"

"I think you did."

"He wasn't wearing a ring that I noticed, but that doesn't mean anything. Not to men. To me, my ring was a symbol of love and trust and commitment. All that is gone."

"Is that why you don't wear any jewelry? You weren't wearing any until you found that ring on the street."

She nodded. "I'm surprised you noticed."

"I notice many things about you." He gave her a look that made her toes curl in her new sandals.

If he was handing her a line, it was a good one. Coupled with that look in his eyes, it was enough to cause her lungs to feel as if they'd collapsed and couldn't hold any air. There were people walking by on the sidewalk, chattering in Italian. School-children were on their way home for lunch, swinging their book bags, but their voices faded into the background. All she heard was Marco's voice in her ear. All she was aware of was his shoulder next to hers, his warm breath on her cheek. He had a way of doing that. Of making her forget everything but him.

She had to pull herself together. This relation-ship, whatever it was, was going to last only until she got to Rome. Then he'd go back to his solitary life, and she'd . . . she'd see the rest of Italy on her own and go back to her own solitary life. Only she didn't want a solitary life. She wanted a life shared with someone she loved. Could she go back to Dan? He hadn't gotten married. Was there any chance they could work out their problems and . . .

Marco put his arm around her shoulders and led her away, and she forgot about Dan. Forgot about everything but here and now and Marco.

"What did you buy?" Marco asked.

"Some wonderful things," she said, feeling the warmth of his arm as they walked toward the car. Feeling protected and feminine and almost natural to be walking down a street in Italy with a man's arm over her shoulders. As if it was natural for a tourist to be picnicking off the beaten track with her so-called tour guide. As if it was natural to fan-tasize about making love to him on a picnic blanket under a tree. "Besides the bread and cheese, I got a roast chicken and some salad."

They got into the car, put their bags in the backseat, and drove out of town.

He shot her a questioning look. "Aren't you going to ask where we're going?"

She shook her head. "I'm in your hands," she said.

He raised his eyebrows and grinned at her.

She hadn't meant that literally. She only meant . . . or had she? Was he surprised? Shocked? Pleased?

She flushed but met his gaze. The look in his eyes was full of questions. Did she know what she was saying? Did she mean she could actually go through with it? Could she do it and not look back? Could she throw caution to the winds and do what she'd come to Italy for? To eat the fruit when it was ripe, to live life to the fullest, every minute, every hour of every day, and not think about the future? To make love to a stranger and not ask questions, not look for guarantees, not worry about the consequences?

He must have read the answer in her eyes. He drove fast without speaking and finally pulled off the two-lane highway onto a dirt road. Some distance down the road, he stopped the car, and from the trunk he produced a plaid blanket. Had it come with the rental car? With their arms full, they followed a path through the woods past fragrant cedar trees, their feet crunching on fallen leaves and needles.

Anne Marie wondered where they were going, but it didn't matter. All that mattered was that they were going together. Somewhere they'd never been before and would never go again. And when they got there, anything could happen. Coming out of the woods, she saw they were on a hill overlooking a valley, verdant with vineyards.

She gasped at the sight. "This is beautiful. How did you know? You have been here before, haven't you?"

Marco shook his head, taking in the view. "No."

He took the bag out of her arms and set it on the ground, along with the white wine he'd bought and a bag of ice he'd stuck it in to keep it cool. He spread the blanket out, and she sat down on the edge of it, cut a wedge of cheese, and tore into the bread as if she'd been starving. Nothing had ever tasted as good as this ripe cheese and this warm, crusty bread. Maybe it was the air. Food always tasted better in the fresh air. After devouring almost half a loaf of bread, she looked up and saw him watching her with an amused expression.

"What?" she asked, startled.

"Nothing," he said. "I was just watching you."

"Watching me stuff myself." She smiled ruefully.

He drank from the open wine bottle and handed it to her.

"You should do that more often," he said.

"Stuff myself? I'd weigh two hundred pounds."

He gave her an amused look, his eyes traveling the outline of her breasts and her hips as if he were imagining her at two hundred pounds. She frowned, and he coaxed, "No, smile. You have a beautiful smile."

"I do?" Maybe she didn't smile much. Maybe she hadn't had much to smile about, until now. Marco not only made her smile, he made her laugh.

He reached across the blanket, across the bread crumbs, and lifted the corners of her mouth with his thumb and forefinger.

"Like that," he said. "It's not so hard, is it?"

She shook her head. Her mouth was so dry that she couldn't speak. She couldn't smile, either; her lips were trembling too violently. The sun was high in the sky. The only sound was a bee buzzing in the distance. Marco smoothed her lips with his fingers, then brushed them with a kiss. It was not enough. It was worse than nothing; it made her want more.

She wanted him to invade her mouth, to press her into the ground and make love to her. She wanted the earth to shake and the mountains to move. She wanted it all, and she wanted it now.

Her clothes were too tight, too heavy, and she wanted to peel them off. She wanted to lie on the blanket, naked under the filtered sunlight, and make love. She wanted to see Marco's lean, strong body above her, to gaze into his remarkable eyes and feel his mouth warm against her skin. Now.

"Anna Maria?" he asked.

"Yes," she said.

He stood and stripped off his clothes. His body was perfect, long and powerful and magnificently aroused. Like the statue of David, only better, made of flesh and blood. She wanted to reach up and touch him, but she was suddenly shy.

She held her breath and lay perfectly still, afraid to break the spell. He went down on his knees and moved toward her, a predatory gleam in his eyes that turned her bones to jelly. He was so close she could see his eyes smolder. She fumbled with the buttons on her shirt.

He yanked at her shirt, and it flew open. She unhooked her bra and tossed it on the grass. Free! The cool air made her skin feel alive, made her nipples pucker. Now for her skirt . . .

Marco put his hands on her shoulders and gently pushed her down against the blanket. One hand moved to cup the back of her head, his thumb stroking the sensitive skin behind her ear.

"Anna Maria." His face was only inches from hers, his voice low and tense. "I've thought about this since the first time I saw you. It was what you call my fantasy. Are you sure this is what you want?"

Anne Marie panicked. She'd never been anyone's fantasy. What if she wasn't up to it? What if she didn't know what to do, how to act? But she'd fantasized about this, too. She wanted it so badly she felt it in her bones.

His hand moved to cup her chin and force her to look at him. "Tell me. Show me what you want." His eyes darkened to the color of chocolate; his mouth promised sensations she'd never known. She'd been waiting all her life for this.

She put her hands on the sides of his face, feeling the slight roughness of the shadow of a beard that lined his jaw. Show him what she wanted? She brought his mouth to her aching breasts. That was what she wanted; that was what she needed.

The smell of his slightly musky skin and the fresh, fragrant air made her gloriously dizzy. When his mouth took possession of one nipple and sucked and tugged at it, she felt as if she were falling through space. His hand went to the other breast, kneading and massaging until she fell into a new and marvelous universe where gravity no longer applied, spinning around.

His mouth trailed kisses down across her rounded belly and to the apex of her thighs. She drew in a large breath and held it, her whole body trembling.

"Wait," she said. "I . . . I've never . . ."

"Never?" He was incredulous.

This was not the time to explain she'd only had sex with one man in her life. One rather unimaginative man.

"Good," he said, sounding unaccountably pleased.

When his mouth found her most intimate spot, she was completely unprepared for the sensations that ripped through her body. She gasped and exploded into a thousand tiny pieces. A voice that didn't sound like hers cried out, then she collapsed and burst into tears. Marco wrapped his arms around her, and she sobbed against his chest.

They lay there under the trees, his arms warm and protective, his shoulder a pillow for her head. When her breathing slowed back to normal and her tears dried on her cheeks and on his shoulder, she opened her eyes and raised her head. Marco smoothed her damp hair and tucked an errant strand behind her ear. And he smiled, a half-amused, half-tender smile.

"I know I promised I wouldn't cry anymore, but I didn't know," she murmured, her cheeks and her whole body flushed. "I had no idea it could be like that."

He kissed the corners of her mouth and the hollow of her throat. He tasted like wine, and his kisses were even more intoxicating. She must be drunk, drunk on his kisses and his touch. Why else would she feel so dizzy, disoriented, wiped out?

Marco rolled over and lay on his back, and she propped herself on one elbow, her adrenaline pumping at the sight of his marvelous erection. Shyly but purposefully, she leaned forward and ran her fingers over his smooth velvet sheath. Goose bumps rose all over her skin.

He shuddered and wrapped his hand around hers. "Yes," he said, his voice as rough as gravel.

She ran her fingers over the silky-strong length of his organ, marveling at the size and the steel strength. He moaned deep in his throat, and she thrilled at the power she had over him, the ability to make him come alive in her hands; thrilled to feel his masculinity, to hold it and want it. She wanted it deep inside her, wanted it to reach into the depths of her, to make her call out once again the rapture and the earth-shaking joy in the stillness of the pure air.

With her hand still around his erection, she shifted so she was straddling him. Her other hand traced the dark hair on his chest, then down to his thighs, exploring the texture of his skin and the outline of his muscles. She followed her hand with kisses, trailing her mouth across his belly, tasting the salt on his skin, delighting in the rough edges and the smooth surfaces. He made sounds so primeval she no longer worried about whether she was doing it right or wrong. Whatever she was doing, it was working.

He grew bigger and bigger, pulsating in her hand until she thought she wouldn't be able to contain all that masculinity. Joy bubbled up inside her throat. She watched his eyes dilate and heard the rough explosion of his breath. She'd never felt this way, never realized she could do this. It made her feel powerful, in control, and yet part of something bigger than herself, bigger than both of them.

He groaned and rolled over, taking her with him, and she knew what would happen next. Her body was ready, moist with the liquid honey he'd already tasted. She was quivering, silently begging him to come to her. To take her over the edge once again.

Though she was slick with wanting him, every nerve, every muscle, every organ waiting and wanting, nothing could have prepared her for the strength and the force of his thrusts. She gripped his shoulders, riding out the storm of passion as he filled the emptiness she hadn't known was there. The emptiness that no one else had ever filled or even tried to fill. The wild pulsations came faster and faster, until the thunder crashed in her ears and lightning struck them both at the same time. In the middle of a warm summer day with the sun shining down on them, a storm struck. Only there was no storm, no storm except the one inside their bodies, in their minds, and in their world.

He shouted. She screamed. Their voices echoed across distant green hills. He lay on top of her, his weight bearing down on her, a welcome heaviness. Eventually, he rolled over again, now coated with a film of sweat. The look in his eyes, the lines in his face, all told her he was sated and at peace.

With a supreme effort, she sat up and looked around. If she expected the world to be a different place, she was mistaken. The blanket was tangled beneath them, still covered with crumbs. The empty wine bottle had rolled away, and cheese and cherries had spilled out of paper sacks. Bees were buzzing overhead.

One landed on Marco's hand.

"*Va via,*" he told it, waving his hand to shake it off. The bee stung him. Marco yelped, jumped up, and grasped one hand with the other, his face contorted.

Anne Marie got to her feet. "How can I help? What can I do?"

"Nothing," he said through stiff lips, getting dressed clumsily but quickly with one hand. "I'll be fine as soon as I get to the car and get some medicine. I'm allergic to bee stings."

"Oh, my God." She grabbed her underwear, jeans, and shirt and threw them on. "My son is allergic. It's nothing to fool with. Come on, let's go." She tossed the remains of the picnic into a bag, seized the blanket, and they ran down the path to the car.

Marco reached into the backseat of the Lancia for his valise and took out a small bottle of pills. He popped two into his mouth and washed them down with a swig of mineral water from a plastic bottle.

Anne Marie glanced at his hands. "We still have some ice. We should wrap up your hand with ice." She took the bag of ice from the trunk, poured off the excess water, then wrapped his arm and the ice in the picnic blanket and knotted it as tightly as she could.

"It's really swollen," she said, trying to keep her voice calm. "It will take a while for the medicine and the ice to make the swelling go down."

"I feel like a fool," he said, looking down at the makeshift bandage on his arm as if it belonged to someone else. "This is ridiculous. How can I drive?"

"You can't. I will."

"You?" He looked at her as if she'd offered to pilot a jet plane. "Do you know how to drive a . . ."

"Stick shift? Yes, of course."

"All right, go ahead." He got into the passenger side.

Anne Marie took the driver's seat, scared spitless. She hadn't driven a stick shift for years, not since Dan had sold their old VW Beetle and bought a Honda. But she had to do it.

She was also determined to show Marco she could take care of herself and him, too, even though there was plenty of evidence to the contrary.

"We'll find a doctor in the next town," she said.

"What for?" he asked.

"To have a look at this and prescribe something else if necessary."

"It won't be. No doctor. I wish . . ."

She waited. He said no more. She could only imagine what he wished. He wished he'd used a condom. He wished they hadn't stopped there to have a picnic. Her hands were shaking; she needed something to calm her nerves before she took the wheel. "Would you be able to reach around and get me the candy in my tote bag with your good hand?" she asked.

He hesitated, then reached for the candy. Before he handed her the box, he read the note.

"Who's Misty?" he asked.

"The cousin of my friend Evie."

"And you're going to eat her candy?"

"I need it now, and she doesn't. I'm going to replace the pieces I've eaten before I give it to her." She slipped her fingers under the wrapping and took out the first piece she came to, a dark chocolate truffle with a swirl of milk chocolate on top. She took a bite and closed her eyes to savor the taste and the texture of one of the best truffles she'd ever eaten. They really were worth the exorbitant prices; no wonder Misty had her bring them all this way. "Would you like a piece?" she said politely, handing him the box.

"I don't eat chocolate." He put it back in her bag and tossed that on the seat behind her.

After devouring the truffle, she felt better. Much better. Sex and chocolate, chocolate and sex. Her body hummed with contentment and a sense of well-being.

"Shall we be off?" she asked brightly.

Marco gave her a reluctant, stiff smile, one she imagined was full of admiration for her courage and her gumption and maybe more, and she put her hands on the steering wheel.

He settled back in the seat, resting his swollen arm and hand on the open window ledge.

Anne Marie took a deep breath and put the clutch in with her left foot. Then she turned the key in the ignition and revved the engine, enjoying the sound and the feeling of power. She'd never been aware that she was lacking in power, but ever since Dan walked out on her, she'd known what it was like to lose it. Now, slowly but surely, she was getting it back. She worked the knob of the gear stick, trying to figure out the shift pattern.

She glanced at Marco, hoping he didn't know she was unsure of herself, but he wasn't fooled. He pointed to the little diagram on top of the knob, and she nodded. Of course, she knew there was a diagram. It was just that she thought Italian cars might be different.

She bit her lip and shifted into first gear, then let out the clutch a little too fast. The car jerked forward and stalled inches from a large birch tree. She was breathing hard, and perspiration beaded on her forehead. She felt Marco's critical gaze on her.

"Give it a little gas as you let the clutch out," he said.

"I *did*."

She restarted the car, found reverse, and raced the engine as she let out the clutch. This time, the car jumped backward five feet before stopping.

"Do you want me to—" he said.

"No," she said shortly. She would start this car, and she would drive it if it took all day. He had his medication; his hand was wrapped in ice. There wasn't anything more anyone could do for him right now, since he refused to see a doctor.

"Look," he said, "it's just a matter of coordination. I don't know why women can't do two things at once. For some reason, they can't operate manually."

Even if pain was making him irritable, his remarks made her burn. "Oh, no?" she retorted. "I think I did a pretty good job of operating manually back there on the picnic blanket."

She started the engine again, shifted into first gear, eased the clutch out as she lightly pressed on the gas, and felt a surge of pleasure as it all came together. The car nosed smoothly back onto the highway, and she shot him a triumphant smile.

*   *   *

Marco smiled back at her, despite his pain and his
fear that she couldn't drive and that she'd either
burn out the clutch or they'd end up in a ditch.
How could he resist her? Her blue eyes glowed, and
her smile lit up her face. She had guts, this woman.
She also had a beautiful smile, and he hoped he'd
given her reason to smile a little more often.

He'd been a boor to criticize her that way. He
also hadn't said anything nice about their lovemaking, but he didn't intend to. He didn't dare. Making
love to Anna Maria was like nothing he'd ever done
before. Her cries still echoed in his mind, and the
image of her body under the dappled sunlight
would stay with him for a long time.

Chapter 13

Marco shifted in the bucket seat, trying to get comfortable, but his mind was in turmoil. He'd done what he thought she wanted. God knew, he wanted it, too. He'd thought once would be enough. He'd discovered what he'd suspected; she hadn't had much experience. Her husband was a *zuccone*, a fool, a cretin who hadn't appreciated her.

She was a passionate woman, one who deserved more. But was he the man to give it to her? Marco was worried. He'd felt something back there he'd never felt before. He'd felt a connection, an invisible cord that stretched between them. He'd also felt it on the boat and that night in the hotel. And now, even with their clothes back on, with her driving his rented car badly and him under the influence of the medication, he felt the connection all over again. What did it mean?

Damned if he knew.

He knew she'd gotten what she wanted; he could tell by the look in her eyes and that smile on her face. That was that; she didn't want or need to go any further.

But he did. Even with his eyes half closed, his brain half asleep, and his hand and his arm useless, he knew he wanted more. He wanted to take her to bed in a real bed, to spend the whole night with her. He wanted to see her beautiful breasts, her long bare legs, and her pale skin in the moonlight and by lamplight. He'd made love to many women, and he thought he understood them. He knew what they wanted, and he was sure he could give it to them.

But Anna Maria was different. He was no longer sure of anything. Except that she couldn't drive with a manual transmission. But that hadn't stopped her. He tried to stay awake, but the vibration of the engine and the effects of his medicine on top of mind-altering sex were too much for him to combat. Despite his efforts, his eyes closed, and he drifted off to sleep, giving up control of the route and the road to her. But that was all, he assured himself. In everything else, he was in total control. Absolutely.

Anne Marie glanced at Marco as she drove. He looked miserable, with his swollen hand and arm propped up on the window ledge and those frown creases in his face. At least, he was getting some sleep, but it didn't look as if he was having pleasant dreams. Maybe he was sorry he'd made love to her. Maybe the sentence that began with "I wish . . ." would have ended with " . . . we hadn't done that."

She wasn't sorry, though she did feel bad that he'd slept in the chair last night. No wonder he needed to sleep. That and the medicine had knocked him out.

As for her, she was enjoying a surge of power and freedom. She'd mastered the controls of the car. She'd had the most incredible sexual experience of her life. And she was now driving anywhere she wanted to go. Marco said he had no plans. He didn't know where they were going, and it didn't seem to matter.

She drove through pine forests. She drove up over modest mountain passes and down through verdant valleys. She passed small towns and vineyards. She passed farmers in their fields who stopped to wave at her, and she waved to children walking by the side of the road. She saw signs pointing to towns she'd never heard of, and she turned onto roads that could lead anywhere. It was exhilarating.

Until the engine started missing. It coughed and sputtered, and she pushed her foot down on the gas pedal until it hit the floor. The engine stalled and jerked to a stop on the empty two-lane road. They hadn't passed another car for an hour.

She muttered a curse.

Marco woke up with a start. Damn, she would have liked to have started it up again without his knowing.

"*Mio dio,*" he said. "*C'e qual cosa che non va?* What in the hell happened?"

"I . . . I don't know. It just stopped."

"Just stopped. What did you do to it?"

"Nothing. I was just driving along . . ."

He looked at his watch and frowned. "*Mamma mia!* Have I been asleep all this time? Why didn't you wake me? Where are we?"

"I don't know. I thought it didn't matter."

He got out of the car and raised the hood with his good hand. She got out and peered at the engine, as if she could possibly know what was wrong. She watched while he yanked on a rubber tube and examined it. "Get back in, and start the engine," he ordered. "Please."

She got in, turned the key, and held it. Nothing happened. She didn't know whether to stay in the car or join him to look under the hood again and pretend she knew what she was looking at. She decided on the latter.

"How is your hand?" she asked, watching him tap on the engine with his good hand, the other arm held stiffly at his side.

"My hand is not the problem," he said.

"What is?"

"See this? This is the fuel line. There's gas in it." He squeezed it, and tiny spurts burst out. "But the fuel pump is cracked. The gas is leaking out and not getting to the engine."

"Oh."

"I'll call a garage. Do you have any idea where we are? Do you remember any of the signs on the road?"

"Let's see. *Benvenuto.* I saw that a while back, and—"

"*Benvenuto* means 'welcome.'"

"I know that. What about *Avalina?* Could that be a town or does it mean 'dangerous curves ahead'?"

He ignored her sarcasm and started punching numbers into his cell phone. While talking fast and loudly, he took a map from the glove compartment and spread it out on the hood of the car. He listened to someone on the other end, then he looked at the map. Then he talked some more. When he hung up, he stared moodily out across the valley below.

"Did you find out where we are?" she asked.

He pointed to a spot on the map. "We could be here. Or here." He pointed to another spot. "I described the landscape, and the man at the garage in Maggiore thinks he can find us."

"What if he can't?" she asked.

"Then we'll wait here until someone comes along."

"But we haven't passed another car for hours. We could be here for days." She looked around. They were on a narrow mountain road, surrounded by fir and pine trees. The air was cool and fresh. It was a lovely spot. But spending days there without food or shelter might present a few problems.

He shrugged. "We have bread and wine. We'll survive."

Yes, they'd survive. Though they might have to make a temporary shelter out of branches and leaves, with their picnic blanket for a roof. After the bread and wine were gone, they could fish from a nearby stream and pick berries. Marco would go out and hunt for wild animals, and she'd stitch clothes for them out of the skins. At night, they'd lie on a bed of pine needles and make love for hours under the stars. It could be days or even weeks before anyone found them. Days and weeks of non-stop passion. Half naked, they'd chase each other through the forest to fall laughing in a pile of dry leaves, where their laughter would turn to cries of passion. It was enough to make her wish they'd be really, truly lost.

Anyone with a shred of romance in his soul would have said, *We have bread and wine and each other*, Anne Marie thought, especially after that incredible lovemaking. But Marco, true to his word, didn't believe in love or romance.

Fortunately, he believed in sex. And sex was what she wanted and needed. She hadn't known that before today. Or, if she had, she hadn't admitted it to herself. Now that she knew what she'd been missing all these years, she wanted and needed it again. Marco made her feel whole. He made her feel desirable and wildly feminine and uninhibited.

But she had the distinct feeling that Marco had had his fling with the American tourist and was feeling only regret. He hadn't so much as smiled since they got up from the blanket. Of course, he'd been stung by a bee, but couldn't he have said something . . . anything?

"Don't look at me like that," he said.

She felt her face flush. Was she that transparent? Could he tell she was lusting after him even now? She had to think about something else. Think about Rome. Think about home. Don't think about the fireworks that had gone off when he made love to her. For him, it was probably just another roll on a picnic blanket with an eager American tourist who'd come to Italy to get unrepressed. She knew he didn't make a living as a tour guide. He was either a gigolo or . . .

"How? How am I looking?" she asked, wrinkling her forehead.

"As if this was my fault. After all, you're the one who got us here."

"You gave me no instructions. You led me to believe we could go wherever we wanted to. I thought the point was to see the countryside."

"Well," he said, leaning against the car door. "Take a look. We're going to be seeing a lot more of it than we planned."

"You mean . . ." Should she start collecting branches for their shelter now? Was it really possible to start a fire by rubbing two sticks together?

"I mean, we probably need a new fuel pump, and fuel pumps for twenty-year-old Lancias are in short supply, especially in some godforsaken village."

"Couldn't we rent another car?"

"I can't leave the Lancia here. It's valuable, and I promised to bring it back. In good condition."

"I have to be in Rome in a few days."

"Don't worry, Giovanni will wait for you."

"How do you know?"

"I have a feeling he wants to see you as much as you want to see him."

Anne Marie didn't know where he got that idea; Giovanni's letter was certainly casual. "Let me see your hand," she said.

He unwrapped it and held it out in front of him, observing it as impassively as if it belonged to someone else. She took his hand in hers and looked at it carefully. His skin felt warm. His fingers were still swollen, but the rest of the swelling had gone down. She felt a rush of sympathy and desire and something else, something that scared her.

"What are you doing?" he said suspiciously.

"Just . . . just checking," she said, rewrapping it for him. "I see it's better. It must be the medicine and the ice."

"And the chance to rest it," he said. "Thank you for driving. I'm sorry I didn't choose a more serviceable car. A Fiat would have done, but I liked the looks of the Lancia."

"It's beautiful," she said, running her hand over the polished hood.

"But not practical. I should have known it wouldn't hold up." Marco wondered if he'd ever learn that with women and cars, looks weren't everything. In fact, the more beautiful the machine or the woman, the less likely they were to be dependable. If he ever found both looks and reliability under the same hood or the same skin . . .

"But it was worth it. We had a great ride," she said.

"Yes, we did," he said with a half-smile and a long, knowing look. They'd had an unbelievable ride, and it had nothing to do with the car. When the words sank in, she bit her lower lip, and her cheeks flushed. He loved seeing her cheeks turn pink. How many women her age still blushed? How many women made love the way she did, shy and bold at the same time? None that he'd ever met.

"And anyway," she said, breaking eye contact and looking away, "we are in no hurry to get to Rome, as long as I have time to see the sights and meet up with Giovanni and Evie's cousin. As you said, we can survive as long as we have our wine and bread."

"And if the tow truck doesn't find us, you wouldn't mind sleeping under the stars?" He swiftly adjusted his fantasy from making love to her on clean sheets in a bed to making love outside with the moon shining through the trees. That ought to satisfy his wildest dreams; then he could let her go. Go back to America, back to her ex-husband, who by now, unless he was a complete idiot, must have realized what he'd lost. Or go off to see Giovanni and give him the diamond.

He'd have to arrest them both, of course, but if

that's what they deserved . . . so be it. By then, he'd be able to handle whatever had to be done. He just needed a few days to get over whatever it was he had. Some kind of adolescent lust or some damn thing. Maybe fate had decreed that the fuel pump should fail, that they should have to spend a few days in some village while his passion cooled. So he could do what had to be done and not look back.

He was waiting for her answer. He didn't know a woman in the world who would sleep outside without complaining.

"Of course, I wouldn't mind. It would be an adventure."

"What about bears?"

Her face paled. "Are there bears here?"

"And wild boar with big tusks."

She bit her lip nervously, then laughed when she realized he was joking. And the tow truck arrived. She smiled with relief. She had the most amazing smile. He couldn't help smiling back at her. He also couldn't help kissing her quickly on those smiling lips while the tow truck backed up to the front of the Lancia.

The driver admired the Lancia and hooked it to his truck, and then they all squeezed into the truck cab for the ride to Maggiore. Anne Marie was crushed against the door. Marco put his arm around her shoulders possessively, as if it was the most natural thing in the world, as if she belonged to him. Of course, it was none of the above; it was simply that there was no room for his arm anywhere else. His hip was pressed against hers, but he didn't seem bothered by their close proximity. She was. So bothered she clenched her hands together and turned her face to the window to catch the breeze to cool her fevered cheeks.

Marco and the driver conversed in Italian, which left her free to go over the day's events, especially the event that had shattered all her notions of what sex was. It wasn't a ritual that had to be performed once a week in a darkened bedroom. It wasn't mechanical. It wasn't boring. Of course, after twenty years with any man, it became that way.

But twenty years of sex with Marco? She sneaked a glance in his direction. He met her gaze, his eyes glimmering with amusement as if he knew what she was thinking. There was no way he could know, yet she felt scared. Scared she'd never make love with him again. Scared she *would* make love with him again.

The small town of Maggiore boasted a garage, a church, a market, vineyards that covered the hills for miles around, and not much else. Still, the streets were full of people.

"They're here for the grape harvest," Marco said.

"These are the workers?" she asked.

"Or tourists. This is an old Roman town. Besides the grape crush, there is a wild donkey race tomorrow to kick things off."

"Then there will be a hotel," she said.

The driver shook his head and spoke to Marco.

"He says it's full. But there's a youth hostel and rooms for rent."

While she wondered just how long they'd be staying in Maggiore, the driver drove through an old stone gate and pulled up in front of a garage on the town square. Marco went with the driver to talk to the boss.

Voices drifted from the garage.

"*Si puo ripararlo?*"

"*Ebbene . . .*"

"*Quanto ci vorra?*"

Anne Marie leaned against a stone pillar that might have been there since Roman times. She studied the cobblestones under her feet, looking for ruts that might have been left by chariots racing through town on their way to Rome.

The people who wandered by, locals or young people with backpacks, speaking German or French, hardly gave her a second glance. In her Italian clothes and Italian hair, she obviously didn't stand out. Maybe having her luggage destroyed wasn't such a bad thing, after all.

Again, she was seeing a part of Italy she never would have seen on her own. She owed Marco in a big way for bringing her on this trip. She owed him for other things, too, such as awakening her sexuality. Not that she was likely to mention that to him.

When Marco came out of the garage, he told her the owner would order a new fuel pump that would take several days to arrive from Rome.

"If you really must get to Rome before that, there is a bus," he said.

"But I'd miss the grape crush," she said. Get on a bus by herself? Go to Rome and track down Giovanni, who may or may not want to see her? Wander around the Coliseum and the Forum by herself with only a guidebook and no guide? She was getting accustomed to having Marco around. She liked feeling as if she belonged. She liked traveling in an Italian car with the world's sexiest Italian. She liked eating outside under a tree. She liked making love.

Yes, that's what it was all about. She wanted to do the things with him she hadn't dared do the last time. She wanted to surprise him. She wanted to please him. She wanted to show him she wasn't as unimaginative a partner as she'd been this afternoon.

"Yes, you'd miss stomping on grapes in a wooden vat with strangers."

"You mean, it isn't automated?"

"Not here; labor is still cheap. Not only that, but the traditional way produces the best wine. Crushing grapes by foot gives the best color, aroma, and flavor without breaking the bitter seeds."

"Can we actually participate?"

"If you want to, along with a few other adventurous tourists and the town people. Most of the women I know wouldn't want to stain their feet purple."

"But it comes off, doesn't it? And if it doesn't,

what a story that will make back home! Wait till my friends hear about this. And my son will be impressed."

She picked up her bag and noticed he carried his with his left hand. The ice pack and the makeshift bandage were now gone, and she could see his right hand was still swollen. As they walked down the street to check out the hostel, they passed what might have been a lemonade stand in America—but at this sidewalk stand, two young men were toasting bread over a small fire. Anne Marie set her new bag down and ordered a *bruschetta* with chopped fresh tomato. At Marco's urging, she accepted a glass of wine, too. She reached for her purse, but she was too late, as usual. One of these times, she'd settle up with him.

"Hmmm," she said. "Very good. I guess the bare feet do make a difference."

Marco swirled his wine around in the glass and nodded. "They want to know if you'd like to see their cellar, where they store the wine."

"Of course. I'd like to buy some from them."

One of the brothers led them around to the back of the house and down steep cement steps to a cool room, where huge wooden kegs lined the walls and a sign said, "Abandon hope, all who enter here."

"Dante," Marco said. "Our national poet. Italy's Shakespeare."

"I know who Dante is," she said.

"Of course," he said. "You probably have his books in your library."

"I wonder," she said to Marco, "if I could leave my candy in this cellar? It needs to be in a cool place. Could you ask him?"

Marco shook his head. "Why don't you just eat it and be done with it?"

"Because it's special, and it's for someone else. I told you. But maybe just one more piece." She reached into her bag and extricated another truffle from the box. Then she closed it again and wrapped it in a plastic bag. The wine maker agreed, she put the box behind some bottles, and someone shouted from somewhere above them. The man excused himself and went upstairs.

"Don't let me forget this." She wouldn't want him to have to drive back to this town as he did the last, to retrieve the lost chocolates. Anne Marie shivered. Marco put his arms around her. She let out a ragged sigh and pressed her face against his chest.

"We should go," she said. "The hostel may be filled up."

"Ah, you Americans, always in a hurry," he said.

The truth was, she didn't want to go anywhere. She wanted to stay in the cool cellar, surrounded by vats and washtubs and kegs and bottles, and eat a truffle with the pungent smell of wine grapes in the air and the taste of home in her mouth. She wanted to slow down.

She ate the whole truffle in one bite, closing her eyes to concentrate on the intense flavor. When she opened her eyes, Marco was staring at her.

"I'll remember the candy for you, but you must remember this day. You won't forget, will you? No matter what happens?"

"No, of course not. I'm going to buy a bottle of wine and take it back with me, for a souvenir."

"When you open it and inhale the scent of oak and grapes, you'll think of Maggiore." He looked so serious she stared at him, wondering what had come over him.

She'd think of Maggiore, but she'd remember Marco more than any town. She'd remember how he looked standing there in the middle of the cellar, his shirt unbuttoned just far enough to expose a glimpse of tanned chest, his sleeves rolled up, showing his muscled forearms. She'd seen his naked body looming above her, but this was how she would remember him.

Would she be happy back in California by herself? Back in her same house, at her same job? Under the same California sun where she'd lived her whole life, where every day was the same? It sounded unbearably dull.

"I wish . . ." she said.

"Yes?"

"Sometimes I wish my vacation would never end."

"It doesn't have to. You could stay here."

"Here?" She gulped, imagining a small house overlooking the sea, done in blues and yellows. Then she came down with a crash to reality. "You sound like Giovanni. He used to tell me to come and live in Italy. Tell me, how would I live, without a job? Unless I win the lottery. What would I do here? I have a job at home, a house, a son, friends . . ."

"And an ex-husband."

"By now, he's probably found someone else to take Brandy's place. Have you ever had a midlife crisis?" she asked, placing her hands on her hips.

"I don't think so," he said. "What does it mean?"

"It means you suddenly wake up one day and realize your life is half over and you haven't done what you wanted to do. You haven't found the job you wanted or the woman you wanted. So you drop everything, quit your job, leave your wife, and act as if you're twenty again. It's especially dangerous if you never acted as if you were twenty when you *were* twenty. Then you have a lot of living to make up for."

"Is it just for men, or do women have midlife crises, too? Have you had one?"

"Maybe I'm having one now. Maybe that's really why I came to Italy, to see a man I hadn't seen for twenty years. Maybe that explains . . ." Explains why she was falling for a man she didn't really know at all. Maybe that explained making love on a picnic blanket with someone whose job was to show tourists a good time. He'd done *that*, all right: she'd had the time of her life. Now the regrets came flooding in, as inevitable as the tide.

Marco asked, "There was another reason, wasn't there? Another reason to come to Italy and see Giovanni again."

"You mean to bring him the yearbook? Yes, but that was just an excuse. I needed to get away from Oakville. Evie suggested Italy. She came here after her divorce, and I'd always wanted to come. So I picked up his yearbook for him. I think he appreciated it; he said it reminded him of the happiest time of his life. I was surprised to hear that. High school was full of anxiety and uncertainty for me."

"Is that all?"

"Isn't that enough? I also felt like an outsider, different from everyone else. I didn't have a boyfriend. It was only later that I hooked up with Dan."

"I mean, is that all you brought? Didn't you bring something else for Giovanni? Didn't he expect something else, something more?" His face was set in a grim line, his mouth was tight, his eyes suddenly colder than the walls of the cellar.

She shivered. "It's cool in here. Let's go up."

"You didn't answer my question."

"The answer is, it's none of your business what goes on between me and Giovanni," she said briskly, and went back out into the sunshine.

Chapter 14

They went to the youth hostel, but Marco immediately knew it wasn't the right place for them to stay. He had something else in mind, a place with some privacy, soft lights, and a soft bed. A place to make love.

He chided himself. Which was more important? Finding the diamond or sex with Anna Maria? Obviously, it was the diamond. But that was hard to remember when she was around. It was only a hard, cold stone, while she was a warm, desirable woman. In the grand scheme of things, what was really more important? If he had to ask, maybe he shouldn't be in the business of catching criminals.

Just one more time, one more chance to do it right, to show her how good sex could be, and then he could forget her and concentrate on his work. He could have her and catch Giovanni, too, if he were careful. But he didn't want to be careful. He wanted to be young and crazy and reckless.

He wanted to make love to Anna Maria because she made him feel young and carefree. No doubt about it, she'd gotten under his skin. He didn't know what to make of her, and that made her irresistible. He'd never known what temptation was until he met Anna Maria.

She wasn't vain; she didn't require or demand his attention. She didn't dwell on past disappointments, such as Giovanni or her room being trashed. She started each day expecting the best, even if the day before hadn't lived up to her expectations. She didn't need fancy clothes or jewelry. She didn't mourn the loss of her suitcase; any other woman would have been frantic.

The hostel was completely unsuitable for her, with its bare-bones dormitories and used linen. Even though she was as low-maintenance as a Fiat, she was as classy as a Lancia and deserved to be treated as well as he would a fine car. Besides, the hostel wasn't safe—they couldn't leave their bags there, locked or not; one never knew who might wander in and out. Wherever the damned diamond was, he didn't want it stolen by some small-time crook. He pictured someone taking Anna Maria's ring off her finger while she slept in her bunk in the women's dorm. And if they couldn't easily pull it off . . . he shuddered to think of what someone might do to take it from her.

Had she really bought it on the street? He had to keep an eye on it, regardless. Certainly, that was why they had to sleep together tonight. Maybe she was telling the truth; perhaps it was just a cheap souvenir. Maybe she was just what she seemed. He wanted to believe that. He also wanted to catch Giovanni.

He himself was an oaf, a *stronzo,* an asshole, for demanding to know what she'd brought Giovanni. She wasn't going to tell him; why should she? Why had he pushed her? Because he was frustrated, that was why. He took a deep breath and nudged Anna Maria with his good hand.

"Let's go," he said.

"Where?"

"Anywhere but the hostel." He pulled a list from his pocket, where the garage mechanic had written possible rooms for rent. Dragging their suitcases, they stopped a half-dozen times to ask directions. They visited two houses. One was full of children with a macho, bare-chested father yelling at them. At the next, a pale, quiet widow proudly showed off her guest room on the second floor. It was spotlessly clean, with a double bed and a small balcony overlooking the vineyards in the distance. The whole scene was bathed in golden light from the setting sun.

"Ask her if she has another room," Anna Maria said.

"Why, what's wrong with this one?" he asked.

"We can't sleep in the same room."

"Why not? We did last night."

"But you slept in a chair."

"I can sleep in a chair again." He looked at a large, overstuffed chair in the corner.

"Ask her anyway."

"*Vorei una altra stanza o una stanza con due letti,*" he said.

The signora asked him how many people were in his party. When he said it was just the two of them, she threw up her hands and professed amazement. She smoothed the bedspread and told him the bed was perfect for a couple, a *married* couple. He nodded.

"No, she doesn't have anything else," he said. "She thinks it's perfect for us."

"Tell her we're not married," she said.

"She's a very conservative old lady, and I'm not going to send her into shock," he said. His gaze was focused on the bed. He hoped it wouldn't be necessary to sleep in the chair. But if he had to . . .

Anna Maria didn't protest any further, and he paid in advance for the room. At least Anna Maria was resigned to sharing the room with him. One step at a time, he told himself. He was beginning to adopt a fatalist attitude: if it was meant to happen, it would. They left their bags there and went out to look around the town.

"I need to make a phone call," Anne Marie said. She wanted to find out how Tim was doing after his first week of college. She also needed a distraction, so she wouldn't think about that bed in that room back there with the little balcony and the fresh air blowing in from the vines below.

She knew she could trust Marco. If he said he would sleep in the chair, he would. But she couldn't trust herself. Making love with Marco in a real bed would be . . . a different experience. Just the thought of how different caused her mouth to go dry. Sleeping together in a bed would definitely be more serious than rolling around on a picnic blanket.

It might, just might, mean something more than it should mean. And she couldn't allow that to happen. She needed to keep this affair casual. Any day, any moment, Marco might disappear from her life. If she'd learned one thing, it was not to get attached to another man. Not for a long time.

Marco took her to a hole-in-the-wall long-distance phone shop. She bought a PIN card and punched in Tim's number at his dorm.

"Tim, how's college?" she greeted him.

"Mom, how are you? Where are you? Dad's been trying to reach you," he said.

"Why, is something wrong?" she asked. Had the house gone up in flames? Had he been fired?

"Nothing except he got stood up," Tim said.

"I can't do anything about that," she replied.

"He wants to go to Italy."

"What for? He's never wanted to go to Italy." She'd suggested it many times over the years, and he was never interested.

"To see you. He's worried about you, all alone in a foreign country."

She choked on a laugh. Dan was worried about her? It was a little late for that.

"And he has the time off," Tim said.

"For his honeymoon, I suppose," she said. "The honeymoon that didn't happen."

"I think he misses you," he said. "Anyway, where are you?"

"I'm in a little town you've never heard of."

"How did you get there?"

"In a Lancia. I've also been on a Motoguzzi."

"A Motoguzzi and a Lancia? Mom, you're livin' large."

She grinned. "At last, I get some respect from you."

"Dad wants me to get your number."

"I don't have one. I'm calling from a phone booth. Tell him I'll call him when I get a chance, but I'm pretty busy. There's so much to see and do. Like wild donkey races and crushing grapes with my feet."

"By yourself?" he asked

"Oh, no. I'm just helping out. The whole village participates, and a few tourists, too."

"I mean, are you traveling by yourself? Who's driving the Lancia and the Motoguzzi?"

"I have done some driving," she said proudly. "But don't worry, I'm not alone. I'm in good hands." Marco's hands were more than good. "Now, tell me about school."

He told her about his classes, his astronomy teacher, and a girl he'd met.

"Mom, I think I'm in love," he said.

"In love? How long have you known her, three days?"

"About that," he said.

"Take it slow," she cautioned, as much to herself as to him.

Tim had a good head on his shoulders, and he wouldn't do anything rash. But what about Dan? Would he really take off and come to Italy? The old Dan wouldn't have. But a man in the middle of a midlife crisis might. Even if he did, though, he wouldn't be able to find her. It was a liberating feeling, knowing no one knew where she was.

She was sincere when she told Marco she'd loved being married, being part of a whole. But freedom was intoxicating. Of course, her feeling of intoxication might have something to do with the wine she'd been drinking and the man she'd been with for the past two days.

She and Marco had dinner together in a small restaurant, where an accordion player went from table to table playing requests. When he came to their table, Marco spoke to him in Italian.

He began to play "That's Amore."

Anne Marie put her fork down and stopped eating her pumpkin-stuffed ravioli in wild mushroom sauce.

"Don't you like it?" Marco asked. "I asked him to play something American. I thought maybe you were homesick."

"You requested a love song."

"For you," he said.

"I don't think you're the cynic you pretend to be."

He didn't answer; he just looked at her across the table, as if she were the sexiest woman he'd ever seen. Of course, wearing an off-the-shoulder, form-fitting red dress of Isabella's, she could almost believe she was.

After dinner, they walked around the town square under a full moon in the cool night air. People were sitting on benches in the square. Marco took her hand, and they walked up a dirt path above the town. Donkeys brayed in a nearby field, and crickets chirped. It was the essence of village life, a never-ending, never-changing cycle. Villagers sat outside on the steps where their grand-parents had sat and where their grandchildren would sit, and they talked about the same things year after year.

Anne Marie wanted to hold the sights and the smells in her heart and mind forever. Maybe on some dull, lonely winter evening back in California, she'd remember this night, this place, and this man. This man who made her feel more alive than she'd ever felt.

Yet his claims of being something she knew he wasn't bothered her. She wanted to keep walking, anything to put off going back to that little room where she'd have to decide whether to sleep with Marco or not. Whether to make love with Marco or not.

When they paused to rest on the footpath, he ran his fingers over her bare shoulder.

"You are so beautiful tonight, Anna Maria," he said, his voice hoarse. Then he kissed her on her bare shoulder. A flame of desire began to burn. His breath was warm on her naked skin, and her heart hammered in her chest. The flame threatened to engulf her. She wanted to think she could make a rational decision about what to do next, but when he brushed her skin with his lips, she was helpless. Her knees buckled, and he put his arm around her to steady her.

"It's the dress," she murmured.

"It isn't the dress," he said. "You look even more beautiful without the dress."

She slanted a glance in his direction, grateful he couldn't tell she was blushing . . . again. In the light of the full moon, with shadows shading his face, she couldn't tell what he was thinking, if he was laughing at her for being embarrassed or using a line he'd used before. Maybe she didn't really want to know.

"Hasn't anyone ever told you that you were beautiful before?" he asked, holding her at arm's distance and giving her an incredulous look. He looked sincere. He sounded sincere. But how could she be sure he didn't use the same line on every woman he gave the grand tour to?

"I . . . not very often," she said.

"What was wrong with your husband, was he blind?"

"Speaking of my husband, my son says he wants to come to Italy. He misses me."

"Isn't it too late for that?" Marco asked.

"Much too late. Now, tell me about crushing the grapes."

"Are you sure you want to join in? Most people are content to watch the grapes being harvested rather than squishing them between their own toes. But if you really want to, then tomorrow morning we join in the grape stomp. It's a competition. The different teams see who can squeeze the most juice during a certain time period."

"How's your hand?" She took his hand in hers and gently ran her thumb over the palm.

"Better," he said, his voice dropping a notch. "That helps."

The only sounds were the faint voices carrying in the night air and music from the village below. Sometimes spoken Italian sounded like music, Anne Marie thought.

"Where's your ring?" Marco asked, his voice suddenly serious. "Why aren't you wearing it?"

"I didn't feel like it. It's back in the room. Why?"

"We should get back." He dropped her hand and led the way down the path back to the village and to the widow's house. She'd left the porch light on for them, but the rest of the house was dark.

Anne Marie wondered why in the world Marco was so interested in the cheap ring she'd bought.

He put her behind him and pushed the front door open with his knee. Anne Marie held her breath. It was dark and quiet inside the house. For a long moment, Marco stood staring into the darkness. Finally, he reached for her hand and pulled her inside.

At the door to their room, he did it again—pushed her back and threw the door open. She could feel the tension in the air. This time, she was so scared she couldn't breathe. The picture of her ransacked hotel room flashed before her eyes. The clothes littered all over the room, the emptied suitcase, the feeling of being violated. There was a tight knot in her chest.

While she waited outside the room, Marco went in and closed the door behind him. She could only imagine what he was doing. Checking under the bed, behind the door, in the closet? For what? Who or what was he looking for?

When he finally opened the door, the lights were on, and the room looked exactly as they'd left it—homey, warm, and welcoming. She breathed a huge sigh of relief and collapsed on the edge of the bed.

"Don't tell me you expected it to be ransacked again?" she said, her voice slightly shaky. "You worry too much."

"Do I?" he asked, turning to give her a cool glance. "Maybe you don't worry enough. Get the ring."

She went to the bathroom and took the ring from her cosmetic bag. She came out and held it out in the palm of her hand for him to see. He nodded, his lips pressed together in a straight line. Where was the good-natured, teasing Marco she'd sat across from at dinner? Where was the romantic Marco who'd kissed her on the shoulder and told her she was beautiful with or without clothes? No wonder he'd never been married—who could put up with this hot-and-cold personality?

"Now, put it in a safe place," he said, "so no one can find it."

"Not even you?"

"Not even me."

"This is ridiculous. I paid practically nothing for this. If I lose it or someone takes it, I'll buy another one."

"Just like that?"

"Yes. I'm not going to hide it. I'm going to wear it." She slipped it on her finger. "Now I'm going to bed. I mean, I'm going to sleep . . . in the chair."

"No, you're not."

"If you don't take the bed, I'll leave." Brave words. Where on earth would she go?

His mouth twisted in a grimace. "All right. You win. Then you get the bathroom first. It's down the hall."

After a quick shower, she came padding barefoot back to the room in Isabella's white cotton dressing gown. Marco had put a blanket and a pillow on the chair and had stripped down to the jeans that rode low on his hips. She swallowed hard and looked away. She knew he was wearing no underwear. She was, just a wisp of silk here and a bit of lace there.

"Sure you don't want to change your mind?"

"Positive." She took a deep breath and looked at the landscape pictures on the walls. Anywhere but at his broad chest. Anywhere but at his hips. Anywhere but at the bulge in his jeans. He took a towel and left the room. She intended to be asleep in the chair by the time he came back. If she wasn't, she'd pretend.

The chair wasn't that uncomfortable, she decided. Not with the pillows. She stretched her feet out onto a small footstool and wrapped herself in the blanket. When she heard the doorknob turn, she closed her eyes.

"Anna Maria?"

Her eyes flew open. It was not Marco standing there in his low-slung jeans, his hair damp from the shower. And it wasn't Dan, her ex-husband who was purportedly on his way to Italy. It was Giovanni, in slim, tapered slacks, a beautiful designer jacket, and smooth leather shoes.

"What . . . what are you doing here?" she asked, sitting up straight in her chair. "How did you know, I mean, where did you come from?"

He laughed softly, as if she'd said something witty. "I couldn't let you go like that. I had to be sure I didn't lose you." He closed the gap between them and took her hand to kiss her fingers. "This ring," he said, his lips and eyes on her new ring. "You didn't have it the last time I saw you."

"No, that's right." It was dark when he'd seen her. How could he have noticed?

He tugged at it, but it didn't move.

"What . . . why?" she asked, impulsively making a fist and digging her nails into her palm.

There were footsteps in the hall. Giovanni pressed his finger to her lips.

"Shhh," he said. "You have not seen me." He crossed the room in a flash and disappeared out the double doors to the balcony. Then she heard a dull thud. The door opened, and Marco came in. He looked around the room, his body tense, his eyes narrowed.

"Who was here?"

"No one."

Marco went to the balcony and spent a good five minutes there. When he came back, he closed and locked the doors behind him. Then he locked the door to the hallway and placed a chair under the knob. He turned and glared at her.

"Where's the ring?" he demanded.

She held up her hand. "Just where it was the last time you asked. You're certainly jumpy. What's wrong?"

"You tell me."

"Nothing. Good night." She closed her eyes. But the image of Giovanni stayed with her. How had he found her, and why? If only he could have stayed long enough to answer a few questions. Whatever the answers were, it was clear he didn't want to run into Marco. Why not?

If she opened her eyes, what would she see? Was Marco undressing? Was he still glaring at her? Was he in bed? She couldn't stand the suspense another moment. She peeked out from under her eyelids. He was lying in the bed on his back, a sheet over his body, his eyes wide open, staring at the ceiling.

"Do you trust me?" he asked, as if he felt her gaze on him.

"Should I?"

His answer was to reach for the light switch and plunge the room into darkness. His calm, regular breathing soon told her he'd fallen asleep.

Ann Marie turned, she twisted, she rearranged the pillow and her blanket, but she couldn't sleep. The chair that had seemed fairly comfortable an hour ago had turned into an instrument of torture.

She sat up straight and looked at the outline of Marco's sleeping body, envying him his ability to forget his worries, whatever they were, and sleep. Of course, he was in a big, comfortable bed. On one side of the bed. There was plenty of room for her on the other side. Did she dare?

He was a sound sleeper. She was such a light sleeper, she'd wake up before he did and return to her chair. He'd never know.

She stood, tiptoed across the room, and gently lifted the corner of the blanket. He didn't move. She slid between the sheets. She held perfectly still, her arms stiff at her sides. He slept on. She exhaled slowly and let herself relax for the first time in hours. But the mattress sagged, and she started to roll toward him.

That wouldn't do. Not at all. She repositioned herself, gripped the edge of the bed with one hand,

and tried to relax. Before she closed her eyes, she glanced at the door. All she needed was for Dan to burst in. But even if he'd hitched a ride on a super-sonic plane, he couldn't be here by now. And if he did arrive, how would he ever find her? Yet Giovanni had found her.

It might have been minutes or maybe hours later when, in the middle of a dream about Dan, the Dan she'd married, the Dan she'd loved and who'd loved her, she backed into a hard, male body. This is what she'd missed when Dan left. The closeness, the warmth, the togetherness.

She sighed contentedly, squeezed her eyes tight, and let herself drift back toward sleep. Even with her eyes closed, she could tell it was early. Doves cooed outside the window. Cool air drifted in through the window, smelling of sage and other wild herbs.

She was half asleep when she felt strong arms go around her and pull her body close to his. With a deep sigh of satisfaction, she drowsily nestled into him. She was at home in her bedroom, happily married and still in love with Dan. She felt his warm breath on the back of her neck. His hands reached under her nightgown and cupped her breasts. His thumbs caressed the round undersides and then teased the nipples, until she was breath-ing hard and wanting more. Much more. With her eyes still shut, she wiggled out of her nightgown and tossed it on the floor. The rough hair on his chest teased the skin on her back, his legs wound around hers, the strength of his erection nudged her toward reality.

This was not Dan. And this was no dream.

Her eyes flew open. She stiffened. "Wait. Where am I?"

"You're in bed with me," Marco said, his voice rough. "If you wanted the bed, why didn't you say so?"

"I didn't. I wanted . . ."

"Yeeees?" His voice held a smile, and she shivered with anticipation. "What do you want, *cara mia?*"

She meant to say she'd come to his bed to get some sleep. But that wasn't what she wanted anymore. She wanted to be seduced. By his voice, his deep, sexy voice, his remarkable hands, and his lips. She wanted to make love to Marco. She wanted to make him feel the way she did, alive and aroused and ultimately fulfilled. She turned to face him, brushing against his naked body. His eyes were heavy, sleepy, and filled with desire. His head was propped on one hand, and he was looking at her with so much heat in his gaze that her skin felt scorched.

His eyes might look sleepy, but his magnificent body was wide awake. He gently pinned her to the mattress, and she reveled in the strength of his hands on her shoulders. His face was so close but not close enough. She remembered his question was still hanging in the air.

"I want . . . I want . . ."

"I know," he said.

He did know. He knew everything. He knew how to make her forget to wonder how many women he'd made love to in how many hotel rooms. He made her forget that she knew almost nothing about him, including what he did for a living. It didn't matter. All that mattered was that it was she and Marco, at this moment in time. A moment he might forget but she wouldn't.

His mouth came down on hers, slowly, tantalizingly. When their lips finally met, she felt the heat and tasted the fierce desire that matched her own. She closed her eyes and matched his kisses one for one. Her tongue met his in a dance that mimicked the lovemaking to come. The tension built, and their tongues merged, and she was frantic to have more. To have his mouth move down her body, to have him kiss her everywhere . . . anywhere.

He broke the kiss and paused for a long moment. His eyes were glazed with desire.

"This is what I wanted," he said, his mouth so close to hers she could almost taste his words, his voice low and raspy. "This is what I dreamed of, to make love to you in a bed. Since the first moment I saw you at the hotel. I wanted to rip off your clothes and make love to you. It was good yesterday—the sun and the grass and you under the trees. But today, in this room, in this bed, it will be even better."

"No bees," she murmured.

"No bees. Just you and me."

His mouth trailed hot kisses down her throat then, down to her breasts. He kissed them, tasted her nipples, sucked them until she quivered and her whole body pulsated.

"Marco," she whispered. Her voice shook. Her arms and legs trembled. Every nerve called out to him to come to her.

He rolled onto his side, bringing her with him. He put his hand between her legs and smiled into her eyes when he felt the slick dampness there.

"Yes, oh, yes," she murmured as his fingers explored and stroked the petals that guarded her most secret erotic place. The sensations built like waves against a shore until they crashed with a huge crescendo, and she fell apart—physically, mentally, and emotionally. She grabbed his shoulders and held on for dear life, sobbing.

He wiped the tears from her face with his gentle, callused fingers. When she stopped crying, she managed a small smile.

"Now," she said. *Now, I'll show you what I wanted to do from the first moment I saw you. How I wanted to rip off your clothes and see what was underneath.* She couldn't say the words, but she could show him.

"What?" Marco needed to make love to her. He needed to come into her slick, waiting body. He needed to be part of her. He needed her to make him whole.

When she began trailing kisses down his body, he

thought he could stay in control, but his whole body was so hard with wanting her he ached inside and out.

"*Basta,*" he pleaded.

"Sorry," she said softly. "I don't speak Italian."

"That's enough. Stop," he said, reaching for her.

Her answer was to take his erection into her mouth. He shuddered as he felt her wet mouth around him. His heart was pounding, and his head had disconnected from his body.

When she began stroking him with her tongue, it was enough to send him over the moon. He wanted to wait. He wanted to get her down on the mattress where he could . . . where they could . . . but if he didn't do it within the next millisecond, he was going to die, because this was more than any human could take.

With a superhuman effort, he rolled over, and she opened her legs, and he entered her, and with one gigantic thrust that must have shaken the whole second floor of the house, he exploded.

She burst into tears again. She buried her face in his chest and sobbed. Marco held her and whispered words of comfort in Italian, words of love and tenderness that he was glad she couldn't understand. He wouldn't want her to mistake what happened here for anything but what it was. Incredible, earth-shaking sex.

He kissed away the tears. He held her tightly until she stopped shaking and his heart settled down to somewhere near normal. Though he wondered in the back of his mind if he'd ever be normal again, ever be able to enjoy casual sex with casual women again.

Whatever happened, whatever he would have to give up, it was worth it. This morning, this bed, this woman. It was all worth it.

After an eternity, after she was calm and peaceful, he got up to open the doors to the balcony. He stood outside and let the morning air cool his overheated bare body. He felt Anna Maria's gaze on him, like a soft breeze, and he turned to see her standing in the middle of the room, wearing the silk nightgown with the tiny straps that begged to be slipped down her shoulders. Her nipples poked at the fabric. The look in her eyes was half shy, half bold, and told him that if he wanted to . . . if he needed to . . . if he wanted her . . .

But there was someone out there who wanted the diamond as much as he did. Whether it was Giovanni or his assistant or his rival, it didn't matter. He had to call Silvestro. He had to stop giving in to his instincts and remember why he was there and why he couldn't trust her.

He walked past Anna Maria, picked up his clothes, and told her he was taking his shower first. She blinked, bit her lip, then quickly arranged her face to hide whatever feelings she had. Shock, hurt, surprise, maybe even anger. He couldn't blame her. He was hiding his true identity from her. But then, wasn't she hiding a diamond from him, hiding her relationship with Giovanni from him?

"Of course," she said. "I'll get dressed. We don't want to be late for the crush."

"Yes, the crush."

He called Silvestro from the bathroom.

"Where in God's name are you?" his boss asked.

"A small town. Does it matter?" he asked.

"Since you're supposed to be in Rome, yes."

"I'm on my way to Rome."

"How, by donkey? It's been a long time since I've heard from you."

"I have everything under control. The woman, the diamond, everything." Everything but his libido, everything but his lust.

"That's good to know. Because the word is that Giovanni is out of the loop. There's a new contact. An American."

"*My* American?"

"Your American and another. They're working together."

"What about Giovanni?" Marco asked.

"He's being squeezed out. He must be angry, and when he's angry, he's dangerous."

"He has a temper." Damn, if Anna Maria had really double-crossed Giovanni by giving him his yearbook with nothing but a "Gotcha" note inside, then he was after her now to get even, as well as to find the diamond. The diamond that Marco now believed was under that fake cheap stone on her finger.

"She could be in danger," Silvestro said. "But when you play with fire . . ."

"I'll make sure she gets to Rome in one piece with the stone," Marco said. Remembering the instinct that told him somebody had tried to get into their room last night, he decided he shouldn't even take a shower without her. Which wasn't a bad idea. While Silvestro talked, he imagined standing in the small glassed-in stall with her. Her smooth, soapy hands on him. She'd lean against the wall, water cascading between her beautiful breasts. He'd kiss her while the water ran down her face. He'd taste her lips, her skin . . . Silvestro kept talking, but Marco's mind was somewhere else.

He heard himself say he'd be on his way immediately.

"Call me when you get there."

Marco agreed and repeated that he'd keep Anna Maria in sight.

But when he got back to the room, she was gone.

Chapter 15

As Marco threw his clothes on, he called himself every name he could think of—*scaricatore de porto*, asshole, fool, and worse. He'd walked out on her after mind-blowing sex without a kind word, and what did he expect? Did he think she'd sit there waiting for him to come back and ignore her again? She had pride. She had guts. And she had no patience with him. The worst part was that he knew women wanted pillow talk, and he easily gave it to them. But Anna Maria was not his usual woman.

He ran down the stairs and out onto the street. He followed the crowd and the noise to the town square and the huge vats where the townspeople were stomping the grapes. The sun was bright, and the air was full of cheering from the spectators and the earthy smell of ripe red grapes.

He scanned the crowd and finally saw her in the center of one of the wooden vats. She was laughing and jumping up and down on the grapes in the middle of a noisy crowd. She was holding hands on both sides with men who looked like villagers, right out of a tourist's dream. His muscles tensed. She was so vulnerable. He should have been in there with her. He should have been stomping grapes and holding her hand. He should have been laughing with her. But he wasn't.

He smiled in spite of himself at her high spirits, picking out her laugh in the din, wishing he didn't have to take her away and put an end to her fun. What if she wouldn't come? What if she insisted on staying there, to flirt with the locals and go to Rome on the bus without him?

When she saw him, she stopped stomping and stared at him until he clenched his fists in frustration. Then she turned away, continued her work, and laughed even louder. She made it very clear she didn't need him to have a good time.

He left her there, went to the garage, and told them he had to have his car. They said the fuel pump hadn't arrived. He said he'd come back another day and get it, but he had to have a car now, any car. The best they could do was to rent him one of their old tow trucks.

"Will it get me to Rome?" he asked. He was in no

position to bargain; he was also in no mood to take the bus.

"*Certo, signore,*" the owner said.

Marco held out his credit card, signed the papers, and went to find Anna Maria. She was still there, stomping and laughing. This time, he walked up to the vat and called to her.

"What?" she said, picking her way through grapes to the edge of the vat.

"We have to leave," he said. "I have to get to Rome today. Business."

"What kind of business?" she asked, her eyes narrowed suspiciously. He didn't blame her; he hardly acted as if he had a job. Little did she know *she* was his business.

"More tourists, more work."

She braced her arms on the edge of the rough wooden vat. "If you need any recommendations, I can tell them what a good guide you are. How considerate, how attentive. How much you do to make sure the tourist has a good time." There was a bitter note to her voice he'd never heard before.

"Look, I'm sorry about this morning," he said.

"Why should you be sorry? Just another day at the office. Just another tourist to entertain."

"No, Anna Maria, you are not just another tourist."

"What am I, then?" she asked, her blue eyes icy cold.

Yes, he'd hurt her. He should never have made

love to her, not yesterday, not this morning, not ever. What was wrong with him?

"You're a wonderful, lovely . . . I don't know enough words in English," he said.

"Let me help you, then. Naive, stupid, deprived, inexperienced . . ."

"No, no."

"Never mind. I'm ready whenever you are. Is the car fixed?"

"No, I've arranged to borrow a tow truck from the garage. I'll have to return later for the Lancia."

"We're going to Rome in a tow truck?"

"We have no choice, except the bus. It's not that far. Where's your ring?"

She held up her hand. "Here. Why is everyone so interested in this ring?"

"Everyone?" he asked, keeping his voice level with an effort. He wanted to shake her, to demand to know who else wanted the ring. Was it Giovanni? Someone else?

"You'd think it was valuable," she said with a nervous laugh. It seemed she wasn't going to answer his question, so he put his hands under her elbows and lifted her out of the vat. She was wearing a short skirt that hugged her hips and a low-cut peasant blouse that, if he strained his eyes, he could see right through to her lace bra. How he could possibly be aroused again this morning, he didn't know. But he was. If she were someone else, just an ordinary tourist . . . if he were someone else, a real tour guide . . . but even then, it could never be more than a flirtation. She would return to the United States, and he . . . what would he do after he caught Giovanni? He tore his eyes from the front of her blouse and looked at her feet. They were purple.

"Do I have time to wash my feet, or are your new clients waiting for you at the two-thousand-year-old Colosseum in the hot sun, standing in front of one of the Greek columns to hear about the gladiators and the lions? Because, if so—"

"*Greek* columns?" he asked.

"Doric, Ionic, and Corinthian, some of each to honor the high culture that came before them. But you knew that."

"Of course. If you know so much, why don't you guide the tour for me? I'll take a nap." He carried her shoes for her as they walked toward the house.

"Why would you need a nap? You slept in a bed all night."

"Until you came over and seduced me."

"I came in to get some sleep, not seduce you," she said, turning her face but not before he saw her cheeks redden.

He grinned. "I didn't mind."

She blushed all the way to the low neckline of her blouse. "It probably happens to you all the time," she said tartly.

"Not often enough," he muttered.

He followed her into the small bathroom back at the widow's house, taking no more chances. As she sat on the commode, he took a sponge from the shower and a bar of soap and held her foot in the palm of one hand and scrubbed with the other.

"Stop," she said. "I'm ticklish."

He put the sponge down, soaped her foot, and used his hand to rub the ball of her foot, to tug on her toes and slide his fingers between them. She closed her eyes and tilted her head back. She murmured something he didn't understand. She was the most responsive woman he'd ever met. The most sensual, the sexiest, and she didn't even know it. She was taking short little breaths. There was a knock on the door.

"Scusi, signora. Apra, per favore."

Anna Marie's eyes flew open. She could still feel it, the building of tension, the thrumming in her body, the awareness of his fingers, those clever fingers bringing her to the brink of delirium once again. Another minute, and she would have gone over the edge. She would have shattered into a million pieces. Just because Marco was washing her feet. Panting, trying to fill her lungs with air, she looked at him. His eyes were brimming with awareness. She tried to speak, but her mouth was too dry.

"Tell her you'll be right out," he whispered.

"Momento," she called.

"I don't know what happened," she whispered as he dried her feet with a towel. She did know; she just didn't know how or why.

"You have very responsive feet," he said softly,

continuing to massage them, only this time with the towel. "Very sexy feet."

"But I didn't know they were . . . I didn't know you could, that I could . . ."

"Just a few more moments, and you would have."

"Yes," she breathed. She stood on shaky legs and opened the bathroom door. The maid was standing there, holding a bucket in her hand, wearing a simple cotton dress, her hair tied up with a scarf. Her eyes widened at the sight of the two of them coming out together. Marco managed a polite smile, and they hurried down the hall. Anne Marie cast a furtive glance over her shoulder. The maid was still standing at the bathroom door, a shocked look on her face. They grabbed their bags and left the house. Fortunately, Marco had paid in advance for the room, so there was no further delay. Obviously, he was happy about that, since he had some overwhelming need to get to Rome that he couldn't or wouldn't explain to her.

The tow truck was an old one. The paint was peeling off the doors, making it difficult to read the name of the garage. The inside was dusty. Marco didn't seem to notice. He was filling the tank with diesel fuel when she remembered she had to call Evie's cousin.

"Use my phone," he said, handing it to her.

She found the number and Misty answered.

"Anne Marie, where are you?" she said. "I've been worried about you."

"I'm in a little town somewhere," she said. "But I'm coming to Rome today."

"Fantastic. You'll stay with me, of course."

"No, I couldn't impose," she said. "Besides, I have a reservation." It wasn't true; she just didn't want to be beholden to anyone. And she wanted a hotel room to herself, a safe haven with a bathroom attached and not down the hall.

"Where are you staying?" Misty said.

"I . . . I can't remember the name of the place," she said. "But I'll call you."

"I'm having a party tonight. Everyone will be there. All my friends want to meet you. What perfect timing."

"How nice," she said politely.

"How is the candy holding up?" Misty asked.

"Oh . . . fine." She'd completely forgotten about it. Again, she would have left it behind. "I'll bring it to the party."

"Just tell me where you're staying, and I'll come and pick it up. You don't know how much I crave one of those delicious Nob Hill chocolates. There's nothing like them in Italy."

There went her plan to replace the eaten candies. "Don't worry; I'll be there soon—with the candy."

She hung up and went with Marco to the wine cellar, where she retrieved the chocolates. The box was cool, so the candy should retain its shape and taste until it was safely in Misty's hands—or mouth.

Once in the tow truck, with her seat belt fastened and Marco at the wheel, she opened the box of chocolates once again. They appeared to be as good as new.

"Don't eat too much," he cautioned. "We'll be in Rome for lunch. Once we hit the *autostrada,* we'll make good time."

"I told Misty I had a hotel, but I don't."

"I have an apartment there," he said. "You could even have your own bed."

She slanted a glance in his direction. His eyes were on the road; his expression told her nothing. Did he not want to share a bed with her? Did he have a girlfriend in Rome?

"Thank you, but no thank you." It was time to break off with Marco before he broke off with her. The more time she spent with him, the more she wanted to spend. He made her laugh, he made her feel like the sexiest woman alive, but he probably made all the women in his life feel that way. And she was going back to America in two weeks.

"You mentioned the convent where your sister is. I think I'd feel safe there, if they have any rooms for rent."

"It is safe, and a good value. I've only been there once, when Isabella first went there. The rooms are simple but clean, and I remember the roof terrace has a view out over the city. I'll be going there anyway to see my sister."

She nodded, leaned back, and closed her eyes.

The next thing she heard was a cacophony of horns blowing. Diesel fumes filled the air, and a cloud of smog hung over the city.

She sat up straight. "This is it? We're here already?"

"This is it. It's a great city, but it's not an easy city.

Not a safe city for a woman alone. I know Rome, and I'll take you wherever you want to go. Not just the Colosseum and the Vatican and the Trevi Fountain; I can also take you to the old medieval city and Trastevere. Unless you have other plans. Someone else . . ."

"What about your urgent plans?"

"They can wait."

Suddenly, he now had time for her? It was too strange. But a tempting thought. Forget Evie's cousin, forget her party, wander the back streets with Marco. Why not?

"There's just one thing. I promised Evie's cousin I'd go to a party at her house tonight. Maybe we could just drop by, if you don't mind. I'll say hello, deliver her candy, and then we can go off to see the sights."

He nodded, and a few minutes later, they climbed a hill and passed a small church. He pulled the tow truck up in front of the convent of the Sisters of Santa Teresa.

Marco looked up at the gray stone building, remembering the one and only time he'd been there, two years ago. How he'd demanded that Isabella leave and come home. She'd refused. She'd just been ditched by Giovanni, who had promised to marry her, and she was devastated, convinced convent life was the answer to her problems. They'd had a huge fight about it. He'd said some things he regretted; so had she. He hadn't spoken to her since.

He had no idea what to expect today. He didn't want Anna Maria to witness another fight between his sister and himself.

The nun who answered the bell gave them an angelic smile and told them she had a room for *la signora,* with a view of the surrounding hills. Marco carried Anna Maria's suitcase to the small, white-washed room with the narrow single bed and sink, and then they went up to the terrace. He knew he was postponing the inevitable meeting with his sister, but he wasn't ready. Maybe he'd never be ready. Maybe Giovanni had already been there. Marco could only guess at what mayhem he could have caused.

The terrace was empty. It was high above the chaos that was Rome. There were graceful cypress trees beneath them and the scent of pine in the air. Anna Maria leaned on the railing and smiled at him.

"It's wonderful. I want to see it all."

"Marco."

He turned. So did Anna Maria.

His sister was wearing a plain gray dress, her hair pulled back behind her ears. She wore sturdy black shoes, but nothing could hide her natural beauty. Her dark curls escaped in tendrils from the scarf on her head; her dark eyes were luminous and shone with pleasure. The cold lump that was his heart softened.

When she smiled at him, he felt a huge surge of relief. Just one look, and he could tell everything was fine, unless Giovanni had something to do with that smile. If he did, he'd have to kill him.

She ran to him and hugged him tightly. Tears ran down her face.

"You came. Nonna said you would."

"Of course I did. How are you, Bella?"

She held out her arms and stepped back. "As you see. Marco, you won't believe what has happened." She peered over his shoulder. "You're not alone."

"Anna Maria, I want you to meet my sister, Isabella."

Anna Maria held out her hand, but Isabella ignored it and hugged her, too. Then she stood back and looked her over.

"My clothes!" She laughed delightedly.

"I'm sorry," Anna Maria said. "I'm going to return them all, but . . ."

Isabella shook her head. "Don't think of it," she said. "Nonna has told me the whole story. You're American. I love everything American—American music and movies. That is, I used to love them before . . ."

"What about candy?" Anna Maria asked. "Would you like a piece of American candy?"

"I would love it."

Anna Maria reached for her box of chocolates and held it out to Isabella. After all the trouble with the damned candy, Marco wished his sister would just polish it off. But after studying the various truffles with their swirls and decorations, she took only one piece.

Anna Maria put the candy box back in her bag and said she would leave them to catch up on family matters while she went down to her room and wrote some postcards.

After she'd left, Isabella motioned to a bench under a tree. "Nonna was right," she said. "She's beautiful, your American."

"I'm afraid she's not mine," he said.

"Since when have you not had any woman you wanted?" she asked with a teasing grin.

"It's not so simple anymore," he said. "She's American and divorced. She has a son in America and an ex-husband who wants her back."

"Pfah," Isabella said. "As if you weren't a match for anyone and anything. She loves you, I can tell. And you?"

"Me? I don't believe in love. You know that."

"I know that's what you say. I also know she's the one for you. You're not getting any younger, Marco. If you lose her, you will end up a lonely old man."

"I may get old, but I've never been lonely. Why should I end up that way?" As he spoke, he thought of Silvestro, looking forward to his retirement with his wife of fifty years. He thought of Nonna and her rich memories of a lifetime of happiness with his grandfather. But she managed fine on her own now, so why shouldn't he? "Enough about me. Don't keep me in suspense. What has happened?"

"Giovanni came to see me."

"What? When?"

"Yesterday. I didn't know how I would feel after

all this time. It's been two years; I have changed. He saw it. Even you see it, don't you? I've learned so much here. So much about life and love. So much about how little material things matter. Giovanni has changed, too—not entirely for the best. He is even more materialistic than before. And he's in love."

"In love? I thought he was married."

"He was. But he's in love with an American. He told me all about her. Someone he met years ago when he was in school in California. Someone who's in the same business as he is. Import-export. It must be something in the air: Italians falling for Americans. Maybe I should go to America to find someone."

Marco felt cold, inside and out. He should have known. He *did* know. He'd known all along they were in it together; he just hadn't wanted to believe it. He wanted to believe she was an innocent tourist, despite all the evidence. *Import-export* meant stealing and fencing jewels. It was clear to anyone with half a brain who this American Giovanni was involved with was: the same American who was downstairs in her room writing postcards. The same American Marco had made love to twice in the past two days. And if he had a chance, he'd make love to her again, even knowing who she was. That was how bad it was.

He suddenly wondered if she'd taken this opportunity to sneak off to see Giovanni, to give him the diamond. Unless she'd double-crossed him and was going to give it to someone else? Marco forced himself to remain seated, to listen to his sister, though he wanted to race down the stairs to be sure she was still there. If she wasn't, he would never find her again. Not in Rome. Not if she didn't want to be found. There was a hollow, empty feeling in the pit of his stomach.

"The important thing is," Isabella continued, unaware of the effect her words were having on him, "that I am no longer in love with Giovanni. I see him for what he is. A philanderer, a materialist, and someone who plays by his own rules."

"You're not angry with him?" Marco asked, feeling as if he'd just run into a glass wall. All these years, he'd hated Giovanni for betraying his sister, and she'd forgiven him.

"Not anymore. It's not his fault, Marco; it's how he was raised. It's how he's always been. In fact, I have to say I am grateful to him. It was because of him I came to the convent. I was a young, immature girl, disappointed in love. The sisters took me in, didn't ask anything of me, didn't pressure me to join the order. They just accepted me. That was what I needed. I've worked hard here, physical work. I scrub the floors, wash the dishes, peel potatoes. While working, I was thinking and learning, and now . . . well, I have much more to learn, but I think I can learn on the outside as well as here.

"That's what Giovanni thinks, too. That's what he told me, anyway. He advised me to return to life. He pointed out that I can do good anywhere I am.

He believes, or he said he does, that I am a good person."

"Anyone can see that," Marco said tightly. "And compared with Giovanni, anyone is."

"Don't be bitter," she admonished, and took his hands in hers.

"Does that mean you are actually leaving, then?" He was amazed and impressed at how mature his sister had become.

She nodded. "In a few months, after I do what I need to do here. Then I'm going back to San Gervase. I'll stay with Nonna until I decide more about my future."

"Does she know?"

"Yes. She's very happy about it. She would like it if you, too, would come back to your house there. She walked by the other day, and she didn't like what she saw. The garden has been neglected. The roof is rotten. The paint is peeling. What are your plans?"

"I have no plans," he said. "I'm here on business. After that, who knows?" But the little house on the cliff in San Gervase, with its overgrown plants and bushes and its leaky roof, called to him. If he didn't want it, it was time to go back there, fix it up, and sell it. If he did want it . . . he had to ask himself why.

"So, we have Giovanni to thank for your change of heart?" Marco said, half disbelieving that Giovanni could accomplish anything remotely good.

"I was already thinking about leaving, but he gave me the push I needed. I know you and he have always been rivals, and people say he's a crook. But he's not in jail, so how can he really be that bad?"

Marco just smiled enigmatically. Isabella kissed him on the cheek and went off to do her chores. Marco ran down the stairs to find Anna Maria exactly where she said she'd be—in her room writing postcards. He'd worried for nothing.

He spent the afternoon showing Anna Maria some of his favorite places, little-known spots not in any guidebook. On their way to the Campidoglio, she wanted to see the Mammertine Prison. Marco warned her it was dark and depressing, and she said she didn't care. Once inside, once she saw the hole through which the prisoners were lowered, she shivered. He instinctively put his arm around her shoulders.

Never before had the thought of the prisoners awaiting their deaths bothered him so much. Never before could he almost smell the rotting corpses, though it had been centuries since the prison had been used. On the wall were lists of prisoners and how they were executed—*"strangolati, decapitato, morto de fame."* Strangled, decapitated, starved to death. "Donation requested."

Anna Maria's face turned pale, and her eyebrows were drawn together as she read the list. Was she afraid she'd wind up in a prison in America? He'd heard white-collar criminals there were treated to country-club prisons with green grass and volleyball. Maybe she'd get a light sentence. Somehow the thought was not as comforting as it should have been.

Once they were outside, the color returned to her cheeks, and they sat down at a small café, ate gelato, and drank tiny cups of coffee. She stirred her coffee but didn't speak.

"Shall we go?" she asked finally. "I want to see as much as possible."

"There's always tomorrow," Marco said. Or was there? Wouldn't Giovanni find her as soon as possible and demand the diamond? Or was it destined for someone else?

"I wish I didn't have to go to that party. I want to see the floodlit monuments at night."

"Where is this party? Maybe we'll pass a monument or two on the way."

She pulled out a piece of paper from her purse and showed him the address.

He whistled softly. "That's a nice neighborhood. What does your friend do?"

"I don't know. You can ask her when you meet her. She's not my friend, anyway, she's my friend's cousin." She looked at her watch. "I'd better call Evie and tell her I'm finally going to see Misty."

He handed her his phone.

"I'm calling America."

He shrugged as if money were no object. Maybe he'd write it off as a business expense.

"Do you always let your clients use your phone?"

she asked. What she really wanted to know was, *Do you always sleep with your clients?*

"Never," he said. "But you're not a client. You're a . . ."

She waited. The words that came to mind were not complimentary.

"Friend," he said at last. "I'd like to think we're friends."

"Is it possible for men and women to be friends?" she asked. She really didn't know.

"Ask me again tomorrow."

Tomorrow. After the party. After a night in the convent. Surely, he didn't think they'd make love in a convent? The thought of their muffled sighs, their contortions on a narrow cot, caused her to forget Evie's number. She had to open her small address book.

"Evie, it's me."

"Anne Marie, I'm so glad you called. My cousin called. I heard about the party. This is so fabulous. You're going to love her house. Do you know how to get there?"

"No, but my, uh, friend does. The one I've been traveling with. Misty won't mind if I bring a date, will she?"

"Of course not. Who is he?"

"No one you know."

"How did you meet him?"

"At the hotel in San Gervase." She glanced at Marco. He was looking off in the distance, his gaze focused somewhere across the piazza.

"Do you know anything about him?" Evie sounded concerned. Anne Marie wanted to hang up.

"Yes, quite a bit. He's a tour guide," she added glibly for Marco's benefit.

Marco shot her a swift glance.

"Anne Marie, be careful. Many of those guides are out to take advantage of you."

"Don't worry," she said. "I have everything under control." *Liar.* She had nothing under control, not her mind or her body.

"Dan's been asking for you. He expects you to call him. If you gave him even a little encouragement, I think he'd fly over there. I wouldn't be surprised if he'd take you back."

"Take me back? How infuriating. How condescending. And you can tell him I said so. Got to run, Evie. Gotta get dressed for the party."

"Are you going to wear that black dress you ordered through the catalog?"

"Not tonight. I'm thinking of wearing a little tie-dyed silk halter dress."

"Tie-dyed? Halter dress? Anne Marie, that doesn't sound like you."

"Sometimes I don't feel like me. 'Bye, Evie."

"Wait, wait, don't forget the candy. You won't, will you? It's okay, isn't it? It hasn't melted?"

"What's left of it, yes." She didn't have time to replace the missing chocolates, but why bother? They wouldn't be the same, and Misty would notice. Instead, she'd send Misty another box when

she got home. Which is what Evie should have
done in the first place. Really, how ridiculous was it
to hand-carry a box of chocolate truffles all through
Italy while they melted, got eaten, or were forgotten
by the wayside?

"Left of it? Left of it?" Evie's voice rose; it was
clear she was upset.

Anne Marie had no desire to explain what had
happened to the candy, and she couldn't believe
Evie had nothing better to do than worry about
some expensive chocolates. She disconnected and
handed the phone back to Marco.

It rang immediately. He got up from the table
and moved away to speak.

"Marco, thank God I got you. I hope you're in
Rome," Silvestro said.

"Yes."

"Giovanni has been double-crossed."

"I know."

"Do you know he's there in Rome and more
determined than ever to get the diamond?"

Marco paced back and forth in front of the café,
his voice low, his eyes on Anna Maria, who was still
at the table.

"Yes."

"There's a party tonight," Silvestro said.

"I know."

Silvestro was clearly annoyed. "If you know so
much, why haven't you taken the diamond? Why
haven't you found Giovanni and arrested him?"

"I will arrest everyone when the diamond is handed off. Don't worry. I have everything under control," Marco said.

"Just in case there's a problem," Silvestro said, "I'll be there tonight, and I won't be alone."

"Good," Marco said, and hung up.

Was it possible for he and Anna Maria and Silvestro all to have everything under control? Tonight would tell.

Chapter 16

Anne Marie sucked in a breath at the sight of Evie's cousin's sixteenth-century villa. Located in a quiet corner of Rome, it was surrounded by lush gardens and statues. In front, a huge fountain spouted water from the mouth of a lion. Floodlights illuminated the pillars and polished marble of the façade.

"This can't be it. It looks like a museum," she said in a hushed voice, suddenly nervous about attending a party like this. Thank God for Marco; she'd have someone to talk to. Though he didn't seem to have much to say in the taxi on the way there.

He hadn't even said anything about her dress. The look he gave her when they met on the terrace told her nothing, either. He merely raised his eyebrows. It was Isabella who'd complimented her when she came to her room and helped her get ready.

"You look wonderful," Isabella said. "Now, with that dress, you should wear a stone pendant. A man I was once involved with gave me one just yesterday, when he came to see me. A farewell gift. I can't wear it now, and I may never wear it, but you can." She reached into the pocket of her apron for the necklace, fastened it around Anne Marie's neck, then told her to wear the patent-leather slingbacks that matched one of the bright rainbow colors in the dress. She stood back, looked at Anne Marie, and nodded happily. "My brother will be knocked off his feet, if he isn't already," she said. "Or perhaps you don't want to knock him off his feet? Don't answer that."

"I have a question," Anne Marie said. "What does he do?"

"Do?" Isabella wrinkled her forehead. "Whatever they tell him to do."

"They?"

"His bosses at the agency. I know what you're worried about, that he takes his work home with him. That's always been a problem. I was just a kid when it happened, but I think that's why Donatella broke up with him. The bad thing is, he didn't take it as a warning. He just got more and more immersed in his work. Not that he didn't always have a woman around, but nobody serious. Not until now."

"Serious? I've only known your brother a few days."

"But you like him, don't you? I'm asking you, just give him a chance."

A chance to do what? Make love to her again? Break her heart? Send her back to the United States an emotional wreck?

"I think, and Nonna thinks, too, that if he had a life outside his work . . . if he had a wife . . ."

"But I haven't seen him do any work at all. Since I met him, he's done nothing but show me around, eat and drink, and . . ." She felt her cheeks burn.

Isabella gave her a knowing smile. "That's why you're so good for him." She looked at Anne Marie with hopeful eyes. "I just want to say that he's a good man. A good man who needs a good woman. I know he's difficult. I know he doesn't always say what he means or mean what he says, but I can tell by the way he looks at you . . ."

Anne Marie waited, but she didn't finish her sentence.

"Go," Isabella said. "I've said too much already. Go and have a good time. I won't wait up for you."

Before they knocked on the massive, carved wooden doors of Misty's villa, Anne Marie turned to Marco. Despite his dark jacket, white shirt, and tie, he was too rugged ever to look suave. Not smooth, either, with his hair a shade too long, his slightly crooked nose, and the shadow of a beard on his square jaw. But he was sexy. Very sexy, with his heavy-lidded eyes on her.

"I have to ask you something." She took a deep, steadying breath. "Who are you, really?"

"I might ask you the same thing." His gaze was dark and fathomless.

"That's no answer. You know who I am. I have nothing to hide."

"Nothing?"

"All right. I didn't tell you, but I've seen Giovanni, and I gave him something. But that's really none of your business. He's an old friend. I trust him."

But I don't trust you, hung in the air. He heard the words just as surely as if she'd spoken them.

"Aren't you going to see him again? Aren't you going to give him something else?"

"I have nothing more to give him," she insisted.

Before he could press her for more information, the huge double doors flew open. Loud music came floating out on the night air, along with loud voices. A woman in head-to-toe gold, a full-length embroidered gold lace coat and gold leather jeans, glittered in the doorway. She was barefoot.

"You must be Anne Marie," she said with a dazzling smile that matched her outfit. "I'm *so* glad to see you. You look absolutely fabulous. What a divine necklace." She reached for the stone around Anne Marie's neck and studied it carefully for a moment. Then she kissed Anne Marie on both cheeks, gave Marco a puzzled, sidelong look, and turned back to Anne Marie. "Where's the candy?" she asked abruptly.

Anne Marie's mind went blank. She'd had the candy. She'd brought the candy. But suddenly, she didn't know where it was. She turned to Marco.

"In the taxi?" he suggested.

"Look, Misty," Anne Marie said, so tired of carrying that damned candy all over Italy, so tired of trying to figure out who Marco was, what he did, why he did it, and how she felt about him, that she couldn't face another problem. It was just candy, for heaven's sake. "Just forget the candy. I'll send you a new box when I get home."

"Forget the candy?" Misty's voice rose so high Anne Marie was afraid it might crack the champagne glass she held in her hand. "I've been waiting for that candy for a week! I came to the airport to meet you, but I missed you because you'd changed your plans and had already left. I called Evie, and she assured me you had the candy. *Where is the candy?*"

"I'll call the taxi company," Marco said, taking out his phone.

"You'll have to do more than that," Misty said, her fierce gaze leveled at Anne Marie. "I must have it."

Anne Marie knew people who craved chocolate, but this must be a serious addiction. Just then, a crowd of guests came up the long stairs behind them, and Misty was forced to turn her attention to them.

Momentarily reprieved, Anne Marie waited until Marco finished his phone conversation. He assured her the taxi driver had been found and would deliver the candy. She hooked her hand in Marco's arm and walked into the huge, high-ceilinged room that was more of an art gallery than a living room. It was filled with well-dressed people, undressed marble statues, and paintings that looked old and valuable. Waiters passed through the crowd with trays of drinks and tiny appetizers. Anne Marie took a glass of champagne and a cracker covered with caviar.

"Thank you for handling the lost candy," she said. "Was it just me, or did that woman seem hysterical about those silly chocolates?"

"I've never understood women and chocolate. She liked your necklace," he noted. "Where did that come from?"

"It's Isabella's. She said it was a present from a man she was once involved with. A farewell gift."

"Really." He leaned forward, his head bent over the pendant, his warm fingers grazing the space between her breasts. She felt her pulse quicken and her heart throb.

"I didn't know you were interested in jewelry," she said, trying to stay composed while chills ran up and down her arms.

"I'm interested in everything you're wearing or not wearing," he said, with a half-smile and a glance down the front of her dress at her embroidered pale green bra.

Her nipples puckered, and she knew he knew. Her eyelids fluttered. The matching lace panties made her feel sexy and wicked. His eyes focused on the valley between her breasts. Her skin was so hot it nearly sizzled. She took a deep breath to try to fill her lungs. This could be her last night with Marco. He'd never said anything about tomorrow or the next day or the next.

If it was the last, then every minute was precious, so why waste time at some glitzy party where she didn't even know the hostess? What a night to be staying in a convent.

Still loosely holding the stone pendant, he looked around the room, his gaze turning cool and appraising. "How did you say Misty got her money?"

"Import-export, I think. I know Evie does some work for her back home. Sends her stuff for her to sell."

Marco turned his sharpened gaze on her. He let the pendant go. "Such as jewelry?"

"I don't know. I never asked. Why?"

"She never even looked at your ring."

"Of course not. It's cheap, ordinary. I'm only wearing it because I like it."

"She looked at the necklace, but what she really wanted was the candy," he said slowly.

"You're as bad as Misty. It's just candy. It's not that important, is it?"

"Yes," he said grimly. "It is."

Marco cursed himself for being so dense. He'd just figured it out, and now it was almost too late. If he could just get the candy from the taxi driver before Misty did or Giovanni did.

But it *was* too late. Misty was strolling majesti-
cally through the great hall with the familiar white
box under her arm. She was laughing and looking
up into the face of the tall man in a tuxedo who
seemed glued to her side.

Marco considered throwing her to the ground
and taking the box from her by force while he
pressed her face into the silk carpet with one hand,
his knee on her gold-spangled back. But maybe,
just maybe he was wrong.

He didn't want to be wrong. He wanted Misty to
be Giovanni's contact, because that meant Anna
Maria was just what she seemed: an innocent
tourist. It made sense.

Anna Maria had had the opportunity and the
means to hide the diamond, and the contact here to
give it to. But she hadn't done it. He'd been watching and waiting, and still Giovanni didn't have the
diamond. Anna Maria didn't have the diamond,
either. From the triumphant look on Misty's face,
she had it. Yes, there had to be something better
than candy in that box.

Giovanni had displeased someone, maybe Misty,
and now he was out of the loop—but not down and
out, if he knew Giovanni. If there was money
involved, Giovanni would be, too.

Marco reached for another glass of champagne.
If Anna Maria wasn't really involved in this heist,
there were even more unanswered questions than
before. It was so easy when he thought it was a matter of a diamond and two people, Giovanni and

Anna Maria. Now it was more complicated. And he needed to be sure, in his mind as well as in his heart.

"What would you do if you had a lot of money?" he asked her. "Would you buy a house like this?"

"A house like this?" Anna Maria shook her head. "It would be like living in a museum. The house I like is your grandmother's house. It's got a big kitchen, a garden, and everything."

"There's no view," he said flatly. His house had a view of the sea. It had a rotten roof and an overgrown garden, with a lemon tree that had long ago ceased producing, but it had a view.

"Oh, well, you can't have everything."

"But you have a house in California. You're not thinking of living in Italy, are you?"

"Don't worry," she said, mistaking his surprise for alarm. "I'm not going to move to your backyard. What would I do? No." She laughed softly. "I couldn't live in Italy."

"Not even if Giovanni asked you?"

"Why would he do that? He's married."

"I'm not sure he takes his vows very seriously."

"How would you know that? You don't even know him."

"I'm a cynical man. You know that by now. What about a diamond?" he asked, looking down at her hands. He looked at the ring she said she'd bought on the sidewalk, at her plain, unpolished nails.

"A diamond?" she said. He caught a hint of wistfulness in her voice. "It's a little late for a diamond.

I've gotten along all these years without one; I don't think I need one now. No, I don't see a diamond in my future."

He was relieved, because she'd told him what he was desperate to hear. He was sure she hadn't stolen the diamond, and he didn't want to believe she was in love with Giovanni. But she didn't say she didn't want a diamond—only that she didn't need one. He'd have to accept that. Along with the good news that Anna Maria had no reason to want a mansion or to live in Italy.

Once she went back home, he could forget about her. He'd misjudged her, but no harm was done, as long as they found the diamond. It would be even better if she never knew she'd been under suspicion. If he'd known it was going to end like this, he . . . what? Wouldn't have made love to her?

No, he would have taken her to his apartment this afternoon, instead of touring the inside of a prison. It would have eased some of the ache in his gut. If she learned the whole story tonight, he doubted she'd ever want to see him again. Even if, by some miracle, she did, even if they walked out of there together, you couldn't make love in a convent.

He glanced around the room. There was a tuxedoed man at each entrance. Damn. Not only that, but across the room, leaning elegantly and casually against a pillar, was Giovanni, dressed impeccably in tux and tie, a glass of champagne in his hand. At this point, Marco was hardly surprised. He didn't hate the man anymore, but he wanted to see him punished.

"There's your friend Giovanni. Don't you want to say hello?" he asked lightly.

"Not now."

"Good, because I want you to come with me," he said, holding her arm so tightly the champagne sloshed over her glass. "We have to find that candy," he said, as they walked toward the door through which Misty had disappeared. "Do you have any idea what's inside it?"

"Of course. Raspberry cream, nougat, caramel—"

"What about a large yellow diamond, about this big?" He made a circle with his thumb and index finger.

"A diamond?" She looked dumbstruck.

"A diamond worth a fortune. A diamond worth risking your life for, worth betraying your lover or your best friend for. It's the Bianchi diamond. Have you ever heard of it?"

"No. How would a diamond get inside a truffle? Where did you get this ridiculous idea?"

"Let's just get our hands on those chocolates."

"And if we don't find a diamond inside one of them?" she asked.

"Then I'm wrong, and I have to start back at zero."

"And if we do find it? What does that prove?" She stopped abruptly. "You don't think I knew it was in there, do you? You don't think I would have brought into this country a box of candy knowing there was a diamond in it, do you?"

He was silent.

Her eyes widened. "Have you been following me all this time because of a diamond?"

Marco still didn't answer. What could he say?

"You have, haven't you?" She blinked rapidly.

Oh, God, she wasn't going to cry again, was she?

"You even seduced me to distract me, to try to get it." Her eyes were ice blue, her cheeks were red, and her voice rose with each word, as the realization of his duplicity hit her. But she didn't cry.

"No," he said, but she wasn't listening.

They marched together across the room. This was no time to have this discussion. The diamond was under this roof, and he had to find it.

They came to a closed door. There was a man standing there, wearing a white shirt and black suspenders, his arms outstretched. He gave them a cool smile. Misty was inside, shouting at someone in Italian.

"What is she saying?" Anne Marie demanded.

"She's calling a servant a filthy parasite. She told her that her father is about as stupid as a chicken."

"But why?"

"It's the chocolates. Someone, a servant, took the chocolates, put them on a plate, and . . ."

The door burst open. Misty stormed out, followed by three ashen-faced, white-aproned maids.

Anne Marie stepped aside. If she hadn't, Misty would have run over her.

"The candy," Misty said. "Help me find my candy."

If Misty was this upset about the candy, maybe Marco was right. But he'd been wrong about her. And she'd been wrong about him. So terribly, painfully wrong. Anne Marie's anger subsided, leaving an aching sadness in its place.

She followed in Misty's wake, Marco at her side, barreling through the grand gallery, going from guest to guest, from table to table, looking under benches, above statues, in alcoves.

Suddenly, a hush fell over the room. Giovanni had stepped up onto a small platform next to a reclining marble nude. In one hand he held a plate of truffles, and in the other he held out a canary-yellow diamond that glittered in the light from a blazing crystal chandelier above. Every eye in the place was on him and on the rare gem. The musicians put down their instruments. No one moved. No one spoke.

"Misty." His voice echoed in the huge gallery. "Is this what you're looking for?"

"Giovanni," she said, suddenly all smiles and good nature. "You found the diamond. Now, give it back to me." She held out her hand.

Anne Marie felt faint. There *was* a diamond. A diamond worth killing for, dying for, lying for, or betraying your best friend for. Giovanni was looking at it with the lust men usually reserved for women. And Misty? With her hand outstretched, she was as still as one of the statues in her gallery, but her eyes glittered with a lust that matched his.

"It's not yours, it's mine," Giovanni said. "Mine

to keep or mine to give. I'm going to give it to someone I love. Now, tonight. To a woman who deserves
it. She has been in my heart from the time I first
met her in America more than twenty years ago. I've
always been in love with her, but I've never told her.
Anna Maria." He came down off the pedestal and
walked slowly toward her, smiling at her the way he
did in her dreams and holding the diamond in the
palm of his hand.

Anne Marie stood watching him walk toward her,
frozen in place. She couldn't move, couldn't speak.
The other people in the room faded away—Marco,
Misty, the guards, the musicians, and the servants.
He put the diamond in her hand, and even in her
state of numb delirium, she knew it wasn't his to
give or hers to get. She closed her hand around it.

Then there was chaos. The huge chandelier
swung overhead as if a giant had given it a shove.
The lights went out. Women screamed. Men
shouted. Heavy footsteps pounded the floor. Doors
opened and slammed shut. Someone grabbed the
chain she was wearing around her neck, and she
choked. Someone else shoved her to the floor, and
her head banged against the inlaid stone. Strong
fingers tried to pry her hand open, but she held on
to the diamond so tightly it cut into her skin, and
she felt blood between her fingers. Shots were
fired, flashes of light in the dark. Someone dragged
her body somewhere else.

When the lights came on, minutes or even hours
later, Anne Marie was lying on an Oriental carpet,

her dress caught up around her hips, her beautiful leather shoes gone. She moaned and sat up slowly. The room was spinning around her.

There were people milling around, talking loudly. Some of them wore blue uniforms. There was no more music, no more party. No more Misty and no more Giovanni. She put her head between her knees for a long moment. When she looked up, Marco was kneeling beside her.

"He's gone," Marco said.

He reached for her hand and gently opened her fist with his rough fingers. The yellow diamond lay there, huge and dazzling and safe in her palm.

"So, it's true. This is what it was all about." She pressed one hand to her head, trying to stop the throbbing. "Is this what they ransacked my room for?"

He nodded.

"But who? Who did it?"

"Who do you think?"

"Giovanni? That's not possible. He's not a thief. If he was, why didn't he keep the diamond, instead of giving it to me? You don't believe what he said about being in love with me, do you?"

He shrugged. "I think he had to choose between getting away and getting the diamond, so he chose to get away."

"Get away from what, from whom?"

"From me."

Anne Marie stared into his eyes, trying to understand, but her head ached, and his face was blurred, and nothing made any sense.

"Who are you?" she asked. "I'd like the truth for once."

"I work for the Italian government. My agency works with other countries to track down international thieves."

"So, that *is* why you've been following me. You really thought I was a thief, and that's why you . . ." Tears welled up in her throat. This time, she would *not* cry. She had been a fool to think he cared about her. Now she knew for sure it was all business. And Giovanni? He had used her, too.

"You had a very valuable diamond in your possession."

"But you didn't know that. How could you? I didn't know it."

"We've been after Giovanni for years. Whenever a famous diamond goes missing, Giovanni's name comes up. We knew he was waiting for this one. We knew he was expecting someone to bring it to him. We thought it was you. I might remind you, it *was* you. You *did* bring it."

"But I didn't mean to, I didn't know—"

"I know that now," he said wearily. "Giovanni knows, too. He thought it was in the yearbook. When he saw it wasn't, he followed us to Maggiore."

"But who put it in the candy?"

"Who do you think did it? Who *could* have done it?"

"Evie gave it to me to give her cousin. But it couldn't be Evie. She's a friend. She's just like me,

an ordinary small-town . . . no, not Evie." And not
Giovanni, either. He might be a careless charmer,
he might be a womanizer, but he wasn't a thief. He
couldn't be. Besides, he was in Italy. Whoever put
the diamond in the candy did it in the United
States.

A man in a rumpled suit walked up to them and
stood looming above them.

"Giovanni is gone," the man said.

Marco got up. He reached for Anne Marie's hand
and helped her to her feet.

"Silvestro, this is Ms. Jackson," he said. He
turned to Anne Marie. "Silvestro Schiavenza is my
boss. He'd like to ask you a few questions. He'd also
like the diamond."

"You must forgive Marco's lack of manners," he
said with a courtly little bow. "Don't make the lady
stand," Silvestro chided Marco.

Marco brought two chairs, one for his boss and
one for her, and Anne Marie gratefully sat down.
Her knees were weak, and she felt cold all over.
Marco put his suit jacket over her shoulders and
stood behind her. His jacket was still warm from his
wearing it. She caught the scent of tobacco and
leather and his soap and closed her eyes for a
moment.

She would not get sentimental. She would keep
her dignity, what was left of it. And she would get
some answers. They might not be the answers she
wanted, but at least they would be the truth.

She held out her hand, and Silvestro took the

diamond. He turned it over in his hand and held it up to the light.

"So, this is it," Silvestro said. "Is it worth risking your life for, betraying your best friend for, dying for, killing for?"

Did this man really think *she'd* done all those things? Why didn't Marco tell him she was innocent?

Marco's gaze met hers. "It's just a rhetorical question," he explained.

She nodded, but she wanted to ask if recovering it was worth making love for, leading a woman on for, or lying for, but she didn't have to. She already knew the answer.

It hit her with the brilliance of a twenty-five-carat diamond that this was the end of her vacation, the end of her affair with Marco, and the end of the adventure of a lifetime. For him, it was just the end of a job. Nothing more.

If they didn't believe that she'd brought the diamond to Giovanni. *If* they let her go.

"Ms. Jackson," said the older man slowly in heavily accented English. "Tell me how you got the diamond in the first place."

"I just got it tonight from Giovanni."

"I mean in America. Let us assume the diamond was inside a chocolate, though it seems a risky place to hide a valuable diamond. Diamonds are the hardest substance on earth. Someone might have eaten it. Swallowed it or cracked a tooth on it."

"Someone like me," Anne Marie said, her voice

faint as she remembered all the truffles she'd eaten. Marco put his hand on her shoulder and pressed lightly. He'd seen her munching on those truffles; he must know by now she hadn't known what was inside one of them.

Silvestro handed the diamond to Anne Marie. "Smell it," he said.

"Chocolate," she said, holding the diamond to her nose and inhaling. "I can't believe it. My friend Evie Barton gave me the chocolate to give to her cousin. It's made in San Francisco; it's very expensive, very famous chocolate. She said Misty was homesick . . ."

"Homesick," Marco said, "for money. It takes quite a bit to keep up this lifestyle." He waved one hand toward the wall hung with paintings.

"I don't know anything about Misty, but Evie? I can't believe . . . why would she . . . ?"

"Why would anybody trade in diamonds? For money. Does she need money?"

"I don't know. She's never said. If it wasn't Evie, I don't know who it *could* have been. She was the one who said I should come to Italy. She'd come to Italy when she got a divorce years ago but she didn't see Giovanni then."

"How do you know?" Marco asked.

"Because she would have told me."

He looked at her as if she was the most naive person he'd ever known. Maybe she was. She'd believed Evie, and worse than that, she'd actually believed that Marco cared about her, that he'd made love to her because he'd wanted to. Knowing that made looking at him downright painful now. His high cheekbones, his mouth that had kissed her, and his strong hands. She flushed and looked around the room, at the statue of Venus in the corner and a copy of Bernini's *David* in an alcove.

"I guess Evie wouldn't have told me she'd seen Giovanni in Italy if she didn't want me to know," she said at last.

"Particularly if she was delivering stolen goods to him," Silvestro said.

"And having an affair with him," Marco said.

"No," Anne Marie said. Her world had turned on end. Her friends were crooks, and her lover was a liar? "That's not possible." Evie was the one who'd told her Giovanni had always been in love with *her*. Why lie about that?

The answer was so clear: she wanted Anne Marie to go to Italy. To take the diamond not to Giovanni but to her cousin.

"Yes," they both said at the same time. "It is possible."

"From the information we've received from the FBI and the messages we intercepted, we think Giovanni broke off with your friend Evie, which made her angry. She sought another fence for her jewels and found Misty, who is not her cousin. She found you to deliver the diamond. But Giovanni was not about to be left out of the loop. He knew you had the diamond with you. When it wasn't in

the yearbook, he came after you, looking for it,"
Marco said.

"So, Evie really did give me the chocolates to give
to Misty," she said, as the truth sank in.

Marco and his boss both nodded as they stood
together, facing her. Everything she said they
already knew. It made her feel dense.

"Giovanni really searched my room?" she asked.
What a horrible thought. Someone she knew, someone she liked, had done that to her while she was
out dancing with Marco. Where he'd taken her just
because it was his job. Where he'd held her close
and whispered in her ear because it was his job.

"Or someone who works for him," Marco said.

Looking at him now, all business, shirtsleeves
rolled up, tie loosened, she wondered how she
could have been taken in so easily.

Because she'd been vulnerable. Because she'd
been dumped. Because she wanted to believe she
was desirable and beautiful. Hah. She may have a
new look, dressed in fancy clothes, but underneath
she was the same boring, predictable librarian
who'd left California only a few days ago.

"At one time, we weren't sure exactly who was in
on this operation," Silvestro said.

"By that, you mean you thought I was a jewel
thief, didn't you?" She looked straight at Marco,
daring him to deny it.

"Yes," he said. "What else could we think? You
came to meet Giovanni. You brought him something. You had an attachment to him going back

many years. We didn't know if you were working with Evie or alone."

"Do you know now?" she asked.

"We have word that Evie has confessed to her part in the heist. But she claims Giovanni was the mastermind behind it."

"If she'd blamed me, what would have happened?" She imagined herself in the prison they'd visited that afternoon, shackled to the floor, scratching the days off on the wall.

Marco's eyes held a hint of wry amusement. "It wouldn't be the Mammertine Prison," he said.

Easy for him to say, she thought. But it could have been Lompoc or San Quentin, if she had to prove her innocence and couldn't.

"She didn't blame you, and we know that you had nothing to do with the theft of the diamond. Even if you brought it to Italy, your innocence is not in question," Silvestro said. "Marco, take the lady back to where she is staying, please. Then meet me at the office on the Via Firenze."

There were guards at the doors to Misty's villa again, but this time they were policemen. They nodded to Marco, and he got into a car that was parked in the villa's oval driveway.

The streets were almost empty. Anne Marie had no idea what time it was. The moon had set, and the sun had not yet come up.

"I didn't get to see the buildings illuminated," she said. "Though I guess I shouldn't worry about it; not everyone gets to hobnob with international jewel thieves." *Keep it light,* she told herself. *Don't yell, don't blame Marco for using you.* Still . . . "I can't believe you thought I was a thief. But you did, didn't you?"

"At first, yes."

His jaw was set. His eyes were on the road. He was all business. She wanted to ask when he'd changed his mind about her, when he'd decided she wasn't a thief, but it was probably best she didn't know. It might have been only minutes ago, or hours ago, at best. All the time he'd made love to her, slept alongside her, danced with her, kissed her . . . all that time, he'd really believed she'd stolen a diamond. That hurt.

"I never really thought you were a tour guide," she said, her chin in the air. She wanted to hurt him, to make him suffer the way she was. But how could you hurt someone who didn't care? The best she could hope for was to show him she wasn't as dumb as he thought.

"No?" he said. "Well, I tried, but you were too smart for me. You know far more than I did."

She shifted away from him toward the door. "Some things, yes."

"Many things," he said under his breath.

She smoothed her skirt and didn't speak until they got to the convent. He stopped the car and looked up at the stone walls and the gate.

"They have a curfew," he said. "I forgot." He hunched over, resting his forehead on the steering wheel. Then he sat up straight. "We can't get in until six in the morning. I'll take you to my apartment."

"I'll go to a hotel." She wanted to get away from him, almost as much as he must have wanted to get away from her.

"I need to know you're safe," he said.

"Safe from what?" she asked.

"From everything and everyone."

"No one would want to harm me. I don't have the diamond. I don't even have the candy."

"I can't take any chances," he said. "I lost Giovanni tonight. I've been trying to catch him for more than two years, and now it turns out I have no case against him. He didn't steal the diamond; all he did was want the diamond. That's hardly a crime. Neither is finding the diamond in a chocolate truffle."

"What now?" she asked.

"I don't know."

He drove to a large building on the Piazza Pasquino, took her up an elevator to the eighth floor, and led her down a wide, carpeted hall and into a small apartment with high ceilings and dusty furniture. He threw the windows open in the living room and bedroom that looked onto a small courtyard. He tossed a few pillows onto a large, austere-looking bed and told her to help herself to his clothes and his toiletries in the tiled bathroom with an old-fashioned tub.

"I'll be back as soon as I can," he said. "Don't open the door to anyone."

He stood at the front door for a long moment, looking at her as if he wanted to say something. What was there to say? *I'm sorry I didn't trust you? I'm sorry I made love to you?*

Anne Marie waited, but she couldn't stand the silence very long.

"Say it," she said. "Say you're sorry."

"I *am* sorry. Sorry I didn't trust you. I wanted to, but I couldn't. Not and do my job."

"And was part of your job to make love to me?"

"No, of course not," he said.

But she didn't believe him. "It doesn't matter. I got what I wanted, a vacation fling. I thought it would be with Giovanni, but you can't have everything. I don't need to tell you that. You got the diamond; maybe someday you'll get Giovanni."

"You don't want me to get him, do you?" he asked, his hand on the doorknob.

He probably wished he'd left before they had this conversation, but she wasn't going to let him off that easily.

"No, I don't want you to catch him. I know he used me; he certainly lied to me. He doesn't love me and never did. But he was once a good friend. He never made love to me to get information from me."

"*Did* he make love to you?" he demanded. "I thought you said—"

"That's none of your business," she said hotly.

"So, I was just a substitute for Giovanni, was I?" he asked, his eyes blazing.

She'd wounded his male pride. Good! At least he wouldn't remember her as some pathetic tourist who'd been used not only by her best friend but by her long-lost Italian boyfriend, as well as himself.

"Yes," she said. "I came here to recover from my divorce. My ego was in shambles. You knew that, and you took advantage of me. Well, I took advantage of you, too. When I saw I couldn't have Giovanni, I settled for you. I couldn't go home without an Italian affair; now I've had it, and I'm going home. My husband is waiting for me." It wasn't a lie; he was waiting for her. She just didn't care.

"Damn it, Anna Maria, I can't stay here and argue with you. I said I was sorry. I never meant to hurt you."

"You didn't hurt me," she said, crossing her arms. A few minutes ago, she'd been so tired and depressed she could barely hold her head up. Now, she was on a roll. Her brain felt as if it had just woken up from a long nap, and her spirit along with it.

"You made my vacation," she said. "I have to thank you for that. I'll have so many stories to tell. Wait till Evie hears . . . well, maybe I'll visit her at the federal prison and tell her. Or maybe I'll just write a book. Don't worry, I won't use any real names. And I'll change the diamond to a stolen painting. It should make quite a story."

"You're going to write about me?" he asked, his eyes glowing like hot coals. He took a step toward her.

"Yes," she said, but her voice wasn't quite as strong as it had been. "You can't stop me." The way he was looking at her and the way he was coming toward her told her he could stop her if he wanted to. He was bigger and stronger than she was. His eyes were narrowed, and his mouth was set; his hard jaw jutted forward.

"I can't stop you," he said. "But I can give you something more to write about."

She took a step backward, then another, breathing hard. She'd never seen him look so furious, so determined. He put his hands on her shoulders and backed her against the wall.

His lips came down on hers, hot and heavy and punishing. His hips pressed against hers, and she could feel the strength of his erection. She wouldn't let herself respond; she wouldn't give him that satisfaction. She kept her arms stiffly at her sides.

His hands framed her face, and he forced his tongue into her mouth and ravaged it. She couldn't take it. Not another minute. Not another second.

She invaded his mouth as he'd done hers. Her tongue wound around his. She pressed back against his assault on her body. She thrust her hips forward and heard him moan deep in his throat. Her nipples peaked and beaded against his shirt.

She was running on pure adrenaline and instinct when she wrapped her arms around his neck and answered his kisses with her own, faster, harder, wilder than anything she'd ever known. Damn it, her body, her heart, and her raging hormones still wanted him, lusted for him, loved him.

At the same time, she wanted to punish him. As he wanted to possess her. It was a duel nobody could win, about love and hate and pride and regret. Somewhere in the deep recesses of her mind, she knew it was also about good-bye.

Finally, he broke away and held her at arm's length, his eyes shut, breathing as hard as she was. So hard she was afraid she'd never fill her lungs again.

He backed his way to the door, his shirt hanging out of his pants, his hair matted to his head, sweat running down his face like a man who'd tried to outrun a hurricane. Before he left, he paused at the door.

"Don't go anywhere," he said, his voice the one he might use on hardened criminals.

"Good-bye." She'd be damned if she'd take orders from him. Not from a man she was never going to see again.

Chapter 17

Marco spent more hours than he wanted to, more than he thought necessary, at the office with Silvestro. It was getting late. He called his apartment; no one answered. He drank cold coffee and popped some aspirin. He and Silvestro called their counterparts in the United States and South Africa and received congratulations on the recovery of the diamond. Giovanni was scarcely mentioned; he'd become irrelevant. He wouldn't like that, but it was better than being in prison. Evie Barton was in custody, and so was her so-called cousin Misty.

"Not bad for a night's work," Silvestro said, rubbing his hands together cheerfully. "On that note, I'm going to announce my retirement. I will nominate you as my successor, of course." Before Marco could either protest or accept, his boss continued, "Now, what's going to happen to the woman? She's free to go, you know. I'm convinced she doesn't know any more than she told us. Any fool can tell she's an honest woman." He gave Marco a half-smile.

Marco wished he could replay the past twenty-four hours and do a better job of it, but it was too late. Too late to make amends, too late to apologize. He had made a fool of himself, let Giovanni get away, hurt Anna Maria, and now what?

"Now what?" Silvestro asked.

"Now nothing," he said. "I'm taking a vacation. A long one. I'm going back to San Gervase and fix my roof."

"And the woman?"

"She's going back to the States to her ex-husband."

"Really?"

"I don't know. With her, there's no telling." He was still reeling from that encounter in his apartment. She was the most unpredictable, beautiful, feisty, honest, sexy, maddening . . .

He reached across the desk to shake hands with Silvestro, then left the building. When he got to his apartment, he knew she was gone before he even opened the door. The bathroom towel was still damp, and the mirror was still steamed up. The bed hadn't been slept in, but he smelled her scent everywhere. On the glass she'd used, on the telephone she'd used, on the window she'd opened.

He was out of the apartment in a few seconds, got into the agency car, and sped through the early-morning traffic to the convent. Dawn was breaking over the convent walls. Inside was an oasis of calm. He asked to see his sister.

Isabella came to the door in her gray dress and apron, her hair smooth and a smile on her face. The convent had done wonders for her sense of serenity, but serenity was not what he wanted right now. He wanted Anna Maria.

"Where is she?" he asked.

"She went to the airport to try to get a flight to California."

"Why didn't you stop her?" he asked.

"Why didn't you?" she asked.

"I didn't know," he said. "I didn't know I'd fall in love with her. I didn't know she'd get under my skin. I didn't know I needed her. I didn't know I needed anybody."

"What's wrong with you?" Isabella asked with a worried frown.

"Everything," he said.

She put her hand out. In it was a small black box. "Take this. It was Nonna's. It is for whichever of us gets married first."

He looked down at the box, then at his sister. "Are you sure?"

"Are you?" she asked.

He put it in his pocket and left. He was only sure

of one thing: he had to find Anna Maria. He couldn't lose her.

At the airport, he pulled out an official card, stuck it on his windshield, and parked in front of the international terminal. He ran through the concourse, stopping to look at departure times for flights to San Francisco. She wasn't in any of the lines at the ticket windows. She wasn't in a lounge. She wasn't anywhere.

That was it—she'd left. She was gone. She must be in the air now, flying over Rome in his sister's clothes, on her way back to her husband. He felt empty and tired and more alone than he ever had. All around him, couples were saying good-bye, families were reuniting, and he was alone. No wife, no family. No one to meet, no one to see off. No one to tease or talk to or wipe her tears away or even kiss good-bye.

Not that he was there to kiss her good-bye. After all, she'd walked out on him. Again.

Anne Marie was sitting at the counter of a coffee bar when Marco came up behind her and sat down next to her. She choked on her coffee and set her cup down with a thump. She clutched her ticket in her hand. She had no luggage. She'd given Isabella her clothes back, except for the stretch cotton pants and linen shirt she was wearing and the cashmere crewneck sweater tied around her shoulders that Isabella had insisted she keep. "For souvenirs," she'd said, after she'd kissed her on both cheeks and sent her off with a sad, worried expression. Anne Marie was also wearing a pair of sunglasses to hide the tears she couldn't stop from falling.

Now that Marco was there, they came faster than ever, running down her cheeks into her coffee. With a loud sigh, he reached for his handkerchief and gave it to her.

"What is it now?" he asked. "Don't worry, I'm not going to arrest you or kidnap you. You won't miss your plane."

"Then what are you doing here?" she asked, making an ineffectual swipe of his handkerchief.

"I came to say good-bye."

"You've said it. Now you can go." She averted her gaze so she wouldn't see his bloodshot eyes, the lines of fatigue around his mouth, so she wouldn't feel sorry for him, so he wouldn't see how much she cared about him. Because if she really looked at him, she wouldn't be able to tear her eyes away. Then he'd see, as he always could see, what she was really feeling. He'd see how much it hurt her to know she'd fallen in love all by herself. How much she didn't want to leave.

"Are you going back to your husband?"

"No."

"Then why are you going?"

"Why would I stay?"

"You haven't seen everything."

"I've seen enough."

"You haven't seen my house."

"You can send me a picture. Give me the address so I know where to send your handkerchiefs."

He wrote it on a napkin, and she took off her sunglasses and looked at it. "This is in San Gervase?"

"On a cliff overlooking the sea. I don't go there much, and it needs work. The lemon trees need pruning, and the roof has to be replaced."

"What about the inside?" she asked, curious in spite of herself. "Is there light wood and yellow and blue tile?"

"Not now."

"Are there tomatoes growing in the garden?"

"Nothing's growing. Not this summer. So, there's really nothing to recommend the place, except the view and the location. Handy for me, since I'll be working in town, but otherwise . . ." His voice was flat, almost morose.

"You could fix it up," she suggested.

"What's the point? Living alone doesn't appeal to me anymore. I'd ask someone to live with me, but I can't."

"Why not?"

"The place is too much of a mess. It needs some tender loving care . . . and so do I."

A small, teary smile tilted the corners of her mouth.

"I need you, Anna Maria," he said, his gaze boring into hers. "I want you. I want you to paint the inside of my house blue and yellow and plant tomatoes and open that bookstore you wanted.

Of course, you'd come home for lunch every day."

"Go on."

"And so will I. We'll eat alfresco, and we'll make love on a blanket under the olive tree. I love you, Anna Maria. Though I never believed in love before, I do now. Don't go. If you go, I'll come after you. I'll stand in your garden in California and sing love songs to you in Italian until you come out. I'll buy your son a Vespa, and he can spend the summers here and be the great-grandson Nonna has always wanted. Say something," he said. "Anything."

She opened her mouth, but no words came out. She was stunned. She was delirious.

"Did you just say . . ."

"I said I loved you. And I'm asking you to marry me and live with me for the rest of our lives."

She'd promised herself she'd never cry in front of him again, but she was so overwhelmed with emotion she couldn't stop. The man she loved had just proposed to her, and she was going to live in a house by the sea in Italy. She thought about Marco on her front lawn, singing songs in Italian with the neighbors hanging out of their windows, and her tears turned to laughter.

Marco slid off his stool, took her in his arms, and kissed the tears off her cheeks. No one looked their way. No one stared in shock when their kisses turned passionate at the coffee shop counter at eight o'clock in the morning. Or when he took out a small black box and put a diamond ring on her finger, the first diamond she'd ever had. And no one would have been surprised if they'd known that the man had just proposed to the woman he loved, and she'd said yes.

After all, this was Italy.

Dear Reader:

Welcome to the exciting world of *Bon Voyage* romances!

Have you ever longed to sail on a luxury ship in the Caribbean, with the wind blowing through your hair, and a steel band playing a tropical beat on deck as you dance with a dangerously attractive man? Or to meander the misty emerald hills of Ireland as a handsome stranger whispers sweet nothings in your ear in a delightful brogue? Or to sit at a cozy table for two in a Roman plaza at dusk, gazing into the eyes of a tall, dark, mysterious man as a singer croons a plaintive Italian love song?

Everyone loves traveling to romantic, exotic destinations—even if only in their imagination—and *Bon Voyage* will take you away to the lands of all your fantasies. Sexy modern English dukes, romantic evenings in Paris, the sun-drenched coast of Greece . . . Love knows no bounds, so we're expanding the world of romance, bringing you irresistible contemporary love stories from all over the world.

Turn the page to get a taste of our next romance, *French Twist* by Roxanne St. Claire, where American Janine Coulter and sexy Frenchman Luc Tremont chase across the French countryside in pursuit of a stolen treasure, only to find themselves pursued— by dangerous men who won't stop at murder to get to the treasure before them. Glamour, romance, danger, adventure—*French Twist* has it all.

So happy reading . . . and *bon voyage!*

Micki Nuding
Senior Editor

POCKET BOOKS
PROUDLY PRESENTS

French Twist

ROXANNE ST. CLAIRE

Available in paperback 2004
from Pocket Books

Turn the page for a preview of
French Twist. . . .

$\mathcal{W}$hat the . . . ? Her Plums were missing!

Janine Coulter blinked against the blinding sunshine reflecting off hundreds of Venetian mirrors. Her precious Pompadour Plum vases were not in Versailles' famed Hall of Mirrors.

"Monsieur Le Directeur, where are the Sèvres vases?"

The museum director sniffed. "How astute of you to notice, Professor Coulter. We are not including them in this area of the exhibit." He lifted a bony shoulder. "We have been advised against doing so."

"Advised?" This would be a battle of wills, and where the Pompadour Plums were involved, her will was steel. "By whom? The vases are the centerpiece of the exhibit, monsieur, and our plans call for them to be in the middle of this hall." Janine turned and crossed the polished parquet, the staccato tap of her high heels reverberating off the marble walls and richly painted ceilings. "They were supposed to be right here."

"We have altered the design of the exhibit because of security issues, Professor," the director said.

Was there a French equivalent to 'I don't give a damn'?

Janine squared her shoulders. "I wasn't apprised of these security issues."

"That's because you were unavoidably detained." The sound of footsteps indicated a new arrival. The English words, buried in a smoky baritone and rich French accent, echoed through the massive hall.

The man approached with all the assurance of the three Bourbon kings who'd ruled from this very room. Those Louis were tall enough to look down on their subjects, dark enough to be the focal point of every portrait, and handsome enough to have legendary libidos constantly satisfied.

This man could be a direct descendant. And then some.

Although his striking features weren't perfect, they were compelling. His eyes, nearly as black as his thick, straight hair, glinted as he gazed at her. A shadow of stubborn beard in hollow cheeks was balanced by a black slash of brow. Everything about him—from the thousand-dollar suit that hung elegantly over his expansive shoulders down to the rich Euro loafers—screamed control, perfection, and superiority.

Not only did he have the drop-dead looks of French royalty, he had the 'tude to go with it.

Janine tilted her face up to him—something a five-foot-seven-inch woman in heels rarely got to do.

He swept a glance over her, lingering a moment longer than necessary on her legs. Maybe her spunky skirt was a little too L.A. hip, and not enough Paris couture?

His eyes narrowed a fraction as he honed in on her face. "Evidently you were unable to be involved

in the last minute decisions, Madame La Curator."
His flawless English was softened by his French
accent. "I understand that urgent personal business
kept you from joining us."

The musical cadence didn't mask the little dig;
he clearly knew that she'd been delayed because
her wedding had been scheduled to take place the
week before. And that although she'd arrived late,
she had no ring, no new last name, and no husband
in tow.

For the millionth time, she cursed her cheating,
lying ex-fiancé.

She held out her hand. "Janine Coulter."

With a slight bow of his head, he engulfed her
hand with his large, strong grip. "Luc Tremont."

"Luc is our *spécialist de securité*," the director
explained. "A consultant we have hired to supervise
the security of the Pompadour exhibit. And yes, Luc,
this is the newly appointed Madame La Curator, our
distinguished guest from the *Univerisité de Californie*,
Janine Coulter."

A shower of resentment sparked at her nerve endings. She hadn't been told anything about a security
consultant.

"The pleasure is mine, madame." A decidedly un-
French smile revealed perfect white teeth. His handshake relaxed as one of his fingers lightly moved over
her skin, and more resentment sparked. *Something*
sparked. She withdrew her hand.

"From California," he said in a tone so soft it
could be considered seductive . . . or mocking. "But
your beautiful name is so French. Janine."

Szha-neen. It sure never sounded like that

before. She shook her head and crossed her arms. This was probably part of their sabotage strategy. They sent this hunk to sidetrack her, to make her stumble on the job, to steal her attention from her responsibilities. Highly effective warriors, these French.

"Monsieur Tremont, where are the Pompadour Plum vases?"

Luc Tremont regarded her from under thick, dark lashes. "It's my strong recommendation that we limit the viewing of the Sèvres in one of the anterooms, guarded twenty-four hours a day. I'll allow entrance by invitation only."

He'll allow entrance? "Not a chance. The vases are the heart and soul of the exhibit."

"There are nearly a hundred other artifacts that have not been seen in well over two centuries," he countered.

"None as precious as the Sèvres." And none as closely tied to Madame de Pompadour, the exhibit's namesake. "They are the whole reason people will come to this exhibit."

"Surely they will want to see all of the treasures of Louis the XV's Versailles."

He was clueless, this big French security guard. "Monsieur Tremont, do you realize that in the history of all mankind, there has never been a piece of soft paste Sèvres porcelain produced in that color, let alone three matching vases, all with Pompadour's image and name?" She purposely used the let-me-spell-this-out-for-you tone that she saved for freshmen. "All three bear Madame's actual signature written in gold. They are *priceless*."

"Precisely my point." A glimmer lit his midnight gaze. "Professor."

A sudden, uncomfortable warmth spread through her, but she continued her argument. "They're the reason more than a million people around the world will file into museums like this one. It would be like exhibiting King Tut without the sarcophagus. We can't deny visitors the chance to see the Pompadour Plums," she insisted.

Tremont took a few steps closer to her, invading her breathing room in that totally French way. But somehow, with him, it was more . . . *invasive.* "There have been very specific threats to the exhibit, madame. I don't think you want to take the chance of losing the vases before they have traveled the world."

Of course not. If something—*anything*—went wrong, her career would end faster than she could say au revoir. But she couldn't let this guy steamroll her. "Why don't you fill me in on the security issues, Monsieur Tremont, and then we can come up with a plan that meets both your needs and mine?"

"Madame La Curator." Was that a tone of condescension buried in that musical accent? "There have been rumblings in the underground world of art trading."

So, word on the street said there would be a hit. "I don't have a problem with armed guards and increased museum security," she responded. "But I refuse to remove the Sèvres vases from the main exhibit."

"I'm afraid you have no authority to *refuse* anything."

"Sorry, but I do." She hoped her glower communicated her anger, just in case the English wasn't getting through. "Perhaps we can discuss this with the Minister of Culture, who *gave* me the authority to do what I want with my vases."

He winked at her. "They belong to France."

Damn. She could have bitten a hole in her lip. "I mean, Madame's vases . . . the Sèvres vases."

With one strong, sure hand on her shoulder, he led her away, leaning close enough for Janine to feel a whisper of warm breath on her cheek. Personal space was irrelevant to the French. "Madame. Professor. What do you prefer that I call you?"

She couldn't resist. "Janine."

"Janine." *Szha-neen*. It was absolutely *sinful* the way he said it. "There is more than I am telling you."

A shiver skated down her spine, but her reaction had more to do with his serious tone than his sexy pronunciation.

He moved his hand from her shoulder, down her back, leaving a trail of heat in its wake. "Surely you understand that there are those who will stop at nothing to own such a magnificent piece of history as Pompadour's vases."

Well, duh. "Of course there are thieves who want them. But hiding them in another room? Offering a viewing by invitation only? Such extreme measures will detract from the appeal of the exhibit."

"Not when lives are at risk, Janine."

"Whose life is at risk?" she scoffed.

His smile disappeared. "Yours."

                    *   *   *

Luc needed her attention, which was why he
pulled out his trump card so quickly. He could think
of a number of other ways to gain her attention,
though—like taking her pretty mouth in a world-
class French kiss. That would satisfy the annoying
itch that started the moment he laid eyes on the
California girl.

"*My* life is at risk?" As the blood faded from
her face, the light revealed the faintest dusting of
freckles. Sunlight suited her; she belonged in the
sun. On the beach. Sparkling on the sand somewhere. She was so bright and fresh and . . . American.

Behind them, other Versailles staff members had
entered the Hall, and there were still many faces he
didn't recognize. Or trust.

"Why don't we walk outside for a few moments?"
he suggested. "We can talk privately."

Her sky-blue eyes flashed, but then she con-
sented with a nod. Luc led Janine through a gallery
to the *Cour de Marbe*, and paused as they stepped
onto the courtyard's intricate pattern of gray-and-
white marble. Beyond it rolled the emerald lawns of
the gardens, dotted with flowers, gushing fountains,
and priceless sculptures.

As always, the singular beauty of France simply
left him homesick. But he held out his hand to share
the scene. "*C'est magnifique, n'est ce pas?*"

She cast a quick glance at the view and barely
inhaled long enough to enjoy the fragrance of orange
blossoms that floated on the breeze. Stuffing her
handbag under her elbow, she crossed her arms and
locked an insistent gaze on him. "I'm not here to take

a tour, monsieur. I would appreciate an explanation of what you just said."

She had no way of knowing he wasn't just another anti-American Frenchman who resented her arrival, so he forgave her the little jutting chin. He knew enough about her situation to understand her air of defensiveness.

"Not a tour, I promise. But I find that hall a bit suffocating, *non*? In May in France, there's never a reason to be indoors."

She gave the grounds a cursory glance, and then trained her blue eyes on him again. "It's beautiful. Now please tell me exactly what you meant in there."

"*Oui.*" A few uniformed tour guides stood smoking a few yards away. Versailles had ears, and eyes; that was his biggest problem. "While we walk, *s'il vous plaît.*" He headed toward the matching pools that anchored the entrance to the gardens.

Although his gut instinct—backed up by a thorough background check—cleared her from any suspicion, he still had no intention of telling the truth. She may have lucked into the curator's job, or she might have been sent as a plant. Or simply a distraction.

He took another surreptitious glance at her long, lean calves. His weakness for a magnificent pair of legs was known to only a few—but those few included at least one man who'd like to see him dead.

"There's a great deal of anti-American sentiment in France, as you undoubtedly are aware. There are those who'd prefer that the curator of the Pompadour exhibit be a French citizen."

A breeze lifted a strand of her platinum blond hair

out of the loose knot at the nape of her neck, and she automatically tucked it back. "I doubt your infamous anti-American sentiment extends to killing visitors, monsieur."

"True, we don't generally kill visitors to France." He smiled at her. "Although we've been known to insult them into leaving."

To her credit, she responded with a soft, musical laugh. "I can handle that."

"I've no doubt you can."

Even in the grainy photo he'd seen on the UCLA faculty website, she was a knock-out.

In real life, she was deadly. Too bad the circumstances weren't different.

"You've assumed a very high profile position in an important and controversial exhibit for Versailles. Indeed, for all of France." He lowered his voice. "And of course, there are those who firmly believe the Plums are nothing but a hoax."

"Oh, God," she groaned. "Save me from the anti-Pompadour crowd. Those idiots would keep Louis' mistress out of the history books completely, if they could."

He laughed softly. "*Mais oui*. A Monica Lewinsky of her time."

Her eyes sparked. "That is *so* wrong. La Pompadour changed the course of history. She was as powerful as a queen, and just as influential as the king she slept with."

"Then you understand why you are the focus of so much attention, Janine."

She shook her head. "But what does all of this—resentment have to do with hiding the vases?"

"That is still being investigated."

Her eyes darkened to match the water in an ornate fountain behind her. "By whom?"

"A small group within the museum and the Versailles' *Directeur de Securité*." He'd never lost his ability to lie with ease.

"Madame de Vries? Simone? She didn't mention it to me and I met with her this morning." She looked sharply at him. "She didn't mention you, either. Wouldn't she be responsible for hiring a security consultant?"

"There are many involved."

"Whom do you work for? The museum director?"

He nearly snorted. "*Non.*"

"But he's the top of the food chain here."

"I was retained from outside the museum hierarchy." She wasn't stupid; in a minute she'd run through her *food chain* and figure it out.

She frowned. "The *Réunion des Musées Nationals* is the only authority over the museums of this country, as far as I know." She stared at him, the stray hair escaping again. "Claude Marchionette."

"*Precisement.*" He resisted the urge to touch that silky strand, watching it dance in the breeze.

Her jaw dropped a little. "You were hired by the Minister of Culture?"

"He has given me carte blanche to protect the exhibit. Even if it means altering it."

"That's ridiculous." He could hear the frustration in her voice. "Security doesn't drive the design of an exhibit; it's the other way around."

He nodded. "I am sensitive to that. I'm a specialist, only brought in for very specific situations such as this major exhibit. I'm well trained to protect priceless treasures."

She shot him a skeptical look. "What kind of training is that?"

He recited his resume casually, glossing over dates and years to appear modest, rather than purposefully vague. He managed to let her know that he had experience in museums all over the world, and enough of an education to be considered "intelligent" by the elite French standards.

"Do you require references, madame?" he asked, unfastening the single button of his jacket and slipping his hands into his pockets.

"I'll talk to the Minister of Culture."

"You do that." Because it wouldn't change a thing.

She held his gaze for a long moment, all pale blonde and blue-eyed determination. If she'd been sent to distract him, then his nemesis knew him far too well.